AIR RACE

A MAX FEND THRILLER

ANDREW WATTS

CHRIS BAUER

SEVERN RIVER PUBLISHING

AIR RACE

Copyright © 2022 by Point Whiskey Publishing, LLC and Chris Bauer.

All rights reserved.

No part of this book may be reproduced in any form or by any electronic or mechanical means, including information storage and retrieval systems, without written permission from the author, except for the use of brief quotations in a book review.

Severn River Publishing
www.SevernRiverBooks.com

This is a work of fiction. Names, characters, businesses, places, events and incidents are either the products of the author's imagination or used in a fictitious manner. Any resemblance to actual persons, living or dead, or actual events is purely coincidental.

ISBN: 978-1-64875-369-5 (Paperback)

ALSO BY THE AUTHORS

<u>Max Fend Series</u>

Glidepath

The Oshkosh Connection

Air Race

BY ANDREW WATTS

The Firewall Spies

The War Planners Series

BY CHRIS BAUER

Blessid Trauma Crime Scene Cleaners

Scars on the Face of God

Binge Killer

To find out more visit

severnriverbooks.com/series/max-fend-thrillers

1

Benton's field agent was buried, figuratively, inside France's cinema community. His phone call to Benton was cryptic, not unlike others she received from agents in her European stable, but the request was out of the ordinary: he wanted to provide his intel report in person instead of remotely.

"It is because I am here, *mon amie*, going through my usual daily routine, that I ask you to *venez à moi*," he'd said. The mangled French that seasoned his request to meet face to face suffered from his British accent. "One must not put *les pigeons* among the cats. I eat my lunches on the dune's beach on days that I can, watching the paragliders circle and the ocean lapping against the shore. Today will be one of those days. Join me for *le déjeuner*, please?"

Benton had caved. "Noon, on the beach side of the dune," she said, and ended the call. This put her on a tour bus from Bordeaux to the Dune du Pilat, a tourist attraction on France's west coast.

The bus followed the winding, packed-sand road to the dune and entered a dirt parking area. The bus driver cut the engine. Benton exited with other tourists, her untucked T-shirt short-sleeved, her sunglasses in place on her face, her backpack over her shoulder. The view across the bay was spectacular and the touristy sand dune was impressive, but most importantly, for their purpose, it was a busy place, assuaging her worry about meeting in the open, but only by a little. The tension from his assessment that he needed to deliver his report face to face intensified with each sandy step.

The Great Dune of Pilat at New Aquitaine, on France's west coast: forty miles from Bordeaux, it was the only desert in Europe. During the summer months, tourism could get heavy. A freak of nature, this sandy patch rose from the coast abutting the Bay of Biscay and ended in a dune so tall it had a stairway to reach its apex. Some people avoided the steps on the return trip down, letting gravity have its way, tumbling forward onto the soft sand for a short thrill. As an ecosystem, it was an oddity. Per the historical record, the dune was moving, advancing inland, slowly gobbling up the surrounding forest and roads over a period of centuries.

Benton spotted her man on the beach's darker, wet sand, the tide moving away from the shore. He leaned against the seat of a three-legged beach chair balanced to accommodate his tall frame. Next to him, a cheap tray table held his lunch in a small vinyl bag. His was a tropical Hemingway look: sunglasses, open-collared linen shirt, long, salmon-colored shorts, and a cocked Panama hat. Nice tan. She arrived alongside and slid her vinyl backpack off her shoulder, setting it in the sand, which was still a little soggy from the retreating tides. She slipped a plastic bottle of water out of her backpack, wet her lips with a short sip, then resettled her sunglasses.

"Trayne," she said to address him, leaning in to kiss his cheek.

He accepted the kiss. "Benton. Good to see you."

Her agent reinterested himself in his small can of tuna fish, stuck a spork into its contents, and placed the can on his table. He found another can of tuna and spork inside his bag and handed both to her. "Glad you could make it."

They looked past each other, their heads on a discreet swivel, to stay aware of and read their surroundings, to calibrate them. Benton remained standing while she consumed her host's offered, modest lunch. Trayne stayed half-seated against his tripod of a beach chair, eating his tuna and sipping from a chilled stainless steel water bottle between bites. Warm day, calm ocean; kites, colorful paragliders, and playful drones flew overhead at different altitudes, soaring above the dune in the crosswinds. A peaceful environment to the untrained eye, yet still a source of tension to the two operatives.

In between bites of tuna fish, Trayne stated his concern. "My organization was passed over."

Benton frowned, not grasping the implication. "Really? How's that?"

"The client found someone better."

Trayne was plugged into a killer-for-hire organization, a group that eliminated people if a criminal gang wanted it done. Occasionally this group targeted someone of political or national security importance. This was why Benton and her CIA employer kept him on the payroll, so they could stay informed when something at that level materialized. They looked the other way when the group performed other wetwork.

"How is that even possible? Who is better than your contractors?"

Trayne had a one-word answer, chewing through a biscuit: "Nomad."

Benton coughed, or rather choked on a piece of tuna fish and disguised it as a cough. She cleared her throat, looked down as she spoke. "That, I'm sorry to say, fits."

"How is that? Fits what?"

"No one's heard from him since Colombia. Two years. Sources said he was out of the game, worried about the narcos after him. Now this, what you're telling me. Plus something that went down ten days ago. We lost an asset."

"Who?"

Benton wrapped her head around what Trayne's update meant, or tried to, making him wait. Then, "That exploding parcel in the Kazakhstan market," she said. "Four dead. One was an oil guy. *Our* oil guy, the son of a Kazakh billionaire. He was the target. We're sure it was Nomad's work. Tell me this. How do you know your client hired him?"

Trayne's eyes darted from paraglider to paraglider, some of them motorized, their engines buzzing like weedwhackers. The dune was a major draw on days like this, the sky saturated with them and other ultralights, plus drones. Above where they picnicked, a hundred feet up, one paramotoring ultralight circled like a buzzard.

"Look, I was chafed that we lost the business. I wanted to know who the competition was."

"No. Tell me you didn't…"

"I did. I called the middleman and met with him."

The CIA officer was now super-vigilant about their surroundings. "Not the right move, Trayne. Never the right move."

"We also never expected to lose any business that interests us. I had to know. There's this, um, connection the middleman says will happen in a few days, a week, I don't know exactly when, but sometime soon. An old-school SRAC thing."

Short-range agent communication, or SRAC. Generated by a high-speed, short burst of encrypted data from one device to a second device, a receiver.

"The details to you about it are, as they say, forthcoming," he said. More spork-fed tuna, with him finishing his can.

"So now you're nervous."

She stuffed her plastic bottle of water into her bag, emptied the tuna can of its water, and tucked it in with the bottle. "Well, you should be. Jesus, Trayne," she said, resisting a chiding headshake.

"You need to help me get away."

"Tell me what you found out."

Trayne watched a pair of men flying a kite at the top of the nearest crest of smooth sand. He spoke, not looking his handler Benton in the eye. "The middleman said the client is a high-ranking official from the UAE. On the staff of the Crown Prince."

"The crown prince of what?"

"Dubai."

Shit. Benton had to assess the impact on the fly. The Crown Prince of Dubai was beloved by the Department of State. If he or someone from his staff was hiring people from her agent's organization, that meant he was into something… undesirable. And if it was the Crown Prince who wanted to hire Nomad…

This would ruffle a lot of feathers in Langley and Washington.

"Not necessarily the prince himself," Trayne said. "At a minimum, it's someone on his staff."

"Close enough. But they'd be dipping their toes into a massive cesspool. Using Nomad sounds like overkill, depending on whatever they had in mind. Which was what?" Or more like who, Benton knew.

"Overkill because of price, and a high price because of Nomad's invisibility and track record at getting things done. But we never got that far. No target info, which means we never got to price, either. But the person I spoke to... the middleman who dropped Nomad's name as the competitor..."

Trayne eyed their surroundings again, the people and things near them, high, low, above them on land, nearby on the sea, his visual sweep more nervous this time.

"... he had an accident the next day." Trayne pushed off from his chair, stuffed his lunch detritus into a plastic bag, then stuffed the bag into his backpack.

"What kind of accident?"

"A deadly one. Paris Metro. Fell onto the subway tracks."

Trayne's nervousness became contagious. Benton made a more severe scan of the perimeter but not overtly, was discreet, her hand shading her eyes from the sun, bettering her sunglasses, with a smile faking her appreciation of the beauty of the sand and the sea, and a sea breeze that kept the airborne tourists aloft, the view so heavenly. But the gliders and the toy drones now deserved her direct scrutiny like the tourists milling past them at beach level. A cold, tingling sensation crept up her spine, belying the warmth of their surroundings.

"I read about the subway accident on a UAE website, Benton. The post was gone when I checked again, a few hours later."

"When was that?"

"Last Friday."

She took a deep breath, eased the air out of her lungs. The smell of the ocean's salt was intoxicating, reminding her of days with her parents and their family summer vacations to southern U.S. beaches.

She was procrastinating, having drifted into two inevitabilities: one, Nomad was back, two, the potential fallout of her British agent's faux pas could be huge.

"You think the murder was because your middleman told you something he shouldn't have."

Trayne nodded. "And if they know about that, they might know who I am, and how to find me."

Exactly. "We need to get you somewhere where you can lie low for a while. I'll get this info back to my boss. You're not still in your apartment, are you?"

"I checked into a low-profile hostel in Marseille."

"Give me the address. We need to get you out."

They agreed to meet near the hostel tonight, late; it could not wait until tomorrow. Things would be tense, but she knew she could get this information to Langley, then put a plan in place to extricate her agent by early a.m. tomorrow.

She climbed back into the bus loaded with other tourists and set to leave in five minutes. These last few moments of exiting a face-to-face were always nerve-racking. Stories of getting so close to a clean getaway, peers letting their guard down, overwhelmed by a clandestine enemy, most times at close range, sometimes from a distance, often immediate, or other times a delayed reaction. Her shaded eyes memorized the face of every tourist now on the bus. One could never be too careful...

She pulled her bottle of water out of her backpack, which left her staring at the near-empty can of tuna at the bottom. Eyes down, she saw what she'd seen earlier while she ate around it with the spork: a thumb drive inside a very tiny plastic bag in the tuna can.

"... *the details are... forthcoming,*" Trayne had said, which meant this gift.

Benton sipped at her water, returned the bottle to the bag, zipped everything closed.

Then she heard the screams.

Bus passengers were leaning out their open windows to see. She looked too, and her mouth dropped open.

A little over fifty meters away, her agent lay in the sand, clutching his neck, blood spurting through his fingers. He must have tumbled, his body coming to rest midway up the dune, his Panama hat blowing away in the wind.

The paragliders and kiters ditched their chutes and kites where they could on the beach, becoming landbound voyeurs like the gathering crowd.

A quick twist of her glasses gave her a clear view of a small drone as it flew away over the bay, gliding above all the pleasure craft near the shoreline, motoring toward a speck of a vessel on the horizon multiple miles distant.

2

The air race in progress on the French Riviera was killing it, a one-day spectacle and a major coup for Fend Aerospace. Max Fend, the flashy son of the old-guard pioneer in aerospace manufacturing, Charles Fend, had pulled it off. The race was a high-speed air sprint around a pyloned course in the Bay of Cannes, held during the Cannes Film Festival. The younger, partying rich knew Max as a ballsy visionary with an unquenchable thirst for the thrilling and the dynamic. The air race community now considered him a god.

At least one other person had a different opinion, she and Max under a VIP tent, peering out at the bay.

"Renee," Max said. It was a plea.

"What?" Renee sipped from a takeout coffee cup. She had no intention of facing him, instead narrowed her eyes at a pair of eighty-foot-tall, colorful pylons sitting atop the glistening blue water.

"Ronny Wright. He is some kind of pilot, isn't he? Dashing—"

It sounded like a question, but it really wasn't, was instead a statement meant to playfully irritate her.

"... debonair..."

A slight dig, with Max hoping she'd still be a good sport about... things.

"... good ol', dependable Ronny Wright."

"You are insufferable, Max."

He didn't include "boring" as a description, it would have been too over the top. No matter, Max knew how Renee felt, yesterday, today, probably tomorrow as well, with them vacationing in so exquisite and romantic a venue, France being *the* place for lovers. He was doing his best to avoid acknowledging it. Renee and he were a couple, there was no denying that. But were they more than a couple? Yes. Renee knew it, so did Max. She was simply looking for him to admit it, which would have been the first step toward them making a decision regarding a longer-term arrangement.

Hell, even here, in the monologue inside his own head, he couldn't be honest, considering he wouldn't let a certain word enter the debate that he was having with himself.

The M word. Marriage.

The married Max Fend. Mr. and Mrs. Max Fend. Max and Renee Fend.

In his cavalier mind she needed to stay Renee LeFrancois, an attractive, once-divorced French Canadian, a while longer. How long? He didn't know. But he also needed for Renee to want it to be that way, too, to have them remain as committed boyfriend-girlfriend only, for the time being at least. Because he was still young, still available, still the jet-setting bachelor. Still having too much fun. Still the carefree, ready-for-anything, jack-of-all-trades, master-of-none, no-tying-me-down, irresponsible, lovable—

"You can be such an *outil* sometimes." She tossed her half cup of coffee in a trash can.

"Wait, what? I know that word. You called me a tool."

"Yes. Rather than the other word, okay? Ronny had a thing for me. It wasn't mutual. Plus, he's now engaged. How about this: you stop talking right now, and I watch the race. Your coveted aerobatic air race, remember? All these people who you paid to come here and entertain the folks at Cannes?"

Max's pitch, made in December to the French Association of International Films consortium at Palais des Festivals et des Congrès in Cannes—the group's title itself was an earful for the impatient—had clinched the deal:

"I'll pay for it myself. All of it. The prize money, the appearance fees, the publicity. Ten air teams. Fend Aerospace's team will anchor it. We will witness the

rebirth of a storied fifteen-year competition that shuttered in 2019, and Cannes will be the site of this resurrection. The ultimate entertainment for the ultimate glitterati. Vive les courses aériennes acrobatiques! Viva la France!"

When the word came out to the air racing public that Fend Aerospace was "putting the band back together," Max easily signed nine additional teams to participate, mostly racing champions from years past, him supplementing the field with a few upstarts.

A tinny public address announcement in French-accented English changed the subject, overwhelming the beach and dockside din of waving pennants, chatter, a slight bay breeze, and Renee's frosty shoulder.

"Next up is the contest's penultimate contestant, from Fend Aerospace, the sponsor of the tournament. Vive les Fend Aerospace!"

Cheers and loud clapping drifted from the tents along the shoreline. At the forefront of the second, third, and fourth generation of bratty heirs in the aerospace industry, Max Fend was the tail wagging the dog, part of the new blood. A breed that enjoyed rubbing elbows, yachting, drinking, sometimes even clowning its way among the genius upstarts, the Musks, the Bransons, the Bezos types, making waves in the staid aerospace and automotive technology space. Inside Max's large VIP tent, he and his friends mixed with the crème de la crème of this year's film and tech community, film producers, directors, and actors, all comingling with other racing royalty to watch the final two runs of the competition.

"Eyes left, everyone. Three-time racing champ pilot Ronny Wright is now banking, ready for his approach to the track."

Air racing—an exotic pastime that ranked somewhere between polo pony tournaments and cricket on the sports pages—was back. A credit to Fend Aerospace's sponsorship, and to Max Fend personally, for its resurrection and its increase in popularity.

The aerial track was designed for high-speed, low-altitude racing, with the action directly in front of an in-person audience. Single-engine, propeller-driven aircraft built to withstand gravitational forces up to twelve Gs produced speeds up to 220 knots. The race "gates" and its chicane stretch were marked by eighty-foot-tall conical pylons, delicate enough to burst if hit by an aircraft but sturdy enough to handle adverse weather. A contestant's run consisted of one pass through the course in one direction, severe vertical and banking for the turnaround, then a return pass in the other direction, with a finish back at the starting gate. Not a wing-to-wing race; each plane instead raced against the clock, the course taking about a minute to run. Jet pilots, stunt pilots, pleasure pilots: all participants might well possess a death wish in addition to an addiction to the adrenalin rush the race provided. Air races could take the most adept pilots in the aeronautics industry and humble them, but it could also do worse: two deaths in as many years shuttered the more recent efforts at bringing the sport back. The prize money for the finishers with the best time net any penalty seconds was substantial, but it would make no difference among the teams' wealthy sponsors. They would turn it all over to their pilots and crew, the ones with their asses on the line.

The Fend plane, an MXS-R lookalike built and refined by Fend Aerospace, with a top speed of 225 knots and a roll rate of 420 degrees per second, buzzed the sparkling blue Cannes Bay, then entered the starting gate at the maximum allowed speed of 200 knots at about seventy-five feet in altitude, with exhaust smoke trailing as a requirement, all part of the spectacle. It slid in and out of the chicane pylons and zipped between the next four gates, then it climbed, banking right for its return run through the course and hitting all the gates at the correct angles. It slalomed through the chicane from the other direction and finished strong. Max had his stopwatch out and knew his plane had had an extraordinary run. He hugged a reluctant Renee, never able to stay pissed at him for long. They awaited the call of the official time from the control tower.

"Sixty-two-point-seventeen seconds and no penalties. The new leader of the race... Ronny Wright of the Fend Aerospace Racing Team!"

High fives ricocheted around the tent among Fend supporters, Max exuberant, Renee a reluctant participant. The run bettered by a full second the prior leader on the board. Max eyed a long table and the many bottles of champagne selected by the Fend family's sommelier from his visit to France's champagne country. Soon, after one more contestant was out of the way, there would be popped corks everywhere. Celebrating their plane's fantastic run petered out when the French public service announcer tap-tap-tapped the microphone to get the audience's attention.

"The last run of the day—our final contestant—is now in the air, mes amis.

Let us give a warm bienvenue to our friends in the United Arab Emirates and their racing team entry."

The speed plane zoomed by the beach in a low pass, rocking its wings through its dramatic entrance. The flyby was a crowd pleaser, the audience cheering in its wake then following its path skyward, the plane gaining altitude and banking wide, ready for its approach to the start gate.

Max's face went slack, his confidence taking a hit. "Oh-oh," he managed.

He pulled out his stopwatch. Whoever this pilot was, he was about to give the course an exceptionally good shake.

The aircraft hit the starting gate pylons and began crushing the course, the demeanor within Max's VIP tent immediately changing. Max clicked his stopwatch; the plane's times bettered the Fend entry at each passed gate.

"Who is this guy, Max?" Renee asked. "He's kicking our butts."

The Emirates team finished the run a full second better than the rest of the field, with no penalties, the Fend team settling for second place.

"Still extremely proud of you guys," Max said to his team members, a brave smile propping him up. "And what the hell, we'll pop open this champagne anyway. When in France, do as the Romans do, or however the saying goes." He uncorked a bottle and began filling glasses.

"Renee." Max handed the first flute to her, a twinkle in his eye. "Honey. I've been a rather rude boy lately. Please accept this as an apology."

"Grrr," she said. She reluctantly smiled and sipped.

Max had a Fend team member gather up two bottles of champagne and find bows for them. He wanted them delivered to whichever tent contained the Emirates racing team.

"And now," he said, "a toast to my team. What a great exhibition and race, folks. You guys were awesome. We'll need to check that last plane for steroids." Laughter. "Or to see if the propeller's governor was legal…" Ha-ha. "And let's save a bottle of champagne for our pilot Ronny Wright," he said, pointing at a steward. "Ronny was outstanding. I promise you we'll get you guys together again. Soon as we can set the next race up. In the mean-time"—he scooted closer to Renee, put his arm around her waist to give her an intimate smile and a gentle tug—"Renee and I would like to invite you all to my canoe this afternoon for some beer and additional celebrating. Right, Renee?"

Renee brushed his cheek with her lips, then turned to the small crowd. "You should take him up on it, people, it will be a good time. You guys know which canoe Max is talking about?"

Their team's buzz-cut crew chief answered, his voice raised. "You mean that big-honking-ass sailing yacht moored with all those other big-honking-ass yachts at the end of the bay?" Ha-ha. "The yellow one named *Fend's Bender*? Yeah, we know the one. Thanks, boss, and thanks, Renee, we'll be there."

~

Early evening, the beer and the barbecue on Max's yacht having been consumed to their fullest, Max and Renee were back on the beach near the Bay of Cannes. They reached a large party tent the size of a circus big top. Cannes' huge, official, post-air race tent shared almost the same footprint as all the individual VIP tents from the afternoon combined, and was filled to the seams with high-profile guests, local dignitaries, and personalities *très chic*. Casual atmosphere, stylish dress, warm weather, and a boisterous crowd, everyone in the mood to party. Max led Renee along the outer edge of the tent, his hand on her elbow, Renee more attentive to her phone than where they were going.

"Here's something interesting, Max," she said, absorbing a chart on her screen.

"Uh-huh." Max's personal radar swept the crowd, navigating the two of them around people, some celebrities he thought he recognized, all jammed against an open bar. A-listers in TV and film, U.S. politicians on holiday, even a few air-race people still in their silk uniforms. "There can't be only one bar in this tent, can there...?" he said, thinking aloud.

"Get this, Max. The pilot for the Emirates racing crew—today's winning plane—was a woman. Wow. Good for you, *ma soeur*."

They stopped at another tangle of people in front of a second portable bar, a swarm of raised hands all empty of alcohol inching their way to the bartenders, an additional stream of them with hands filled with mixed drinks, wine, and beer on their way back out.

A man and his thirst could not be denied. Max waded in, Renee attached to him with Max's hand around her wrist, she cooperating without complaint, preoccupied by her phone.

"Listen to this, Max. The UAE team brought the pilot in at the last minute. Ever hear of a Camille Gagneux?"

"No." He raised his hand to get a bartender's attention. "Sounds French. You know her maybe?"

"My *Québécoisin* home and France are eight hours and an ocean apart. No, I don't know her. It says here she's an aerobatic pilot. She's also former French military. Wow, she's competed in at least fifteen of these races. I'm looking at her racing résumé..."

"Uh-huh..." Max half-listening to Renee's news, was scanning the room, a hazard both of his training as a DIA intelligence operative and as a moon-dogger. He glanced over her shoulder at the info on her phone's screen, grunted an agreement, then handed her a flute of champagne. He took a healthy gulp from a beer bottle, then continued his visual sweep.

Someone nearing the tent held his attention. Tall man, tan skin, dark hair, Middle Eastern. A large group of people surrounded him, and in his wake were more of the same. Max chin-pointed at the group for Renee's benefit.

"That guy over there—the one in the flight suit—is he wearing the same insignia as the Emirates race team?"

A horizontal tricolor of green, white, and black alongside a vertical red bar on the hoist side; the patch sewn above a breast pocket displayed what Max knew to be the Emirates' ensign.

"Looks like it," Renee said. "Seems like a popular guy."

The large troupe pulled up short at the edge of the tent. The man in the flight suit scanned the tent crowd, gave short hello waves to a few people, then scanned the interior of the tent until he settled on eye contact with Max. An older man in traditional loose-fitting, white Islamic robing whispered into Mr. Tall, Dark, and Middle Eastern's ear. He acknowledged the input, then smiled in Max's direction. Max read a lot into that smile. Its gist was *Hello, nice to meet you, Mister Man of Common Noble Origin. We shall catch up with each other shortly.*

Max returned the smile and nodded. "Check it out, Renee. That's the Crown Prince of Dubai. No one from the royal family was supposed to attend the race. How about that..."

Renee moved in closer to Max, pouncing on his distraction. She spoke lightly into his ear. "Interesting, yes. But Max, about what we were discussing after the barbecue today—you know, when we were alone—"

"Uh-huh..."

"About our future..."

The Crown Prince was on his way through the tent crowd. Max soon realized the prince was on his way to see him, Renee still talking into his ear.

The prince arrived, wide smile, great teeth, tightly trimmed beard, bodyguards at each elbow, other Muslim-dressed males in tow. He was in his late thirties, if Max's memory served him. A good-looking guy. He made no attempt to greet Max yet, out of respect to the conversation that Renee was having with him.

Renee wrapped up her pitch. "... I'll have to think about your, um, suggestion, Max dear. But you and I with four kids? You know what that would do to this body..."

Max finally turned to her, out of sorts. "Wait. You what? Four what?"

She pinched his arm. "Next time pay attention so I don't embarrass you. Now stop being rude and let this nice gentleman introduce himself to you, then you can introduce me."

The Crown Prince nodded. "Thank you, mademoiselle. Max Fend, I am Sheikh Khalil Bin Saeed Al Abbar, but my friends call me Ja-*seem*, spelled J-A-S-E-M. This is my uncle, Sheikh Saeed Bin Rashid Al Abbar." Jasem spoke to Max and Renee simultaneously, with only a slight deference to Max. He remedied the deference with a shake of Renee's hand first, before he shook anyone else's, which she was delighted to accept, then came a turn to Max for a heartier handshake.

"So, Max Fend," Jasem said, "son of the esteemed Charles Fend. It is my distinct pleasure to meet you."

During negotiations for the race, the Emirati reps had been adamant with Fend Aerospace that none of the royals would attend. Surprise.

Max heard "*Sheikh*" and the extended name that followed, was busy doing the math in his head. Jasem had multiple bodyguards and an entourage of beautiful people including some very attractive women, plus a noble-sounding name. Charming, charismatic, His Royal Highness came across as easygoing and comfortable among the masses, plus he was friendly toward Renee. Far from a given was his willingness to shake Renee's hand, considering his cultural background as a Middle Eastern male, and yet he had. It was something the sheikh's older uncle didn't do.

"Nice to meet you"—Max would err on the safe side—"Your Highness."

"Jasem. Call me Jasem. My social media persona. I have a lot of Instagram friends out there who know me as Jasem, but only a few of them ever get close enough to me to use the name in person, for security reasons, of course. I'm hoping to be able to count you among my in-person friends, Max Fend."

"I'm flattered, Jasem. Thank you."

"You're welcome. And let me introduce you to the hero of the day. Or I suppose I should say heroine..."

Jasem turned, opened one arm wide enough to gather in it someone from behind him while not quite making the embrace physical. Immediately a male paparazzi pushed up front, iPhone in hand, and snapped a picture of Jasem and the woman, the photo at a compromising angle. The paparazzi abruptly turned to leave and got about three feet before one of Jasem's bodyguards tackled him, slammed his face into the brown asphalt, and relieved the man of his phone. The bodyguard led him out of the tent with the paparazzi's arm bent at an odd angle, him screaming in pain. Max was familiar with the drill from his own experience, the bodyguard perhaps intending to walk him off a nearby pier, into the bay. A replacement bodyguard appeared immediately at Jasem's elbow. Max could tell now that several of the males following him were part of a security detail. At closer inspection, enough of his entourage appeared to be muscle, not hangers-on.

"Ah, Jasem, you're not going to actually toss him—"

"No, no, of course not, just scare him enough so that he perhaps soils his pants. This is a common occurrence for me, unfortunately, with many of my countrymen trying to associate me romantically with non-Muslim women all the time. Mademoiselle Gagneux here is, of course, French, and an attractive French woman at that, but we are not a thing. The UAE tabloids would have had so much fun with that..."

Short stature, auburn hair swept to one side, and pretty, she was dressed in tight capri pants, a form-fitting but untucked blouse, and spiked heels. Aviator sunglasses. Not in a flight uniform, her outfit showed off a toned, athletic physique, just not stunningly gorgeous.

"Please meet Camille Gagneux, our pilot. Not a casual pilot like you and I are, Max. She is the shining star of our racing team, and I'm sure you will agree hers was the most incredible performance in your wonderful aerobatic race today. Kudos again, Camille. Camille, this is Max Fend and Renee LeFrancois, both pilots like me..."

"Everyone's a pilot," Max said. "Doctor, doctor, doctor... *and* doctor." He was pleased at his movie reference but no one else seemed to get it. Renee rolled her eyes.

Intros finished, Max, Renee, Jasem, and Camille settled into airplane and cinema talk. Max accorded Renee's discussion items their due with smiles and comments but spent more time analyzing Ms. Gagneux. The race showed her skills as a gifted air pilot, and she seemed okay standing quietly and listening, a thin smile on her face, often in the direction of Jasem. His first impression: a tough cookie who'd experienced a lot in life already; strong; confident, and had learned to survive in the male-dominated aerospace industry.

If Jasem and Camille were a couple—something Jasem and his PR team had to regularly deny—Max couldn't see it. Jasem, as a royal, could have anyone he wanted, and the private jets and yachts of the Emirati royals were no doubt stocked with the most beautiful women that money could attract. Still, to protect his brand, his reputation, his path to the monarchy, he couldn't be seen sharing any intimacy with a non-Muslim Caucasian.

They moved outside the tent, bringing their conversations with them, the evening sun over their shoulders, setting just above the coastline. Exotic oceanside performers on the promenade—sword swallowers, jugglers, snake charmers—reinforced the film festival's indulgent, eccentric, almost sideshow atmosphere. Max and Jasem's talk moved to aircraft—aerospace, military, experimental, pleasure. Renee and Camille trailed them, speaking more casually, Renee fascinated with Camille's aerial accomplishments, gushing a little, Camille a good sport about it. Renee took the conversation deeper, the two already on a first-name basis, pressing Camille.

"Your time in the air, Camille, piloting a fighter jet—what's it like for someone of your... stature?" Renee had her pegged for around five-two in height, one-twenty in weight. An athletic physique, but in no way imposing. The G-forces in jets could be debilitating, or so Renee had heard.

"Ah. *Tres bien*, not a gender question, a size question." Her English was perfect. "I have piloted armed jets weighing more than sixty thousand pounds, plus petite racing aircraft with only three to four thousand pounds displacement." She raised her head. An early moon hung soft and weak in the evening sky, the sun not fully set. She removed her sunglasses, found space in her capris pocket for them. "The G-forces can be formidable based on the maneuvers an aircraft makes regardless of the plane's size. They are manageable, without blackouts and headaches, or temporary loss of vision, only if the G-suits and headgear are up to the task. But so, too, must be the pilot. Good conditioning, no alcohol, good general health. But *mon Dieu*, I am boring you with G-forces talk, am I not, *mon amie?*"

A sensitivity here, a slight chip on her shoulder. Renee picked up on it, Max, too, but he was otherwise engaged. The message: *Do not ask if a smaller person can do the job, or worse yet, if a smaller woman can do the job. Give me the right gear and get out of my way.*

Max had found a kindred spirit in Jasem at Cannes; perhaps Renee had, too.

"*Mais non*, Camille, of course not. *Vous prêchez à la chorale.*"

Camille studied Renee. "Let me mention this here, for the record, Renee. His Highness the Crown Prince has been the perfect gentleman. We met at the last Red Bull air race, in Abu Dhabi. The condescension of the male pilots before that race, his own pilot included... it was shameful and stupid. The public dressing-down the prince gave his pilot was gratifying, and he did so even before I won the race. I believe that pilot is now teaching flying lessons to *les seniors.*"

They reached a section of the beach with games of chance and other distractions along the promenade. Max's personality sparked up. A shooting range with firearms, an archery range, even a gamehawking exhibition by a local falconry club, all temporary demonstrations that had sprung up as entertainment for the audience generated by the festival. They paused at the archery exhibit.

"Jasem. An idea." Max picked up a longbow, felt its heft, tested the bowstring's tightness. "But first, let me double-check. Have you ever shot apples off anyone's head?"

"Can't say that I have, Max."

"Me neither. Good. So—"

"I do, however, know my way around archery," Jasem said. He sipped from his champagne flute, gave a patronizing nod. "A hazard of being a royal. I've been trained in many exotic weapons, past and present. Uncle Saeed here has helped with this training."

The trailing sheikh uncle offered a head bow and a smile in Jasem's direction. The uncle's bodyguard remained stoic, a big guy but with an Omar Sharif face, angular and handsome.

"I see. Well, there goes my idea," Max said. "I was about to suggest we wager on a few arrows. It would have given me a chance to regain some respect after having been bettered by your air sprint team. Anyway—"

"To be specific, Max, I know the long bow, the recurve bow, and the barebow. What I know nothing about—" He used two hands to lift a weapon that had a bowstring, a stock wooden frame, a trigger, and a scope. "Is this. The crossbow."

"A compound crossbow," a large Frenchman, one of the exhibiters, offered in French-tinged English, a row of bows on the table between him and the prospective archers. "More of a twenty-first-century weapon. It operates on the rifle principle. A trigger means less effort on the part of the archer to keep the bowstring drawn and the bow steady."

Max lifted a second compound crossbow off the table and fell in love with it immediately. A magnificent weapon in appearance. He leaned in closer to Jasem, but not too close because, well, bodyguards.

"Five practice arrows, Jasem, after he shows us how to use it, then we give it a go, you and me. One arrow each. Closest to the bullseye wins. How about it?"

"And what would be the prize for the winner?" Jasem asked without hesitation.

Max sensed a thrill-seeker persona in Jasem. Or maybe it was the champagne, wine, and beer talking between them. He could see the two of them hanging out together far into the night, testing each other's limits, upping the antes, best two out of three, best three out of five, etcetera, with Max primed for competition while hoping there wasn't an alligator wrestling contest farther up the beach.

"The most valuable non-currency in the world. Bragging rights, Jasem."

Jasem's smile widened.

From behind them, Renee spoke up, dripping with snark and a mock check of her wrist, empty of a wristwatch. "Well, would you look at the time," she said. Her impatient, wary eyes narrowed at Max, who didn't budge.

"Okay then," she said. "You stay. Mademoiselle Gagneux, would you care to join me in a screening of a French entry to the film festival? It's playing at the Cinéma de la Plage, an open-air theater. I hear we'll also get to taste the local cuisine."

"*Mais oui*," Camille said.

"Max, you're not invited. While you two boys play with your bows and arrows, the mademoiselle and I are going to the movies where we'll also ply ourselves with food and alcohol. *Au revoir, messieurs.*"

~

Slow-boiling angst on the theater's outdoor screen, two hours of it, supplemented with trays of canapés and other hors d'oeuvres that Renee and Camille split between them, and only a few glasses of wine. They returned to the large party tent after the movie, food-satiated but still thirsty. The tent occupied a parking lot next to the beach and was raucous with a hundred people or more dancing, drinking, swaying, and yelling, the music loud, a French DJ playing American rock 'n' roll.

The first clue for Renee was the song blasting through the DJ's speakers: Kenny Loggins' "Danger Zone," an '80s classic worldwide, and the theme from the movie *Top Gun*.

"Oh no," Renee said to herself, wincing.

"*Pardon?*" Camille said.

"That song. I often hear it when Max has gotten very intoxicated." Renee sighed. "Men."

Camille shook her head. "They are not men. They are aviators… boys in adult bodies."

Mixed throughout the crowd were people in their colorful flight suits, the colors of today's air race teams. How many of each team's crew members were there was difficult to tell, but most of the air race teams were represented, including Fend Aerospace and the Emiratis. A middle strip of the big top tent's floor was empty of people, a lane cleared from end to end, the width of the path enough for a car to negotiate or, worse yet, a small plane to land. On the floor were orange miniature pylons inside a straight path that mimicked today's racecourse gates.

"This isn't good," Renee said under her breath.

Max did crazy things, sometimes full-moon crazy, when prompted by this song and alcohol. Renee's eyes searched the tent's rafters. Earlier in the afternoon in true avant-garde fashion, the tent had had circus performers on high—gymnasts on hanging ropes, trapeze aerialists, tightrope walkers, a unicyclist on a wire—all in the name of film festival fun. At this hour the professional performers were gone but their hanging apparatuses were not. A zipline trailed from the highest rafter and ran the length of the tent and beyond, ending in a sand dune fronting a hotel pool filled with partiers. Drunk men in flight suits stood, more like swayed, in a queue at the bottom of a tent pole, the young pilots waiting their turn to climb twenty-five feet to a small platform surrounding the pole, Renee confirming that Max wasn't one of them. She squinted, eyed each wobbly man in line at ground level, found Jasem at the head of the line but not in it, acting like a chaperone or coach. She pointed him out to Camille and the two of them began excusing their way through the crowd, heading in Jasem's direction.

They got closer. Renee raised her eyes to focus on the platform in the rafters, or rather who was on it. A man wearing a Fend Aerospace flight suit teetered there, his arm wrapped around the pole.

The crowd started a chant. "Fend, Fend, Fend…!"

"Shit," Renee said, her jaw clenching. "Max, you moron," came out more in resignation than chastisement.

The zipline was crude, a trapeze bar hanging below a pulley, a hundred or so feet of straight cable with the angle just enough to let gravity do its thing after a short push-off from the platform. Some of the pylons that were arranged as gates along its path, Renee now realized, were made of stacked plastic flutes and desserts in plastic dishes, and table flower center-pieces left over from the day caterers. At the end of the line a short flagpole rose out of a sand patch outside the tent, inserted loosely in a dune, the Festival De Cannes blue and white pennant attached to the pole and waving under the lights in the late-night breeze. Beyond the dune, a swimming pool.

"Max!" Jasem called through a bullhorn, his smile broad. "As our first contestant of the evening, are—you—ready?"

Max gave a wobbly thumbs up.

Renee stopped excusing her way through the crowd, began shoving her way through, Camille behind her somewhere. The *Top Gun* music was loud, in a loop, the refrain's lyrics whipping the crowd into a frenzy of hoots and hollers.

"Remember," Jasem called to Max, "you must avoid the pylons, then catch the flagpole with your knees or your thighs. It will bring you great joy and kudos as a true competitor. But a slight miscalculation," he said, snickering, "could bring you great pain and embarrassment, and the need for two bags of ice in a sensitive area..."

Guffaws from the crowd. Renee reached the front of the line of drunks at the bottom of the tent pole, her eyes ablaze. "Max! Get down, damn it, you're going to kill yourself up there."

"Renee! You're back. Wonderful. You will be a witness to my triumph and glory—"

"Get down *now*, Max!"

He hesitated, entertaining her demand, a shred of sobriety second-guessing the stunt, the noise quieting, the crowd wary of their exchange. One voice, anonymous, clearly male, clearly intoxicated, came from the back of the line and was heard above the remaining din.

"*Chicken.*"

The chant started. "*Chicken. Chicken-chicken-chicken,*" with "*bawk-bawk, ba-gawk,*" clucking and additional taunts rising up, bettering the DJ music.

Jasem raised his arms. "Enough," he said through the bullhorn, the crowd quieting. "Our contestant is clearly having second thoughts about this game of skill, this... test of his, um, bravery—"

"And his manhood!" came another anonymous call.

"Ha! So let me do this," Jasem said. "My dear new friend Max. If you capture the flag, I will extend to you, and Fend Aerospace, an invitation to *another* air race. This one is very exclusive. A chance for redemption after today's defeat. All arrangements will be handled by Emirati royalty, all expenses paid. A white-glove event of decadent proportions. We've just had an opening. What say you, Max Fend? Are you up to this task?"

Renee lost her composure, glared at Jasem. She closed her hand, readying her knuckles for a clean right to his chin; she was going to straighten this man's royal ass out. She leaned her shoulder into the punch but never got to extend her arm, her hand lost inside the massive paw of a bodyguard. He relaxed his grip after he moved between her and the prince and shook his head *No, dear lady*, this was not going to happen, blocking her access.

Above them, an oblivious Max responded, to Renee, not Jasem.

"Renee, my love, I have been challenged... by a prince!" His voice was raised, his speech sloppy, but he sounded dramatic and sincere. "Jasem questions my bravery, and the honor of Team Fend. It's an offer at redemption. Jasem! Good sir!" he called.

"Yes, Max?"

Max cleared his throat, raised his hand with flair. "On behalf of Team Fend, good Prince, I accept your challenge!"

The tent crowd roared and clapped and chuckled. Max gripped the trapeze in both hands, ignoring Renee's protests. He shoved off from the platform, his legs dangling. The zipline dipped from his weight, Max swaying left then right then clearing the first pylon gate, two bookended stacks of cubed Jell-O shots above stacked plastic chairs, no contact with the gate, no damage. The second gate was two adjacent towers of crème brûlée dessert cups, with less separation between them than the Jell-O stacks, and lower to the ground. Max's body swiveled but he held on, took out one of the dessert towers buttocks-first, which sent him into another spin into the third gate, the champagne-filled flutes, lower yet and even closer together, with both flute stacks jettisoning into the crowd. Still on the trapeze, still on the move, still spinning, he slammed crotch first into the film festival pennant, uprooting the flagpole. When he hit the sand he lost his grip on the sliding trapeze and flipped over the dune, into the swimming pool.

Two of Jasem's bodyguards leaped into the water. Max's head broke the surface, the two men helping him to the pool's edge where he made a point of showing, rather crudely, that he was astride the flagpole as he staggered up the steps under his own power. The tent crowd roared its approval.

A delighted Jasem was there to congratulate him. Max climbed the last step, the pole discarded. "Quite a performance, Max. You, sir, are a hit."

"Jasem, my good man," Max said, the water sobering him, "I do believe you owe me entry into your esteemed air race. What say you?"

"I believe I do, Mister Max Fend. Welcome aboard."

Renee arrived, her face pinched into a fist, her eyes laser-focused on catching up with a grinning, clueless Max poolside, soaking wet in his Fend flight suit. She elbowed past Jasem so she could get up into Max's face.

"Renee honey, see, I, ah—"

She shoved Max back into the pool. "Save it, Max honey, you're flying solo tonight."

3

____

The deck below Max rocked, the low wake of a yacht navigating the inlet passing beneath it. The sound of the waves lapping against the dock awakened him.

A kaleidoscope of images from the previous evening flashed through his mind. What time was it, where was he, why did his head hurt so much, is there a bucket, did he already use it, where's Renee, oh my, was he really that crazy last night...

Cannes. He was still in Cannes, docked in an inlet in the Bay of Cannes, in his own sailboat, more correctly, his Concorde yacht, a sloop. Max moved out from under the pillow but wouldn't open his eyes because he felt the heat of the sun on his face, and that meant it would be blinding to a person with a common hangover and excruciating to someone with a hangover of this magnitude, and why were all these thoughts stringing together like this, they needed to stop, oh God, where's that bucket...

Then a noise next to his bed made it all stop, a jolt to his beleaguered senses. A footstep. It wouldn't be Renee, she'd ditched him last night, and with good cause, but had she come back to the boat? Could it be his deck crew, they had the night off...?

A hard squeeze to his eyes closed them tighter to clear his senses before he moved another muscle. He needed to open them, swivel, and assess the danger—

"Max," came a male voice. "Relax. It's Wilkes. Get back to your hangover."

A squint through the blur, to focus.

Wilkes. Specifically, the ever-business-suited Caleb Wilkes, his CIA handler. At least his suit wasn't dark, was instead tan, showing some fashion sense in deference to the locale and the season. Max was bare-chested but still pantsed, and still with his deck shoes on.

"You need to quit these surprise entrances, Wilkes," Max said, rolling over in his bed, then trying to raise his head, feeling like it was full of bricks. The sun was over Wilkes's shoulder, so bright, *ouch*, Wilkes sitting across from him in an armchair. "Why are you here?"

"Here, take this." Wilkes retrieved two mugs from a fold-down table next to the latrine, handed one to Max. "Tell me what the hell went down last night after the air race. I heard you behaved boorishly."

"*Boorishly*? Seriously, Wilkes, listen to yourself. You looking to join the jet set, since you can't seem to beat it?" Max sipped at the cup, grimaced. "What the hell am I drinking?"

"Bouillon. Best thing for a hangover." Wilkes tossed a single-dose pill packet at him. "And Tylenol."

Max tore open the packet. "And you are drinking...?"

"Coffee."

Max dry-swallowed one of the pills, stomached another sip of the bouillon. "It was all that prince's fault."

"The Crown Prince of Dubai."

Max eyed Wilkes with new interest. "Yes. I need to apologize to Renee." He shook his head. "I'm telling you it wasn't all my fault. That prince... he was pressing my buttons all night."

"How so?"

"Subtle conversational implications. Better pilot, better marksman, better archer, better alligator wrestler... wait, that one didn't happen... but his team did beat Fend Aerospace in my air race."

"Kicked your butt, right?"

Wilkes. Always up to date.

"We lost by a full second." Max frowned, trying to remember a conversation from the night before. "I think I might have agreed to participate in another race. Something he's sponsoring. It's all so fuzzy..."

Wilkes let him ramble.

"... so I'll need to take care of that today, need to catch up with the guy. Renee says he's got a million social media followers. I'll tell him, gracefully as I can, that it was all a mistake. Hopefully I won't look like an ass."

Wilkes shook his head. "Too late to worry about that."

"Yeah, well, I wasn't looking for your feedback, Wilkes."

Wilkes's smile faded. "About the prince's race, Max. We need you to do it."

"I'm sorry? Say again?"

Wilkes was dead serious. "Fend Aerospace needs to be in that race."

"Why does the U.S. government care?"

"He's the Crown Prince, Max. He'll be the King of Dubai someday. He stands to inherit a lot of power and influence in the region." Wilkes leaned in closer to reinforce a point. "You familiar with the Abraham Accords? The Middle Eastern peace treaty signed in 2020?"

"Vaguely."

"The U.S. was a witness to those declarations, helped foster them, and was plenty happy about them. Also plenty happy about what the Crown Prince did to shepherd them through, especially the normalization agreements between Israel and the UAE, and between Israel and Bahrain. But there's more to them..."

Max's head was throbbing like someone had taken a chisel to it. The bouillon and migraine pill hadn't done enough to ease him out of the hangover, but now, his stomach... "Sorry, Wilkes, I need to—"

Max stumble-rushed the latrine, closed the door, first found the sink for his stomach, then the commode for his lower half. The day-after joy of excessive alcohol consumption. Wilkes paused his lecture, Max not having a good time of it on his side of the latrine door.

Wilkes started up again, the door still closed between them. "You ever hear me talk about someone called Nomad?"

Max focused. Nomad was a ghost who operated both inside and outside the espionage realm. A mercenary contractor, a zephyr, never fully materializing, but wherever the agency could trace him, he was always deadly. Once Wilkes began this briefing, Max knew he was officially back on the CIA clock.

"Refresh my memory," Max said, still seated in the latrine.

"A dangerous, powerful assassin. Responsible for a lot of high-profile killings. There are no good photos of him, but plenty of his work. Some of his kills were really gruesome stuff that showed he's as crazy-good with a knife as he is with firearms. Intel agencies, the Colombian and Mexican cartels, large corporations. No allegiances, doesn't care who he kills. Prolific, successful, anonymous. A big-money contract killer. And..."

Max stood at the latrine sink, cupping cold water to his face, his blood-shot eyes greeting him in the mirror. Shirtless, his six-pack was still there but it was losing definition, blurred, he knew, by too much partying. For now, he'd succeeded in expelling from his body, fore and aft, what he could of the alcohol demons that entered it last night. He could go for a quart of orange juice if the galley had any. And he needed more headache meds, considering he'd puked up most of his stomach contents.

"... we think he took out an operative's agent on France's west coast just before you arrived in Cannes. A long-range shot of some kind. We don't know how he pulled it off. Either an extremely competent sniper or an extremely sophisticated gun or both. Interpol investigators are looking into it. We'll have more soon."

"Got it. Nomad. Bad guy."

"Problem is, your friend Crown Prince Jasem's been talking with him, Max. Jasem's going to inherit the kingdom someday, but word has it he's been a little erratic lately. Uncle Sam doesn't want this young prince screwing up any peace deals in the Middle East, even the ones he negotiated himself. The CIA needs to find out what he's up to with Nomad."

Max pulled open the latrine door and stepped out, more focused now. He found a chair and dropped into it. "And you know all this how?"

Wilkes pointed at a pint carton of OJ and another package of Tylenol on the pull-down table. Max didn't ask, didn't argue, didn't want to hear Wilkes recite the Boy Scout motto to him, would simply accept the nicety. Wilkes spoke while Max helped himself, gulping down the juice.

"Some chatter across the agencies out there. If Nomad's involved, it's usually for one reason only. The questions are who is the target and where and when will it go down? And if there's an assassination in play, it will probably be in spectacular fashion. Our intel has it that Jasem will deliver the details about the target in person to Nomad. We might only be chasing a what-if here, but we're thinking it's more of a who, when, and how. Flipside is we're also looking to neutralize Nomad. Forever. Hopefully all this goes down without causing a major international incident embarrassing the UAE or their royal family. Or the U.S., for that matter."

"Okay, okay," Max said, "but hold on. I see this as a poor use of resources, Wilkes, me in particular. I've got things to do, places to go, and a company I run with my father. Get your intel drones to surveil him. Easypeasy. And I'm having trouble thinking my new buddy Jasem is into what you say he's into. Hell, he's got like a billion social media folks out there following him. They think he's a real mover and a shaker and a genuinely good guy. What am I supposed to do, put a bell around his neck?"

Wilkes squinted at the mangled metaphor. "His followers know only what he wants them to know, Max. His social media accounts are great public relations, and they support his image as a progressive. Smart on his part, of course, but they're cosmetic and contrary to some of the things we're hearing. That's why we need you. Those other CIA assets—they *are* gathering intel, but it's not nuanced enough, and definitely not specific enough. No known meeting location, unknown target, invisible contractor. We don't know when or where Jasem and Nomad will meet. The only way to monitor Jasem effectively is shoe leather surveillance. Which brings me to his uncle. You also met him, right?"

"Traditional Muslim wear, not a modern guy like Jasem, older. Stuffy, but he seemed nice enough. His bodyguard looks like Omar Sharif. Great mustache."

"Maybe he's nice, maybe he's not. You'll need to pay attention to when the uncle is around. He's an advisor to the prince, and he's one of Jasem's dad's—the king's—brothers. He had eyes on the throne but finished second in the running for the Crown Prince title. Point is, he and Jasem together make a powerful team. That would be something to look for. When they're together."

Max drank the rest of the pint of OJ, then crushed the waxed carton in one hand, beer-can macho-like, for Wilkes's benefit. "So that's it? We watch Jasem? Watch him and his uncle together, see if they dance around the campfire at midnight after his air race?"

Wilkes sent a text while he was still talking. "The prize here isn't the uncle. Jasem will talk more with Nomad, we think meet with him, too, somewhere between here and Dubai. It will happen during the air race he's sponsoring, during one of the legs."

"You lost me. Legs? What legs?"

"The air race. It's transcontinental."

"It's just a flight around some pylons," Max said. "Transcontinental would mean days. I don't think so."

Wilkes shook his head, smiled. "You have no idea what you agreed to, do you?" He tossed Max a tan manila envelope, unclasped. "Here. This arrived on your deck this morning. From the Crown Prince."

"So you're opening my mail now."

"The race will be underway in forty-eight hours and take about a week. You've got some work to do, Max. It looks like it will be quite a production."

Max removed the contents. A few pages of instructions in English and other languages, timetables, pictures of aircraft, and brochures. "This is out of control. Renee will lose it, me gone for this long."

"Read the fine print. Not now, later. And no, she hasn't seen this. She knows nothing about any of it. You'll need to do more than talk with her, considering her... history. Be gentle, but be firm. So. Here's what we know." Wilkes dropped a yellow legal pad onto the table. "I'm going to draw it for you. We have intelligence saying Nomad will communicate with Jasem via short-range, line-of-sight encrypted comms somewhere along the flight route, we think between Rome and Egypt, we just don't know where."

The only way the CIA would be able to intercept the message—Wilkes drew a cone rising up and spreading out from a single point on a line representing the ground, where the contact attempt would originate—would be to have someone fly over the same ground location as Jasem around the same time. Now Max understood why they needed him.

"Jasem flies through this area." Wilkes drew an *x* inside the cone. "You fly through the area behind him." A second *x* signified Max's plane. "When the message is transmitted with both planes in the cone, we—meaning you

—intercept it. We expect it will be encrypted, but our guys are confident either they or the NSA can break the encryption."

Concentrating on Wilkes's chicken-scratch Sharpie drawing between them, his headache came roaring back. He rubbed his eyes, the painful pinpricks forcing him to shut them. "You guys, ah, figured all this out between yesterday and today? I'm supposed to buy that?"

"About that. No. In motion longer than that. The original plan was to work with the other U.S. team in the race, of course, but they're out. Food poisoning, or a crazy bug they picked up. The pilots, some of the crew, they all got it. You, on the other hand"—Wilkes threw some metaphorical salt in Max's wounds while Max rubbed his temple—"are suffering from self-inflicted abuse of a more temporary nature, so you're up."

A long-range air race. Multiple days of flying, and now spy work on top of it. Max's lurching stomach and pounding head begged him to find an alternative.

"Why can't you just hide something inside Jasem's plane? A listening device. A bug with a transmitter?"

"Nice try. The prince's guys are on top of that. They already sweep his personal planes looking for rogue electronic surveillance. We can't take the chance they won't do the same with all the planes in the race. Nope, better that we bug *you*. Something on your person. A dual-purpose device. It will sweep the airwaves looking for this hot spot and will let you know when it picks up the signal."

"And this device is... what? Designed to look like something else, right?"

"An earbud. More specifically, an AirPod."

Max nodded his approval. "Sweet. But wait. Will it need to be in my ear the whole time?"

"We'll work on narrowing the window. My guess, no."

"That would be good. How much of a range will it have?"

"Ah. You have arrived at the finesse part of the operation. Something that would be a challenge for any less of a pilot, but for you, Max Fend, aerospace wunderkind, not so much."

"Cut the patronizing, Wilkes, my hangover can't tolerate it. Net this out for me please. What's the range, and why does Nomad need to communicate this way?"

Wilkes launched into it. The short-range encrypted burst transmission would come from a remote area, great pains taken by Nomad to keep it from being intercepted, plus to keep his location unknown. Nomad's communication M.O. per Langley. It would also protect Jasem as its anonymous recipient, the expectation that he wouldn't know when and where to expect it either, other than it was on this flight route. For Jasem, here would be anonymity plus plausible deniability as the person commissioning Nomad.

"So the device will give you a heads-up by way of a beep or a pulse," Wilkes said, "to let you know the ground level transmitter is operating. Set it on beep if it's in your ear, and pulse elsewhere, somewhere you can feel it, like your pocket. Same as your phone."

"Why not have it be a phone, then?"

"Phones need Wi-Fi. Do the planes have Wi-Fi?"

"Don't know yet."

"Hence the AirPods. You'll have maybe five minutes to close the gap after the signal starts, to catch up to Jasem's plane. You'll need to get within a mile of him while he closes in on the origin, too, before the communication transmits and the device can intercept it."

"It's a goddamn race, Wilkes," Max said, his patience waning. "What sort of magic will I need to catch up to him? We'll both be flying with our throttle near red-line. You've seen *Star Trek*, right? Scottie can only give so much power..."

"Not for me to say. Check out the weather, the winds, maybe test the lower versus higher limits of your altitude, you figure it out. A chance to impress the hell out of Renee, right?"

As if on cue, the stateroom door opened. A breakfast tray entered, Renee behind it, she in running clothes.

"Good morning, cupcake," she said. "Wilkes texted me while I was on my run and said you need more hangover remediation. Wow, that's an understatement. You look like what the dog threw up."

"Renee. Honey. So where did you—"

"A different stateroom. Your yacht sleeps ten, remember?" She lowered the tray to a table.

Max looked at the tray of food. "I can't eat this."

"You get the dry toast and the juice, honey, the rest is mine. And stop giving our guest a hard time. Wilkes didn't drink the whole bar last night, you did."

"So Max, sir, I believe you're up to speed now," Wilkes said.

"Yeah, well, thanks for nothing."

"You're welcome. I best be going."

But Wilkes's serious stare belied this welcome, sobering Max up a little more, and playing the next bit of business he expected from Max close to the vest, no hint that a certain romantic third party would need to be majorly finessed into agreeing to participate.

4

———

Max laid his request for forgiveness on thick, ate the dry toast, groveled more, sipped more orange juice, then administered a second round of eyedrops. Renee ate from the plate she brought herself—yogurt, eggs, bacon, and a cup of coffee—while she listened nonplussed to his multiple apologies. They were fifteen minutes into their breakfast together after Wilkes's exit.

"Watching you eat that isn't helping my hangover," Max said.

"Watching you last night," she said, swallowing, "I don't really care. What does Wilkes want?"

"In a minute. I'm getting a shower. Care to join me?"

"You're funny, Max Fend, really. You need a hazmat scrub. Plus, I've got some work to do. But tell me this. All that life-of-the-party BS with the sheik last night—did you get that out of your system? Are we going to have a few nice weeks together on the French Riviera, like you promised?"

"Sure. Yes. Absolutely."

Her eyes narrowed. "Why do you have that look?"

"It might need to be a different few weeks."

She put her knife and fork down, stared at him. "Damn it, Max—"

"Fend Aerospace is going to be part of that prince's air race. It's in a couple of days."

"No. Call it off. Tell the prince you were mistaken. Tell him the truth, you were too drunk and should have kept your mouth shut. You just sent your team home, Max. What are you going to do, fly them all back? They've been away from their families for weeks."

Another sheepish look from Max. "Yes, but…"

Renee's eyes narrowed. "What don't I know?"

"It's a different kind of race. The aircraft type, the other contestants, this won't be an aerobatic sprint around pylons, it has multiple legs. A few thousand miles, and the makeup of each plane's pilot crew will be different. The Fend aerobatic flight crew won't be a part of it. What we need is…" Max's eyes darted to Renee's, held fast.

"What? You need what? What's different about the flight crew for this?"

Max cleared his throat. "You know how you've wanted me to take you on more trips? Here's an opportunity for that. The flight crew—one person on the flight crew needs to be a woman, and you're going to be her."

Max filled her in. Jasem was into promoting gender equality at home, was looking for worldwide publicity for UAE, wanted to foster tourism, deemed himself a visionary, etc. Renee's expression changed from shock and anger to surprise and excitement.

"The other major stipulation," he said, "is the woman needs to be a full co-pilot. She'll need to do a lot of the flying and will handle a significant portion of the multiple legs."

"Wait, what? A woman actually sharing the flying?"

"Yeah, like how they do co-ed sports teams. Everyone gets a member of the fairer sex on their team. To make things even," Max said, grinning.

"To make things even," she repeated.

"Well, yes."

"You hear yourself, right? You know I can beat you at every sport ever invented."

"I'm quite aware, darling. They probably think they're being progressive. Give them a pass, okay? Think about the fun we'll have. You'd be flying the aircraft hundreds of miles at a time. You, plus me. Co-pilots."

"Max, look, this sounds like fun, but… *me*? I don't have that many flight hours. Are you sure…"

"Absolutely. This will give you plenty more."

Renee still looked skeptical.

"If not you, then I'd need to find another female co-pilot."

"Or quit the race."

"Too late. We can't do that."

"And why's that?" she said, indignant. Then she answered her own question. "That's why Wilkes was here."

Max nodded. "I wanted out, but Wilkes wants me in. Wants *us* in. Something's up."

"Damn it, Max Fend! No. Just… c'mon, Max, no…"

"The CIA's hearing rumors about the Crown Prince, that he's interested in contracting with a certain assassin. Why, how, where, when, they're a little light on the specifics. Including who the target might be."

Max paused, evaluating his girlfriend, clear to him that her interest was tinged more with disgust than eagerness.

"We come over here," Renee said, "looking to relax a few weeks, to enjoy each other…" She tossed her napkin onto her tray. "This isn't what I had in mind, Max."

He stayed on message, knowing the rest of it would make a difference. "Wilkes thinks they know who the prince wants to engage."

"I don't care. I'm disappointed."

"Renee, it's Nomad. They think he wants to contract with Nomad."

She frowned, squinted like she hadn't heard right. "Nomad," she repeated.

"Yes."

She gulped down whatever was in her mouth, stood, went to a porthole, blankly stared outside at nothing, chewed on her spit, then said, "I'm in."

"Hello-*o*? Mister Fend?"

Someone calling to him from dockside. A text had come from a person on Jasem's staff, and now this person and one other man stood astern of Max's sloop, at the end of a short gangplank. A strap lay on the speaker's right shoulder and reached across his chest to where a laptop bag rested on his left hip. He was otherwise dressed in traditional Islamic garb but no turban, and no other accessories. Trim gray-black beard, chubby cheeks, short stature, and older than his boss the prince by at least twenty years, he stood there at attention, waiting. A second man, bulky, in a business suit, stood next to him. A bodyguard. A limo was double-parked at the end of the dock.

"Jundiin, I assume?" Max called, then left the shade of a canopy and walked aft, toward his presumptive guest. Renee followed.

"Yes, at your service, Mister Fend," he said, waiting. "I am here with what you will need to know about the race, with some simple documents you will need to sign, and some trinkets. Permission for me and my associate to come aboard?"

"Granted."

Greetings and pleasantries aside—a handshake for Max, a head nod for Renee, the bodyguard ignored—Max led his guest to an outdoor table under the canopy.

"Jundiin. An interesting name. What does it mean?"

"Yes. It is my Instagram name," he said, his smile a bit forced. "I have carried it forward from my days in the Dubai military. It means 'soldier.' Our young sheikh has opened our eyes to the world of social media, as you know. I have entered it tentatively, reluctantly perhaps, but regardless, I am out there now, something he wants us to do. I have twelve thousand followers. Ha! Twelve thousand of my closest friends," he said, winking. "I suppose I should feel blessed. Let us talk about the race and your aircraft, Mister Fend and Mademoiselle LeFrancois. Let me fill you in..."

The race would begin in two days, starting at Cannes's Mandelieu Airport and terminating at Dubai's Al Maktoum International Airport.

"You are team number nine, Mister Fend, replacing the other U.S. team. They came down with a case of—"

"Food poisoning, as I understand."

"Yes. You are correct. They will not fully recover in time. You impressed His Royal Highness yesterday, you and Mademoiselle LeFrancois both. You will see from the brochure that each team will compete in the race in an FW50-RG aircraft. You are familiar with the plane?"

"Yes. Fleetwings Europe makes it. Never flew one; I own something comparable. The FW50's an excellent single-engine prop. A composite. Pricey."

"It is all relative, is it not, Mister Fend? The specs for all nine planes are identical. I have the title for yours here. The plane is here already, at the Mandelieu airport. It's been refueled and is ready for you to take for a spin. Please, you will need to sign here... and here..."

"Sign for what?"

"To accept transfer of ownership of the aircraft. You didn't know? The UAE—Jasem, actually—is providing all aircraft for the race, free of charge. That is, of course, only if you would like a free luxury airplane as a parting gift, Mister Fend, when the race is over."

"He bought nine airplanes? They're free to each team?" Max said, repeating the offer. A quick glance at Renee.

"Yes. No strings attached. Yours to keep after the race is over. If you don't want it, you can sign the ownership back to His Royal Highness and leave it in Dubai. Or wherever, depending on wherever the race ends for your team."

"*Wherever the race ends for your team*?" Renee repeated. "What does that mean?"

"I will get back to that," Jundiin said.

The paperwork, now in Max's hands, read as described. Two pages only, a few quick sentences including make, model, manufacturer, and a serial number, and the cost of $0.00 to the purchaser.

"My father would have a team of lawyers review this first," Max said. "I, on the other hand"—he signed the paper, returned it to Jundiin—"am a bit more seat of the pants opportunistic. Never look a gift airplane in the mouth, I always say."

"Thank you. Now, here's a release that you and Mademoiselle LeFrancois must sign allowing the event to be recorded live, then streamed later. The only modification to the original specs for the plane is a camera has been installed in the cockpit, with facial recognition software, plus full SATCOM connectivity with Wi-Fi hotspots. Streaming video from it will be uploaded after each flight for viewers in our country and around the world, wherever there's an interest. This is not negotiable. It is necessary to prove to the audience that the original participants who start the race finish the race."

"So no team brings in a secret ringer pilot partway through," Max said.

Renee bristled. "And it presupposes that your co-pilot selection," she said, her anxiety showing, "has the requisite flight experience. Ha."

"Renee, relax, honey, we've got this. Or we will, by end of day tomorrow."

"I am not familiar with the term 'ringer,'" Jundiin said, "but I can guess what it means. Yes, no swapping pilots at any of the stops to bring in more experienced flyers. Who you start the race with is who you must end with, or you will be disqualified. Now, about flight planning, travel logistics, and the maintenance of the aircraft during the race..."

All incidental arrangements would be handled by Jasem, the sponsor, by way of Jundiin's administrative team including a ground crew of maintenance professionals at each stop, to recertify the airworthiness of each plane overnight. Tighten rivets, kick the tires, engine spot-checks, refuel. Perform all safety protocols. They would have the plane ready to return to the sky by ten a.m. sharp next morning. One leg per day, all contestants flying to the same airports at the same destinations across three continents and terminating in western Asia in UAE, at the eastern end of the Arabian Peninsula.

"... and lodging. All flight crews will stay at the same hotel at each stop."

Jundiin's laptop was open, showing pictures. "Here are the accommodations. See, these hotels are quite comfortable. And here are the airport destinations, all within reach of the FW50's fuel tank capacity for each leg."

Renee's laptop was also open, a common occurrence when Max attended meetings with her, with Renee always multi-tasking, always on top of things even when it looked like she wasn't paying attention. "Jundiin. Send me the list of airports and the hotels, please," Renee said, "and a list of the other teams and their pilots. My email address is..."

"Certainly, Mademoiselle LeFrancois... There. Now, I will explain the actual race, and how it will work."

Staggered aircraft departure times twenty minutes apart. Short of an emergency, GPS usage would not be allowed, each team needing to rely on the navigational skills and cockpit decisions of the pilot and co-pilot, otherwise the GPS would make things too easy. Team eliminations would be at the end of each leg, one per destination based on clocked arrival times, all except for the first leg, where two teams would not advance. Wing-to-wing racing on the final leg only, when all but two racing teams would have been eliminated. The last leg would be a head-to-head start with the two planes next to each other on the runway. Touchdown would be on the destination tarmac in Dubai with a painted finish line bookended by electronic pylons, the winner being the first to cross.

"Mister Fend. Mademoiselle LeFrancois. Let me add this. Every other flight crew has been training for this for weeks. The race rules are inside this binder. Your navigational chart will need to be approved by the judges selected for the race. They are all pilots. Missing waypoints will add time to a leg. Learn the plane, pull together your flight plans, then rest up, the both of you. You have a long race ahead. Please do not overextend yourselves. This race is important to His Highness, to the Emirates, and to the region. We do not want anything untoward to happen to any of our contestants. We expect this to be a celebration of good sportsmanship, camaraderie, and goodwill between all the nations who participate. Finally, Mademoiselle LeFrancois, you have my contact information in the email, and Mister Fend, you also have it on your phone. And now, my associate and I must be going. *Au revoir*."

"Jundiin, wait," Max said. "First, let me thank you for your input and your guidance. You will be a good facilitator for the race."

"My pleasure, Mister Fend."

"Call me Max. Second..."

Max's grin turned tiny, sophomoric, but it was also expectant. "Renee sent me a text a moment ago. It's about your nickname. 'Jundiin' appears to carry a few different meanings."

"Yes, it does."

"Soldier, man of arms, knight, for example."

"Yes. I earned it when I was in the Emirati military many years ago."

"It also means 'batman.'"

Jundiin smiled. "Yes, Mister Fend—Max—it also means that."

"So you're Batman."

"Yes," he said. "Nothing to do with your American comic strip hero, of course, and everything to do with providing custom service as the personal assistant to His Highness, the Crown Prince. But yes, to verify," and with an impish grin that anticipated Max's pleasure, he said, playing along, "I'm Batman."

A second round of Cannes films were must-sees, according to Renee. "Let's go to the Palais des Festivals tonight, Max. Tarantino's latest is showing on the roof. I need to put a dress on after all this sun and sand and rid myself of all the 'dirt' swirling around us." Her reference to the intel dump from Wilkes. "Maybe see if we can rub elbows with some movie A-listers…"

Sure, Max would do what Renee wanted, but, "We've got so much to do for this race and no time as it is. I wanted to see our new plane tonight before we show up there tomorrow to train in it. Besides, didn't he lose the top director award, the, um…?"

"Tarantino? Yes, he didn't win Cannes's Palme d'Or."

"Lost to that subtitled Korean movie."

"So that's your play, Max? The movie didn't win? Finishing second makes the performance bad? That's not what you said yesterday to your racing team, remember? And one more thing: that dog in Tarantino's film, the pit bull, *he* won an award. Best canine performance in a film. The 'Palm Dog' award. A real thing. We're going to see it. Get yourself ready."

The Soixantième, a temporary theater, had sprung into existence on the roof of the Riviera section of the Palais des Festivals as a venue for special film screenings and Cannes classics. They went, they watched, and they waited for the last movie credit to scroll by before standing to leave, proper etiquette for Cannes film attendees. Max's phone buzzed with a text. He checked their surroundings after he read it, beyond a sea of heads all looking for the open-air theater's exits from the roof.

"A text from the Crown Prince. He's… back there," Max said, looking up, "near a potted plant. Him and his group. He wants to know if we can join him for drinks."

"One drink, that's it," Renee said. "Remember what's on our plate for tomorrow. And who we're surveilling."

"Sure, there's that. One drink only."

"We need to be careful with him, Max," Renee said, squeezing his hand. "The picture looks different now. A whole lot different."

"Yeah. Leave it to Wilkes to kill a budding friendship."

Jasem was gracious, charming, sheepish even, because of their shared poor behavior last night. "I am happy to see you in one piece, Max, my friend." Jasem gestured into the middle of a crowd behind him. "Camille!" he called. "Camille Gagneux! Can you come here, please?"

His female pilot friend left a conversation and was soon alongside. Five minutes later the four of them plus Jasem's troupe had swarmed the outside seating of a bar on the street, grabbing the high-top tables. Some conversation about the movie, some conversation about the movie's dog. Max mentioned Jundiin's visit to the yacht, then asked Jasem more about the race.

"... the route, the cities, the contestants. Give us a quick primer on what to expect."

"Very well. One day for each leg. The first leg will be Cannes to Rome, not quite five hundred miles. We'll stay at a wonderful hotel, I am friends with the owner. Two teams will be eliminated with that run, so that evening we'll throw a party for them both, whoever they turn out to be. Do your best to not be one of those teams, Max, otherwise the rest of the race will be a bore for me."

"You will not be rid of us that easily," Max said. "If we get knocked out of the race, we'll keep pace each day and finish it anyway. You'd just need to keep me from distracting you."

"Excellent," Jasem said. "Bravo. The second leg..."

Jasem went over the remaining stops. Rome to Athens, Athens to Cyprus, Cyprus to Cairo, then to the southern tip of Egypt's Sinai Peninsula for refueling only, not scheduled as an overnight stop. Sinai to Buraydah in Saudi Arabia, then Buraydah to Qatar, and finally Qatar to the race's terminus in Dubai.

"The longest leg will be Rome to Athens, almost seven hundred miles. The FW50s take seven hundred fifty gallons of jet fuel, so we'll all be good for that. The shortest leg will be the last one, a two-hundred-twenty-four-mile sprint from Qatar to Dubai, where we'll finish with a little ceremony, and my father the king will bestow prizes and an award. Local and world-wide news people will be there for the presentation. We'll follow it up with a large party, all race participants invited. Would you like to hear who comprises the teams?"

Max and Renee knew about them already, courtesy of Wilkes and validated during Jundiin's visit, but to hear Jasem gush about having assembled them was enjoyable. Hard for Max to see this man as a malcontent, or the enemy, listening to him describe his tenacity in pulling this race together. The prince had kind words for each country's flight crew and was ecstatic their governments had allowed them to participate. Adding to Jasem's Emirati team and Max and Renee's U.S. entry was a Greek team, the Saudis, the Swiss, the Pakistanis, the UK, and Qatar, plus one team Jasem was most excited about, the Israelis. Israel was the jewel of the race, the feather in his cap, considering the new normalization agreement between the two countries, with "... the race a wonderful manifestation of our steps forward together, fostering peace in the Middle East."

"A bravo to you as well, Jasem," Max said. "No small endeavor pulling that off."

"Thank you, Max. So now, I propose a toast, after which we will need to make our exits. To a safe, sane, and thrilling air race, Mister Fend, and Mesdemoiselles Gagneux and LeFrancois. To quote French pilot Antoine de Saint-Exupery: *'Je vole car cela libère mon esprit de la tyrannie des choses insignifiantes.'*"

Renee managed a smile and placed a hand over her heart. Camille grinned her appreciation.

Max didn't have to translate it in his head, he already knew the quote from his early days while learning to fly, heard from his father. "*I fly because it releases my mind from the tyranny of petty things.*"

5

The hired car took fifteen minutes from Max's yacht dockside in the Bay of Cannes to reach Mandelieu Airport at seven in the morning on a Sunday. They went through airport security and snagged a skycap cart ride to hangar seven. Jasem's assistant Jundiin met them inside the hangar.

"Good morning, Mister Fend, Mademoiselle LeFrancois. What a great day for flying. Your airplane is on the tarmac. Please, give it a close review, and then I will have you meet our maintenance crew." He gestured at a corner of the hangar, where twelve men in work uniforms stood at near attention. "These are the men who will travel ahead of each leg of the race and will await each team's arrival at the next stop. They'll work through the night to ensure airworthiness of all nine planes for the next day. When you are through doing a pre-flight check of your new plane, I can have them join you on the tarmac for a meet-and-greet."

Max gave a casual salute to the maintenance guys. On the flight line sat the newest addition to Max's stable of toys, a white Fleetwings Europe FW50-RG single engine airplane with gull-wing doors and an orange stripe running fore to aft, the upswept wingtips accented in the same orange. Forty-four-foot wingspan, thirty feet long, ten feet tall with its landing gear down. Sleek and sexy.

"I like the tail number," Max said. "Renee, our callsign ends with RJ. That works, right? Romeo and Juliet?"

"How romantic," Renee said, gazing at the plane's tail, unimpressed. She rattled off more of the specs with a quick read from the manufacturer's website. "A five-passenger personal aircraft. Retractable landing gear. Range, seven hundred fifty nautical miles at low air speed, reduced if running at higher speeds. Carbon fiber body. Parachuted aircraft failsafe installed for the plane itself, plus passenger parachutes. Full GPS and Traffic Collision Avoidance..."

Max grunted an interruption. "TCAS, too? Nice upgrade."

Renee resumed her read. "Jet fuel engine with three hundred horsepower at the top end, two-seventy maximum continuous horsepower. Turbo-charged. Fuel consumption, nine gallons per hour. Maximum takeoff mass, forty-four hundred pounds. Prices start at—" Her eyebrows tented. "My goodness. Never mind. Sorry, Jundiin. Rude of me to bring up price."

Jundiin spoke over his shoulder as they walked, unfazed. "It lists at one-point-two million U.S. dollars, Mademoiselle. However, having ordered nine of them, all identical to each other, even the colors..."

"So Jasem worked a quantity discount," Max said, "on a million-dollar product. Shrewd businessman."

"Yes, he is. But as he often does"—they arrived alongside the plane—"he allowed me to do the deal on his behalf. Suffice it to say that after some hard negotiations with people less visionary than His Royal Highness, it became a better deal. I present to you your transportation for the next ten days, Mister Fend. I will leave you and your co-pilot to your new acquisition. When you finish here and are through with the maintenance crew, you are free to give it a spin. I have taken it upon myself to clear it with the airport controllers that you will depart the airport and return to it twice, to give Mademoiselle the full experience of takeoff and landing also, if you so desire."

"Thank you for all your help here, Jundiin," Max said.

"My pleasure." Jundiin beckoned the maintenance staff assembled at the front of the hangar. "A quick chat with the race support team, Mister Fend, and then we'll leave you to it."

The tarmac finally empty of Jundiin and the support team, Max and Renee climbed into the cockpit. With the gull-wing doors open they absorbed their surroundings, Max in the pilot's chair, Renee next to him. The yoke controls were centered in front of each seat, between their knees.

"He's odd, Max," Renee said.

"Jundiin? How could he not be? He's Batman." Max's smirk didn't give Renee's perception its due. "Seriously, though, sure, he's a little off, but I'm not worried about it. What I am worried about is getting someone in addition to his UAE maintenance crew to certify this rig for each leg. I need someone I know I can trust will keep it in the air."

Renee leaned between their seats to get the full impact of the interior, checking out the second row of passenger seating. "And who might that person be, Max?"

"You know who I mean."

"Don't you dare. He's on a European vacation."

"Sorry, but it needs to be Lou."

Luberto Dotto, Lou for short. An Italian transplant living in the U.S. for twenty-plus years, Lou was Max's ageless lead mechanic, perpetually shrouded by an aroma of engine oil and hydraulic fluid. He was also Max's mentor and cover back when Max was still cultivating his public-facing image of decadent playboy, an image needed to mask his role as a government intel asset, whenever the need for that role arose. Lou led the pit crew for the Fend entry in the Cannes aerobatics race. Now that the race was over...

"He's vacationing where? Italy? Is he solo?"

"Yes, Max, he's solo. Italy then Greece. The guy's looking to cleanse his palate after his divorce. Leave him alone."

"I'll make it up to him, I always do."

Fifteen minutes and one phone call later, it was done. Burly Lou Dotto would board a shuttle in three days, would arrive in Cyprus, the end of the third leg. Max continued his perusal of his new plane.

"Beautiful aircraft, but I like my Cirrus better. Mine is lighter and has more range. Let's taxi her some then take her up, shall we?"

In the air, with Max piloting, his *ooos* and *ahs* accented her various mentions of the instructions and protocols Jundiin's binder contained.

"It would be nice if we had what's in that binder on our phones," Max said.

"Done," she said, her thumbs and fingers still ablaze on her phone's keypad. "Check your emails for the link he gave when your hands are free."

"Great. We'll need to put this all on paper charts tonight, do research, come up with our own navigation waypoints in addition to whatever the race has. Navigation can be visual only, no GPS. Them's the rules, and we'll have that little camera capturing our every move to make sure we comply. This is where you'll pick up some pointers, Renee, because things can get interesting. An example..."

Winds aloft potentially gave very different results on the speed over ground, could blow 180 degrees differently when separated by a few thousand feet of altitude. A rare occurrence, Max explained, but it could happen, and even a minor difference in wind direction could be a big difference in ground speed, and that would be the ballgame in an air race like this.

"Uh-huh," Renee said, nodding.

But to fully understand, she'd need to experience it. Max passed the plane's controls to her. "Your aircraft," he said.

Renee was still reading, not ready to fly the plane. Race rules, the visual flight rules or VFR navigation charts, each leg's waypoints, Jundiin had it all covered. "In a minute. It says here the recommendation is to fly something close to a straight-line route for better speed. It will also make the waypoints easier to see..."

Max returned an uh-huh.

Renee read more. "'Each navigational chart must be approved by the judges...'"

"We'll get our chart over to Jundiin."

"... 'the teams need to fly within one mile of the waypoint. The judges will look at GPS and transponder history after each leg to make sure the team's aircraft hit each one.' That's why we need to see them easily, per the notes. 'A missed waypoint adds ten minutes to the flight time as a penalty.'"

"Are you ready yet?"

"Almost. Finally, 'The winner of each leg gets a certain point value. First leg serves to eliminate two teams, every leg thereafter eliminates one team, reducing the number of teams to two for the final leg, a wing-to-wing sprint to the finish line.'"

"Fine. Got it. Tell me this, Renee. How do you feel about really trying to win this thing? You know, go all out and capture the flag, for us and for our country?"

"Feeling patriotic, are we? Look, we win if we do the job Wilkes gave us to do and not die trying to do it. And we want Nomad. Give me the controls, Max. I'm ready to do some flying."

"Okay then. Your aircraft, Renee," Max said again.

"My aircraft," she said, accepting the controls.

"Your aircraft," he said, confirming.

The thing about Nomad: he was a monster of an assassin, the CIA profile said. No allegiances to anyone except maybe his middleman, another ghost. A planner, not a pantser. And according to the CIA playbook, generally speaking, when a contract strayed—if an assassination attempt needed to incorporate collateral damage—hesitation wasn't an option. Specifically speaking, when Nomad ignited the blasting caps he'd arranged as a surprise near an Acapulco, Mexico, mayor's residence, the nail bomb took out the mayor and half the Acapulco police department as his protection, but it also blew to bits two French-Canadian transplants.

Renee's godparents.

"*Keep Renee's fever regarding Nomad to a low grade,*" Wilkes had told Max. "*It's good to want revenge, but you must manage her need for it. No loose cannons.*"

"The plane handles beautifully, Max," she said. "One favor. Can I name her?"

"Go for it."

"Rose," she said, a reverence in her voice. "After my godmother."

"Rose it is."

Max's phone vibrated in his pocket. "Good, this proves the plane's SATCOM is working." He checked the caller ID, took the call.

"Wilkes? Your ears burning? We're in our nifty new toy right now, at eight thousand feet. Very comfortable. Here are the call letters..."

Max filled Wilkes in on the UAE maintenance crew and quirky little

Jundiin, plus the person from Max's own staff who he'd lined up to keep the maintenance crew honest at each stop.

"My lead air race team mechanic Lou Dotto is a part of this thing now. I promised him a few more weeks' vacation, and a bonus large enough for him to get a new RV. What?... She's doing fine piloting. She hasn't hit anything yet..."

Renee pushed the yoke forward. The plane dipped and Max lost his breath a moment, then she eased it back again. "Oops, my bad," she said, glaring at him.

"Okay, I earned that. Wilkes, I gotta go. We need to bring Rose back to the stable and tuck her in for the night. The race starts ten a.m. tomorrow. Call me later, we'll talk one more time about all this."

"Hold on," Wilkes said. "Who's Rose?"

Max glanced at his co-pilot before answering, Renee flying the plane, her headgear on, her contented smile reciprocating his glance.

Back to the phone call. "Do I really need to explain, Wilkes?"

A pause, which led to more dead air between them, Max wondering if Wilkes was still there. "Hello?"

"No," Wilkes said, "no need to explain."

Max and Renee FaceTimed with Wilkes on Max's phone from their hotel room, Wilkes out there in the EU space somewhere. Renee munched on the macadamias that came with the room. She had a question.

"You promised me a handgun, Wilkes. Where is it?"

"I did? Look, Renee, I understand where this is coming from, but I don't think it's a good idea. You hate guns."

Wilkes was speaking into his phone's camera from a breezy hotel balcony while seated at a table, a clear, starry night sky behind him, a full beer bottle in his hand.

"I hate them, but it's Nomad, so I want one. Make sure it has a laser sight."

"Which brings me to the reason I called. I've given this a lot of thought, guys, and I know this is extremely last minute, but... I decided to make a switch. Renee, you're out. I'm sorry."

"I'm out? Out of what?"

"The race. We can't take any chances. I'm going with someone else. Max, I have another pilot lined up. An Air Force captain who just became available. Fully cleared. She's already at your hotel."

Renee exploded on screen, French and English curses blending together. She soon turned her anger to Max. "Did you know anything about this?"

"No, I—just take a breath, honey, we'll get this cleared up. Wilkes, this isn't going to happen. Not now. Too last minute. Renee stays, or I'm out."

Wilkes rubbed his forehead, regrouping. "This is extremely high risk, Max. Renee, I never should have put you in the middle of it. You'll be way too invested in taking down our target, too... intense. You're also not fully instrument-rated and you need more hours in the air. When I got wind of this other resource... sorry, Renee, she'll be more objective, plus her piloting skills are lights out."

"Really? Too intense?" she said into the camera. "Not enough skills? Damn it, Wilkes—"

Max intervened. "Renee, honey—"

"Quiet, Max. Wilkes, get that pilot on this chat with us. Do it. I want to meet her—right *now*."

Wilkes balked. "Look, Renee, please understand—"

"NOW! If you give me that, I'll talk Max into staying with this little excursion of yours. I promise. If you don't, he leaves with me tonight."

"This is blackmail."

"You're damn right it is. Make it happen."

Wilkes picked up a phone, made a call. Renee paced the room behind Max, hurling French Canadian insults that ricocheted like hockey pucks off an ice rink's boards. Max's cellphone screen split into two camera shots, a carrot-topped woman on the left, Wilkes on the right, who was now broadcasting from inside his hotel room.

"Max, Renee, this is Captain Pamela Enders, USAF. Folks, this conversation is on a protected line. Renee, what can Captain Enders help you with?"

"The captain can answer some questions for me. Ready, Captain?"

Wilkes objected. "Renee—"

"Our deal, Wilkes, or Max is out."

"Captain Enders, I'm sorry, you'll need to bear with me please," Wilkes said. "We're getting some last-minute details worked out. Miss LeFrancois here has some questions."

"Your rodeo, Wilkes," the Air Force captain said, "no worries. Fire away, miss."

"Captain. You're aware that in-flight airplane computer systems can be hacked, correct?"

"Yes."

"Does it happen much?"

"Um..."

"Yes or no is fine, Captain. I'll answer that one for you. Yes, it happens enough to cause the FAA to be concerned. Ever seen or heard of any instances?"

"I know of one hacker who got into a commercial jet's system via the plane's entertainment system."

"United Airlines flight to Syracuse, 2015," Renee said. "He was on the plane. He'd done it before. He claims to have issued a command that made the plane climb. The FBI took him into custody after the flight. Others?"

"Well, no, I don't know of any others..."

"There are vulnerabilities on large commercial aircraft as well as small aircraft. Would you as a pilot know if something like that was happening to your aircraft?"

"I fly fighter jets, miss. It's not going to happen on a fighter jet."

"Interesting. Would you notice it if you were piloting a small plane?"

"Not unless the hacking made it so I couldn't operate the controls."

"The cost to change one line of code in an aviation system is about a million bucks and can take up to a year to implement. I know hackers who can get into airborne assets from the ground due to security weaknesses in satellite communication technology. Many have done it already, on a challenge, no money involved, and with no long-lasting effects. When money is involved, with hacker mercenaries, it's much more serious." She chin-pointed at Wilkes's face onscreen, her eyebrows knitting. "No, I'm not giving you names, Wilkes. Just know that it's possible."

"This... what the hell is this, Wilkes?" Captain Enders said. "What's happening here?"

"Sorry, Captain," Renee said, "I'm just pontificating a bit. I'll be done soon. Wilkes, I don't need to know everything about flying a plane to accompany Max on this junket. We have Max for that. But I can tell you this. I know a helluva lot about what hacking can do to *unfly* a plane. Just a few more questions for you, Captain. What chemical element is not allowed on an airplane?"

"What the what? What *element*?"

"Metals, non-metals, chemicals, the things you see listed on a periodic table. Which one is banned?"

"I—" The captain tightened her face, was getting highly annoyed.

"Mercury," Renee said. "It eats aluminum, and a plane's skin is made of aluminum. Planes exposed to mercury get quarantined. How about this one. In safety tests, which kinds of birds are thrown into plane jets and against windshields. Geese, ducks, birds of prey, or what?"

"This is bullshit. Wilkes—"

"WHICH ONE, CAPTAIN?"

"Geese. I hate those bastards. I'd say geese."

"It was a trick question, Captain. It's chickens, even though they can't fly. Dead chickens to be exact, shot from a 'chicken gun,' something that looks like a small cannon. Last topic. Do you know what cryptocurrency is?"

"Of course. Digital money."

"Which crypto is ranked number one based on total amount in circulation and price per unit?"

"I know that one. It's Bitcoin. I own some. Two Bitcoins, actually. It's so damn expensi—"

"Super. Good for you. Why might we care about cryptocurrency in the spy game?"

"Dark money, sales on the deep web," the captain said. "When it's below the radar, it's unregulated. It's how some bad guys get paid for their wetwork."

"Correct. How much Bitcoin is out there?"

"How much? Millions and millions."

"There's a finite number, Captain. What is it?"

"I don't know."

"Twenty-one million Bitcoin, no more, no less. Why that number, you ask? The world is waiting for the answer to that question, the currency's anonymous creator not telling its significance. It's important to know that there is a maximum amount of some cryptocurrencies, in case someone tries to pull you into a deal for more crypto than exists. Wilkes, I'm done with my questions here. I need to use the bathroom."

Wilkes abruptly closed out his call with a "Goddamn it. I'll call you back."

"Was it something I said?" Renee said to a blank screen.

She took her bio break and returned. They waited. She again paced the room, but Max could tell she now felt enormously better. "You saw that, Max. Wilkes has chosen poorly. She'll be a train wreck if you ask her for anything other than spelling you at the throttle."

Max's phone rang. Another FaceTime call, Wilkes only. This time he was sipping clear liquid from a small glass, a bottle of tequila behind him.

"I'm disappointed in that *My Cousin Vinny* stunt you just pulled, Renee." Wilkes ran his hand through his thinning hair. "You're lucky the person I picked didn't have a hacking degree in addition to her degrees in military science and aviation."

Renee mumbled, "It's not a hacking degree, Wilkes, it's a degree in computer science..."

"Just stop. She's gone, and I've got some egg on my face for having recruited her."

Renee smiled broadly. "Does that mean—?"

"Yes. Your other credentials are formidable, Renee, and I should have given more weight to them. You're back on the team."

"Great, Wilkes. Wonderful. Now about that gun I asked for..."

"Renee, please stop asking. In the meantime, let me check on something, on a different phone. Max, you good with your handgun?"

"I am."

"Good, then let's go over your flight routes."

Renee opened her laptop next to Max's cell. She had the VFR sectional map on the screen, showing the obstacles, terrain, and airspace along their intended flight route. Max viewed the navigational waypoints, checkpoints like road and railroad intersections, church steeples, lakes, and other landmarks easy to recognize from several thousand feet above ground level.

"Renee, I forget, is it east or west that we add 500 feet to our VFR altitude?"

Renee shot him a look. He was toying with her, pretending he didn't know simple rules.

"We'll need to feel these out as we go," Max said to Wilkes. "Watch our speed at each altitude, see how well we're doing. But I don't like that they'll know where to find us at every point for every route. They need that info for the race, sure, but it comes with exposing our locations to all the Emirates government officials and the royal family, too. Wilkes? You there, Wilkes?"

"I had to check on something again. Okay. Good, Max, fine, I get it. Renee?"

"Yes?"

"Counting down... five, four, three, two, one—"

A tap at their hotel door. Max and Renee traded glances.

"He will ask for a Hack Wilson," Wilkes said.

Max left the FaceTime screen, went to the door, checked the peephole. An African American male in a cycling helmet stood on the other side. He stared into the peephole with a full facial.

"Package for Hack Wilson," the cyclist said through the door.

Package in hand, Max brought it to Renee, who was pleased with the alias. She opened the wrapped box and lifted out a smallish Styrofoam container with a taped edge. Renee slit the tape with her fingernails, pulled off the top, and removed its contents. She admired the handgun in the presence of her FaceTime audience.

Wilkes, with a satisfied expression, onscreen: "A Ruger pocket pistol, laser sight, small clip, six shots, ammo included. For protection only, Renee, you got that?"

"Understood."

He raised his glass of probable tequila onscreen, gulped, and grimaced. "You're welcome. Safe trip tomorrow. And guys?"

"Yeah?" they said in unison.

"Don't get eliminated on the first leg. It will make us look bad."

6

Jundiin, Jasem's admin person, held out an upturned French beret in two hands as he approached each team, jostling its contents. Each female pilot closed her eyes, reached in, and removed a poker chip. The heads side of the chip read *United Arab Emirates Transcontinental Air Race* with today's date. The tails side had single-digit numbers from one to nine and would determine takeoff order for the race.

Renee, eyes closed, selected the chip from the hat and handed it back to Jundiin. "Six," Jundiin announced to the crowd, the teams clapping. Over the next three hours at Cannes' Mandelieu Airport, all nine air race teams would be airborne, spaced twenty minutes apart.

Their overnight bags loaded, Max and Renee posed for official photos next to their airplane looking trim and trendy in their gray and red Fend Aerospace flight suits with white AirPod accents. Two hours later, five teams already in the air, their takeoff as the sixth contestant was flawless, Max piloting. A half hour into the flight, Renee took over the flying. Max busied himself with different flying tasks, receiving radio traffic calls, reviewing the navigation to their waypoints, checking fuel consumption, and testing the streaming video connectivity and recording. Their destination, Rome, Italy, was 295 miles away. One hour, fifteen minutes in the air. It would leave a large chunk of the day open for sightseeing in the destination city.

Below them, the Mediterranean Sea was magnificent, the azure water meeting the clear, cloudless, cornflower blue of the sky. Their approach to the northern tip of Corsica abruptly changed the scenery, clouds beginning to engulf the island.

"This was not on the meteorological survey. Take us up five hundred feet more, Renee," Max said through the headphones. "Corsica is one big mountain range. Let's give ourselves some distance so we don't find any of its peaks the hard way. First checkpoint is a water tower south of a campground in Olzo. I don't see it yet."

"Well, then, you'd better be finding it, fella. I'm busy here, you know, flying the plane."

"We should be coming up on it." Max removed his AirPod and stuffed it into a uniform pocket. No attempt at contact was expected during the first leg per Wilkes; he'd give his ear a rest and set the AirPod on pulse. "These trees here—campgrounds can have a lot of trees. We should be over the campground right... now."

Multiple copses of trees peppered the light elevation, a great location for a campground, but no visible water tower, to its south or anywhere else.

"I didn't see it. Take us around again, Renee. We can follow that east-west road back, we're lost."

Renee circled and approached the trees that should have given up a water tower on their first pass. "Instrumentation said I was where I was supposed to be the first time through, Max, so none of this *we're* lost BS. *You're* lost."

"Ha-ha, funny, but last time I checked, you're flying the plane."

"And you're the one with the eyesight problem. There," she said, pointing, "right there, two o'clock—one water tower, in green. I'll bring us back around again to get back on course. Maybe it's time for some corrective lenses, Max, my dear?"

The tower peeked above the treetops, painted a forest shade of green. "Not a good waypoint, Jundiin," Max groused aloud, invoking their race contact. "A green water tower near a green miniforest? Too easy to miss."

"Excuses, excuses. So what did it cost us?"

"Four minutes," Max said.

"If you get some drugstore eyeglasses in Rome, maybe we're not having this conversation again, sweetie."

"I started the clock for the next checkpoint. It's a set of church ruins in a large vineyard. My turn to fly," Max said, "and your turn to eat crow." Yoke back, Max took them up. When they hit three thousand feet, a crackling radio transmission jolted them. "You get that, Renee? What did he say?"

"I missed it. Corsica's a French island, but that wasn't French. Maybe Italian...?"

Another transmission, the speaker more urgent. "... *commerciale...* *Ryanair...*"

"It's neither, it's mangled Italian," Max said, eyeing the sky around them. "Corsica's own language. It's an air traffic controller. So much for English being the international aviation language. Go ahead, answer him. In English."

"Okay, okay, I got this." She took a breath, gathering her thoughts. "Approach, this is November Three-Six-Eight Romeo Juliet with you at..."

Max nodded, pleased. "Romeo and Juliet. Ha. That is so never going to get old."

Renee shot him a fiery look as she continued transmitting. "...with you five miles west of the navigational beacon at three thousand feet with information Bravo. We are inbound for a full stop to..."

A white dot appeared onscreen at ten o'clock just as the plane's TCAS blasted its aural warning. A resolution advisory, from the collision warning system. Another aircraft was in close proximity.

Max spotted it first.

The behemoth silhouette of an Airbus A380, sporadically masked by the scattered layer of clouds.

Max instinctively placed his hands on the controls. "Traffic... twelve o'clock... level..."

Renee saw it. She finished her radio transmission with an *oh-no* on the internal comms circuit...

An accented voice came over the radio. "*Aircraft calling Corsica Approach, five miles west of the navaid, you have commercial traffic at your twelve o'clock, do you have him in sight?*"

Max pushed the yoke forward, eyeing the mountains below getting closer and the jumbo jet above them. Renee's voice shook delivering her answer. "Yes…"

Max depressed the transmit button. "November Three-Six-Eight Romeo Juliet has traffic in sight."

"Roger, November Three-Six-Eight Romeo Juliet, maintain VFR clearance."

Renee spoke. "That means he doesn't want us to climb into the clouds."

"November Three-Six-Eight Romeo Juliet, wilco," Max said to the controller. *Will comply.* Then, to Renee, "Well I don't want to go into the clouds either. I think we can make it…"

"You *think*?" Renee was looking down. "That mountain's getting closer."

The aircraft's terrain avoidance alerts were sounding.

Max was looking up. "So is that jumbo jet."

A tall ridge of rock formed Corsica's northern coast, and Rose was too damn close to it. Renee's view outside her window had her stressing. "Max, honey, please, I see mountain goats. The goats are scattering!"

Above them, merely a few football fields away, Max could make out the double rows of seats in the commercial airliner as it passed them. He felt his heart tick a few beats per minute slower as it passed.

"Mountaintop." Renee was pointing.

Max banked their aircraft hard left, seeing the radar altimeter tick way lower than it should have been. "Not quite sure if we're going to get in trouble for this…"

"Clear of traffic…" the Corsican air traffic controller said a moment later.

"… and this is only the first leg," Max said to Renee. "Isn't this fun?"

Renee responded with an expletive. When calmer, "You think anyone else has had trouble with these clouds?"

"Like who?"

"For one, the Crown Prince and Camille."

"Damn, that's the first I heard them mentioned together that way. Wasn't there a recording duo back in the seventies…?"

"Max—"

"Sorry. No, no messages from anyone. If it was an issue for any of them, maybe it wasn't worth putting the word out." Max was interested, but not enough to investigate it right now. Maybe over drinks tonight at the hotel with the other teams.

Renee was at her laptop now, keying, Max watching the horizon in their path. He side-eyed her. "You ever not have internet connectivity?" he said.

"Rarely. It depends on who and/or what I connect with. We know people, remember?"

"Fine. Wiseass."

She pressed the laptop's return key with a flourish. "Captain & Tennille. The name of the pop singing duo. Before my time. You're welcome."

"Right. Good for you, genius."

"It says here the Captain's gone. Tennille is in her eighties. It also says that, in her autobiography," Renee read from an internet link, "their relationship was never all that physical."

"Great, honey, more info than we need right now. Let's start prepping for our landing, maybe put that away..."

"You're just going to cancel me? You know, Max, sometimes..."

"Okay, no, sorry, Renee..."

She stuffed the laptop into a backpack, set the backpack under her seat. "Because I know Jasem doesn't cancel Camille like that. I'm convinced Camille doesn't put up with any BS regardless of who her boyfriend is."

"They're not boyfriend-girlfriend. Jasem's too, um, committed to his culture."

"Sure, whatever. But it could be more like Camille is too committed to her independence."

She went into the Frenchwoman Camille's digression on the topic, how Jasem had stood up for her before selecting her to pilot his race team entry. "That earned him some goodwill in Camille's book. In my book, too. Max? Hello?"

"Hold on..."

The comment the Corsican controller made about talking so many other small planes through negotiating the clouds and the mountains made more sense now. Max concentrated on what he was hearing from a different controller on their approach to Rome's Da Vinci International. Max could hear him, but he couldn't understand him.

"Sir. *Signore. Inglese*, please."

A switch to accented English came but it wasn't much better than the Italian. Max and Renee exchanged looks, snickering some, but his mispronunciations became an issue when the directions came faster and faster.

"*Le due, le due...!*" the controller said.

"*Inglese, per favore...*"

"*Eh, at deuce—two—o'cock!*"

They didn't have time to laugh. The calm of their flight turned into a lot of planes converging on one of the airport runways at once, the controllers giving their landing clearances in Italian to some, English to others, some of the directions only a speech therapist could have understood. The first jumbo jet was where the controller said it was, at two o'clock, but more were filtering in left and right.

"*'leven o'cock, one o'cock, quattro o'cock...*" their controller said.

Max didn't pick them all up, but TCAS did, the jets, the smaller planes, a helicopter, the traffic jam like a powerful magnet pulling at all this airborne metal, dragging it groundward, the quick descents, the abrupt turns, increasing the airspeed, decreasing the airspeed, up, down, the aircraft distances shortening by the second. Radio calls in multiple accents were stepping on each other, the controllers passionately advising the pilots of the smaller aircraft—

"*... nessuno, no, your left, a sinistra, no, no, signora, your other sinistra, left, si, yes, bellissimo, beautiful, eccelente, now clearing you for a runway at terminal three, report a sinistra—left—base to runway...*"

A quick reach across the console and Max connected with Renee, squeezing her arm. His questioning look gave her the go-ahead to land the plane if she felt up to it. They switched their duties up, and after a wind current jostled them, the tower cleared them for landing, and Renee took them in, Max backing her up.

"Keep her stable, no lift, yes, good, there it is, Renee, the finish line..."

"You mean those two eighty-foot red and white pylons on the tarmac that say 'finish line' in six languages?" she said. "*That* finish line?"

The roar of jumbo jet engines on all sides compounded the pounding in their hearts as Renee raced the plane between the pylons and touched down for the official end to this leg. A harrowing, exciting, and eventful first day. Renee took them to the taxiway where they both eyed an Emirati maintenance team guy directing them to a landing spot not far from the airport terminal, the fifth plane in the sequence, the landing spots close to each other.

"Count 'em, Renee. We're the fifth team to land. That looks like the Swiss team disembarking next to us, so we landed just behind them. We did good. Wow. We did real good. Started out sixth, so we made great time. That little maneuver we made over Corsica minus those four minutes—"

"Max, stop. I almost wet my pants going over those mountains, and this landing here took a few years off my lifespan." Renee shut the plane down and did her best to regulate her heavy breathing as she took off her headgear. Max squeezed her shoulder gently, affectionately, then rubbed it. Her return smile said she was relieved and would be okay. He leaned in for a nuzzle, their respective tensions dissipating.

"I owe you a glass of wine, *mi amore*," Max said. "You did great today."

"If you think speaking French to me will make a difference, it does tickle me a little."

Her hands reached and found the back of Max's head, bringing his face closer to hers. She offered a more deliberate kiss than the one he had initiated.

"But the wine is more what I had in mind, sweetie, and one glass is not going to do it for me tonight."

7

______

Terminal three, Leonardo da Vinci–Fiumicino Airport, early afternoon. Unofficial flying time for Max and Renee per the airplane clock, 1:36 hours, average air speed per Renee's calculations, 161 knots/185 miles per hour. They retrieved their belongings, one bag of luggage each, one backpack each, and exited the plane. "Good show, young lady," Max said, patting the plane's engine compartment. "You did great, Rose. Thank you."

A legion of twelve Emirati techs, grease monkeys, and detailers awaited them in uniform, here by way of an Emirati jumbo jet, ready to spend the rest of the day and overnight checking each plane's rivets and readouts and flaps and cockpit controls and fuel tanks—all systems—to guarantee the utmost in safety and performance, plus do a fore to aft spit-shine spruce-up for the next leg scheduled to start at ten a.m. tomorrow. And leading the team of professionals at the front of the line on the tarmac—

Max nudged Renee, whispered to her. "Batman, straight ahead."

"I think he prefers Jundiin, Max."

Jasem's right-hand assistant stood awaiting their approach with the broadest of smiles.

"Max Fend, Renee LeFrancois, welcome to Rome! You have competed very well during this first leg. Here." He handed Max and Renee two sheets of paper each. "Let me give you an introduction to our judges serving as arbiters for each leg. They will review the cockpit recordings and video, and they will produce the finish-line statistics per the data collected by the pylons. Official landing times and accumulated points less any penalties will be available this evening. They will send all the results via text to your phones after His Royal Highness announces them. You've already met the men on our maintenance team in Cannes, but the second sheet gives you their photos, their credentials, and their areas of expertise. They know this model aircraft inside and out. Extra parts, special lubricants—they have brought all this with them. Take note also that you now have their cell phone numbers, in case you think of something you want them to check during their review and tune-up of your aircraft. I hope you can relax during your overnight stay knowing your aircraft will be in the best of hands. You are good with your reservations for the Baglioni Hotel Regina, I presume?"

"We're all set, Jundiin," Max said, stifling his urge to address him otherwise. "Thank you."

"You are welcome. Mister Fend, Mademoiselle LeFrancois, I will have you know that His Highness has booked you into the second-best suite in the hotel. You will both rather enjoy it."

"I will offer my thanks to Jasem when I see him tonight after dinner."

"Very well, Mister Fend. May I switch keys with you then please, the keys to your plane for the keys to your rental car?"

They swapped, with Batman volunteering they could still trade in their rental car for a car service instead, Max again declining the invitation. They headed into the terminal.

"Sandwiches are reasonable in here, the baked goods and desserts are not," Max said. "Four bucks for a muffin. What's that all about?"

"I don't care about the muffins, I care about wine."

"Copy that. Let's get to the hotel."

~

Baglioni Hotel Regina was a thirty-five-minute drive from the airport, a sumptuous, decadent hotel carrying a five-star rating. A beautiful location in the heart of Rome on Via Veneto. Italian marble lobby. Original Italian art deco motif throughout. After Max and Renee checked in, the concierge held an elevator door open for them. Inside the elevator, a tall, buff man well-tailored in a three-piece suit nodded at their entrance and pushed the button for the eighth floor. Their destination as well, their room the Roman Penthouse suite. Max received a text halfway through their quiet elevator ride, Renee busying herself with furtive glances at the other passenger.

"Is that from you know who?" Renee asked about the text.

"No," Max said. She meant Wilkes. Max eyed the other man, then quickly read the first part of the text in silence.

Mister Fend, please know that the Crown Prince has passed along a few special hotel perks that he does not intend to use. They came with his suite. He thought you might enjoy them. First, by now you have probably met Signore Joccobattzi...

Max stopped reading. "Renee, did we meet a Mister Joccobattzi downstairs?"

Mr. Three-Piece-Suit, the button-pusher, bowed slightly at the waist at the mention of the name. "*Signore*, I am *Signore* Joccobattzi. Jocco for short. I am at your service."

Max and Renee shared looks. Max spoke. "This text says *Signore* Joccobattzi comes with the room."

"*Jocco, signore, per favore.* Yes, I am your butler, in your service for this evening and tomorrow morning."

The elevator elevated, floor five, six, seven...

Max read more of the text to himself.

Second your suite is provided with a free bar and a barman who has access to any liquor for any drink you can conjure.

They reached the eighth floor. Jocco seized their two luggage pieces and exited the elevator first, the double-door entrance to their suite directly across the hall.

"*Signore?*" the butler said, expectant.

Max unlocked the door. Jocco swung the doors open and marched into the suite ahead of them, Renee following first, Max trailing, still distracted by his phone. He continued his silent read of his messages while Renee drank in the space, Jocco going from room to room swinging doors open, ending by doing the same for the terrace.

And third at 4 pm this afternoon world-renowned Chef Lucille Scalzi-Santori will arrive at your suite and prepare for you a five-course dinner that will as you Americans say knock your socks off. She will have it ready by six pm and she will serve it to you on your terrace. Enjoy. Then His Highness Sheikh Jasem would greatly appreciate if you could join him in a private party room off the lobby at nine pm

Max read who the text was from, blurted a *Ha!* before he could stop himself.

"What's so funny?" Renee said.

"This text," he said, re-reading it. "Jundiin signed it *Batman*. Outstanding."

Good for you, Batman, a delighted Max thought. "I'm liking you now, Jundiin, good buddy."

Renee's smile got larger as she walked from room to room. "This suite is lovely, Max. So romantic. The art deco accents, and this view..."

"I can take him, you know, mano a mano," Max said under his breath, grinning. "The bigger they are..."

"What are you talking about?"

"Jocco. He might look like he's put together, but he's too light on his feet. You were checking him out."

"Max, you're insufferable. But he is kind of cute..."

"I knew it."

She kissed Max on his cheek. They both stepped through a set of doors onto a sun-drenched terrace that gave them a 180-degree look above the rooftops of Rome, the Eternal City. Renee sighed her appreciation.

"I know. Absolutely breathtaking," Max said.

"Yes. Wow. But... who is *that* guy?"

Another three-piece-suited attendant stood at attention at the end of the terrace. The barman uncorked a bottle of red and poured an ounce into a wine glass that he placed on the bar for Renee's inspection.

"I am Nicodemo, *Signorina*, and I am at your disposal. The concierge let me into your room. He said the *signorina* wishes some cabernet before her dinner. Please, you must try this cabernet, it is of excellent Bordeaux vintage..."

~

Unpacked by Jocco and unwound, and their inhibitions undressed by a bottle and a half of Nicodemo's vintage cabernet, Max dismissed both butler and barman for the rest of the day, with Max hoping for some alone time with Renee before the chef arrived. He returned from seeing them out. Renee reclined on the settee in the bedroom, her head down. She might have dozed off even before the help had left. Regardless, she was now asleep, a vision under the sunlight reflecting off the crystal prisms thrown by the chandelier. He draped a blanket over her, then hopped into the shower, letting the heat and steam wash away the day's travails.

They would make time for intimacy before things turned… busy. Before they were forced to sink their teeth into the reason for them being a part of this air race, their "mission," their gather of intel on Jasem, an ultra-wealthy Emirati playboy whose potential duplicity about his country's role in keeping peace in the Middle East worried the U.S. government. Emirati royalty, he was destined to be UAE king. But was Jasem working against his own family, against his own country? Against the U.S.?

Max towel-dried his hair and slipped on a hotel robe. He would wake Renee soon, in time for her to shower and ready herself for Chef Scalzi-Santori's arrival, for the preparation of their fabulous dinner on the terrace. Then they would make an appearance at Jasem's party, where they would learn how each team did today, learn which two teams would not advance to the next leg of the race, maybe learn more about their target, a smooth, charismatic enigma beloved by social media. Max sat at the end of the settee watching Renee, a lovely, relaxed visage just now stirring.

She opened her eyes and stifled a yawn. She raised her arms in a stretch, became aware of the light cover Max had pulled over her, smiling at his effort.

"What time is it?" she asked. "Where are…?"

"Jocco and the bar guy are done for the day. It's a little before three. You have about an hour to ready yourself for our chef. I hope your rest—"

She sat up, inserted her arms into his robe where they found his waist, and pulled him toward her.

"I'll make do with half an hour, as long as you don't mind needing to take another shower…"

~

They ate their magnificent dinner on the terrace with only the slightest of breezes needed for their comfort in the early evening heat. The chef was not a solo act, having arrived with one sous chef, one dessert chef, and two waiters as her attendings, creating an Italian surf and turf extravaganza, its wine pairing light and unobtrusive.

Nine p.m. Time for them to learn the results of the first leg of the race. Downstairs, two turns off the lobby, they found Jasem's large, private party room where about thirty people had gathered. Jasem spoke into a wireless handheld microphone after Jundiin called the room to attention.

"Hello, everyone. I welcome you to Rome, the Eternal City, and I congratulate you all for completing the first stop of my country's first transcontinental air race."

He bowed, and when the clapping subsided, he continued. "I won't be long. The race results will be sent to your phones, in whatever language you requested, immediately after we read them here. And now my assistant will read the performance times and the points earned for the first leg of the race. Jundiin, please proceed."

Max already knew they'd bettered the Swiss team, and when Jundiin read the results, the Swiss's performance put them at the bottom, eliminating them. Second from bottom were the Greeks, also eliminated. Max and Renee had survived the first leg, had done well enough for a third-place finish behind Jasem and Camille at number one and the Israelis at number two.

The Crown Prince worked the room, glad-handing and backslapping his contestants, and confirming his promise that even though the Swiss and Greek teams were eliminated, their planes were theirs to keep. Max and Renee, champagne in hand, shared their flight experiences for the day with the UK and Pakistani teams. Jasem and his bodyguards arrived at their sides, with Jasem politely waiting to insert himself into their conversation.

Max had no time to speak up, Renee the first to address Jasem. "Sheikh Al Abbar—"

"*Jasem*, please, Renee. Hello, Max. Hello, Colonel Tuttle, Sahib Zaman," he said, bowing to all four of the other pilots in the conversation, two of them female. "It's so good to see you all here tonight. A good showing for all our teams today as well, was it not?"

Nods and verbal acknowledgments followed, then they all deferred to Renee, who had addressed Jasem first.

"Yes, Jasem. Our accommodations here at the hotel, they are wonderful. I just want to say bravo to you and your support team."

The *hear-hears* reverberated, glasses raised in agreement.

"Well, thank you, Mademoiselle, and thanks to my friends from the UK and Pakistan, and to you, too, Max, for attending my party at this hour, all of us needing our sleep to make tomorrow, the longest leg in the race, even a better day. I trust the smarter ones among us"—he glanced at Renee—"napped a few hours this afternoon in preparation for this, the first of the after-dinner chats I expect to have with all the participants at each destination."

Jasem's co-pilot Camille wandered up and Jasem re-introduced her, and before long, all had lifted their glasses in good cheer to each other multiple times. When the crowd thinned, Jasem was with Max, Renee with Camille.

"Max, I have a question," Jasem said. "Do you know what happened to the first U.S. team in my race? How it was that they'd disentangled themselves from competing?"

Max frowned his puzzlement. "Disentangled? You make it sound like they poisoned their own food, Jasem. Not just the pilots, the others on their team at the Cannes aerobatics race got sick also. Your admin Jundiin told us all about it. I have no idea about the specifics. Maybe he has more info on it?"

"No, no, sorry, just wondering if you had any insights. It is fine you do not." His glance past Max made Max check over his shoulder. Behind him, Camille and Renee shared a small chuckle together.

"Your co-pilot and mine are becoming fast friends, Max. What is that American phrase, 'worse things could happen?' It is good Mademoiselle Gagneux finds comfort in the company of other female pilots. Camille is a tenacious pilot, is so very intense when it comes to flying in a race. She is intense with everything, as I'm led to believe. Quite the driven person." He flashed an admiring smile at the two women talking. "It would do her good to relax more. I am happy to see this."

A yawn closed out his commentary and Jasem checked his watch. "Max, I must take your leave so I can get more rest. Another long day tomorrow, another leg up for grabs, another leg I intend to win," he said, winking. "I'm extremely fortunate to be able to entertain myself with distractions like this race when I'm not performing my princely duties."

"Like negotiating peace agreements between countries," Max said. "You are commended for your work in the Israeli normalization agreement. You and your country should be proud. Quite a feather in your cap."

"Yes, yes, we all did some good with that one. At least most of us in the royal family believe so. But that is a topic for another discussion. Max, I bid you a good night."

With Jasem's departure, a third of the room emptied. Max made the rounds preparing for his exit, sipping, not gulping, his champagne, aware that he, too, needed rest. Qatar's team, the Saudi team, the Israelis—he congratulated them all, pilots and co-pilots alike, for having survived the Cannes-to-Rome leg. His feel for the room was that the party was about to change, about to move to a higher pitch. Something he'd normally enjoy, but tonight, no, he couldn't. He found Renee with Camille and one other female pilot, the co-pilot for the Pakistani team, the three of them conversing in French, the Pakistani pilot the most animated.

Max's hand on Renee's shoulder got her attention. "I need to make a call so I'm heading up."

She squeezed his hand, a caring gesture, but her smile said she was staying. Max found the elevator.

Upstairs, Max grabbed a burner phone and dropped heavily into a sofa. He dialed a memorized number.

Wilkes picked up on the first ring. "Waiting for you, Max."

"I'm honored. Look, I just left Jasem's party downstairs, on the first floor of the hotel. The Swiss and the Greeks are out, eliminated. We survived the first leg. Finished third behind UAE and the Israelis. Hurray for Uncle Sam."

"Any issues?"

"The Corsican mountains were a distraction for us, but the real fun kicked in at Da Vinci Airport."

"Go on."

"Nothing to report, really, just crazy chaotic. A lot of air traffic controller chatter in poor English. Renee landed the plane. She did great. But I do have one concern. It came from the time we spent in our suite this afternoon."

"Yes?"

"Jasem made an odd comment tonight at his party. Two comments, actually. First, he knew Renee took a nap before dinner."

Wilkes stayed silent, then, catching Max's drift, "Did you sweep the room?"

"Yeah, little by little, in fits and starts. One butler, one barman, a chef, and three of the chef's associates were in and out. That made it difficult to do it and stay discreet. We got after it much better after I sent them packing just before dinner. We found nothing. It made me think the rooms and the terrace were clean, but then Jasem mentioned Renee's nap. Something he had no business knowing about."

Wilkes, silent again, finally exhaled an assessment. "You had people in. People who knew Renee took a nap. Who were they?"

"Good point. The butler and the barman came with our penthouse arrangement. The special chef, too. Okay, it makes sense. I'll let it go, the place probably isn't bugged. But then Jasem asked me about the food poisoning, about what took the first U.S. team out of the race."

"What about it?"

"He wanted to know what I knew. Kind of an insinuation, like I might have had something to do with it. Like *we*, the U.S., might have had something to do with it. I told him I had no idea how it went down."

"We're looking at it, Max, but so far, nothing. I do have other info. First, the analysts narrowed the likely area for the encrypted radio transmission. It should happen sometime before the race reaches the Middle East."

Max did the math. Next stop was Athens, then Athens to Cyprus, then Cyprus to Cairo. "Before the Cyprus to Cairo leg?"

"Yes."

"They decided this why?"

"Classified info at the moment as we piece this together. Sorry. Just know that it's expected to happen between Athens and Cyprus."

Good, Max thought. Not tomorrow's leg to Greece, the next one. A breather for them. An AirPod to the pocket day, not in the ear day.

"Here's what else, Max. There are other players in this race."

"Players? You mean—?"

"Other intel agencies. Britain's MI-6 for one."

"You know this how?"

"I'm texting you a picture."

A pilot in a Royal Air Force uniform. A glamor shot, something a book agent might put on the back of a military pilot's debut novel. A smiling face above a RAF flight suit in front of a fighter jet. Shades of a Prince Harry, Duke of Sussex photo op.

"He's a former fighter pilot, Max. That's an F35B Lightning."

"Huh. Colonel Tuttle. I met him tonight. So he's a former fighter pilot, no big deal. Did I mention I flew Piper Cubs? Does that make me a big deal, too? Anyway, what's odd about him?"

"Max, he retired just last month," Wilkes said. "We're not even sure he's not still RAF. We think that's too quick, him retiring then showing up in this race. Plus, there's also this."

The first photo was gone already, having disappeared into the espionage ether, replaced by the next photo showing a man exiting a French hotel. Superimposed onto the photo, pointing to his image, was an arrow. Next to the arrow, *MI-6, Menke, Thomas, officer.*

"That was taken in Cannes the day of your aerobatics race. We're looking into it. MI-6 hasn't responded yet. See this next one also."

With the second texted photo also gone, a third one was in its place. Another pilot, this one female, a long-range telephoto showing her climbing into the pilot's side of a small commercial jet prop.

"Meet Bibi Memona Qureshi, Pakistani ISI."

"Inter-Services Intelligence," Max said, absently translating. "Damn, I do recognize her. She and the MI-6 colonel both. Renee's with her right now, downstairs. And I spoke with the colonel tonight as well. He's using his real name. But the Bibi person, I dunno, she might have introduced herself as something else. Something-something-Mizka. This is turning into a spy convention, Wilkes."

"She's a wild card here, Max. We know she's been cut loose by ISI; she might now be freelancing. FYI, Bibi isn't her first name, it's an honorific, it means 'miss' or 'wife,' but Bibi is how she identifies herself. Be aware that we don't expect much help from Pakistan on her."

Max was anxious now, looking through a set of glass doors at Rome's illuminated nighttime skyline. He rose from the sofa, his upright posture deferring to the holstered handgun in the crook of his back. Nearly eleven p.m. He removed the gun, uncomfortable where it was, and set it on a coffee table.

"I know it's a lot to swallow," Wilkes said, "but I'm not done. There's work you need to do. Tonight."

"Christ, Wilkes, it's after eleven. What's the problem?"

"We've had our eyes out, and something's going down right now, in real time. Is Jasem still at the party?"

"No, he retired early. His co-pilot Camille stuck around. Renee and the Pakistani ISI woman are with her."

"Don't bet on Jasem being in his room, Max. You need to do some recon. Leave the hotel, head over to the airport. To the maintenance hangar."

"But Renee—"

"Leave her out of this. Go, *now*. Call me when you're in the car."

Max's hundred euros to the valet brought his car to the lobby pronto, tires screeching. On the phone with Wilkes again, on speaker, on the way to the airport, Wilkes filled him in on the fly.

"... find the service drive for the private side of the airport. Go to the hangar where all the FW50s are being serviced."

Binoculars, night goggles, a phone with a telephoto lens, water bottle, all stuffed into a backpack. Jeans, dark jacket. His loaded Sig on the seat. Eleven forty-five p.m. Renee hadn't gotten back yet. He'd left a note for her in the suite. *Company business, back soon, rest up. Max.*

"When you get to the hangar, we're looking for a large private jet to make an appearance. It's on its way. Tell me who climbs in or out of it."

The parking spaces near the hangar were out in the open. Max found space in a lot one hangar and a hundred yards away, his view unobstructed, his rental one among many vehicles sitting in relative darkness, the hangar's spotlights off. It was quite dark out here, and quiet.

Car engine off, with no need for him to exit. He powered the passenger window down and leaned across the seat. Binoculars up, AirPod in, Wilkes chattering again.

"What do you see?"

"Nothing out of the ordinary. Wait. Another plane. Smaller, is taxiing up, closing in on the maintenance team's jumbo jet."

Max snapped the telephotos. "It stopped next to it. The engines are shutting down. A black SUV is there, four doors, idling, is now pulling in closer to the private plane."

"Markers on the plane?"

Max put on the night goggles, squinted, and read the plane's call letters to Wilkes. He waited for feedback.

"It's who we thought," Wilkes said. "It's an Emirati aircraft, and it's registered to Sheikh Saeed Bin Rashid Al Abbar."

"Sounds familiar."

"Jasem's older uncle. One of his private jets. This is what tonight is all about. His visit here. Not sure yet, but we think—"

Max interrupted him, the night goggles and binoculars in tandem now in front of his face. "No shit. Jasem's here, too. He just got out of the SUV, shadowed by bodyguards. So much for him needing his beauty sleep."

"Exactly. Anyone leave the plane yet?"

"No one leaving, but someone's at the top of the jet's steps. Looks like a man in Islamic clothing. He's waiting for Jasem."

"I want more photos, Max, whatever you can get."

Photos of Jasem, in casual clothes, climbing the steps. Of Jasem embracing the man in traditional Islamic dress, Jasem entering the plane's hatch, the hatch closing. Then came the silence, whatever going down inside the plane conducted in privacy.

"Wilkes?"

"Yes?"

"We assume Jasem is tapped into his own intel agency, right?" Max said. "And is up to speed on... things around the Gulf?"

"Sure. Why?"

"He probably knows more about me than he's letting on. You follow?"

"I follow."

"And knows more about Renee, too."

"Look, don't assume that, Max, just... don't. The UAE has been doing better, but they're still not all that progressive with women."

"How does that comfort me?"

"Women there are less... consequential. Not considered threats."

"Not threats aside from their sexuality," Max said. "Jasem does seem different. He champions women's rights. I heard and saw it with my own eyes."

Wilkes didn't respond until, "Sorry. Reconfirming that it's the uncle's jet, and it was the uncle in the hatchway. A midnight meeting with Jasem."

An exasperated Max was still processing Jasem's subterfuge. Who would even care if he had to meet with his uncle? Why would he lie?

"Any idea what this is about?" Max said.

"Something urgent, and maybe they don't want the world to know they're meeting, so they're doing it at midnight. We're concerned Jasem has something to hide. You can't leave yet. You need to wait to see how long they..."

"Don't need to," Max said, "the jet hatch just opened." He raised his phone to snapshot Jasem's exit. "He's down the steps, walking fast, heading to his SUV." The doors to the SUV opened and closed quickly. "He's back inside."

No screeching tires, no urgent exit, just the car's calm departure from the hangar's parking lot.

"... And he's outta here. I want to be outta here, too, Wilkes, I'm tired. We done for the night?"

"Yes, Max, we're done. Thanks."

Another set of headlights came on, something behind the hangar, unnoticed until the lights reflected off the tarmac. "Hold on a second, Wilkes."

Jasem's SUV had left, was already a distance down the service road, his taillights becoming small red BBs until they disappeared. The second set of headlights was for a sedan, now pulling out from behind the hangar and moving close to the steps for the private jet.

"There's another car…"

Max took telephoto shots as fast as the phone's camera could capture them, *click, click, click, click,* until he lowered the phone and spoke while watching who was exiting the car.

"Driver's side door opened. Looks like no one other than the driver inside. It's… *what* in the flying fu… what the hell is she doing here?"

"I need more than that, Max," Wilkes barked. "Who is it? Send me pictures."

"It's that Pakistani pilot, that Bibi person."

"What? *Qureshi?* Former ISI?"

"She's… yeah. The jet's hatch is open again. She's heading up the steps. She's—"

Bright overhead amber lights switched on, big, nasty spotlights atop the hangar that housed their race planes. Illumination so bright that the parking lot for the nearby hangar, where Max was parked, was also bathed in amber. His phone down, a nervous Max eyed a retreat route, would need to do a vehicle about-face to get to the airport service drive. He checked his immediate surroundings. No repercussions yet, no airport security, apparently no harm done. A few more camera snaps before he'd need to retreat. He raised his phone again, aimed it at the steps leading to the uncle's jet, adjusted the telephoto, would take more pictures, except—

The Pakistani woman stopped mid-stairway, stared directly at the distant hangar, at the cars in the lot next to it. She held her stare.

Could she see him, like he saw her…?

He raised the binoculars. She couldn't possibly see him well enough, but he felt she was memorizing everything she could, the cars, his dark silhouette inside one of them, maybe light glinting off his glasses. She abruptly looked away, finished ascending the stairs, and entered the uncle's plane.

"Weird, Wilkes. The hangar's exterior lights switched on as soon as Jasem left. It makes me think he'd had them turned off for his meeting then had them turned back on. Weirder that our Pakistani pilot found this lot to stare at, a sixth sense kind of stare, maybe at my car, from a hundred yards away. The uncle's plane's hatch just closed with her inside. I might have spooked her. I need to be leaving…"

"I want those pictures, Max. Send them to me now. And Max?"

"What?"

"Nothing's going to happen to Renee. We won't put her in danger, got that?"

Max eyed the Sig Sauer on his seat and scanned the general vicinity for anything that looked threatening, then he put the car in drive.

"Damn straight nothing's going to happen to her."

8

———

Nearly two a.m. Max took a shower, slid under the covers next to Renee.

Renee stirred from her wine buzz, her form looking wonderful under the silk sheets, moon shadows slanted across their bed.

She dropped her hand onto his chest. "You want to talk about it?" she said.

Max stared at the ceiling, wrapped his hand around hers.

"Nah," he said, going for cavalier, to keep from making her anxious this late. "It can wait."

~

Daybreak. Max filled Renee in on last night's recon at the airport, the highlights only: Wilkes, the service hangar, binoculars, photos, the uncle's large private plane, Jasem's blink-and-you'd-miss-it visit with his uncle, then the longer visit by Qureshi, a lesser-known player.

"*Who?*" Renee said.

"You know her as Bibi Mizka. The Pakistani co-pilot."

Renee's forehead wrinkled. "That big-mouthed little sweetie? Never in a million years... wow. A late-night rendezvous? Props to you, Bibi, girlfriend."

Max shook his head. "Stop. You want to hear about her or not?"

"Okay."

"First, Mizka's not her real name, and..."

And her visit at the uncle's plane maybe wasn't a booty call either, or maybe wasn't even about the race. It could have been a debriefing of some kind, but more likely it was a job interview.

"And she's no longer working for her government," Max said.

"Private intelligence contractor?"

He nodded. "Her aviation skills are real. She got this gig as a legitimate co-pilot, but her real reason for being here might be to do freelance work for the highest bidder. That's Wilkes's take."

"Any other skills?"

"We don't know. Wilkes is running her down. We'll need to be careful around her, Renee, and not volunteer anything while we keep our eyes and ears open."

Max stroked her dark bedhead, ruffled her hair, so silky and soft on her pillow as it slipped through his fingers. He kissed her cheek, gave a sly smile. "Enough about this bad operator. Know what I'm thinking about right now?"

"Yes, I do, and no, we need to get ready. We need to order breakfast, fuel up, and get over to the airport for our preflight inspection of the plane. Today's the longest leg of the race. Let's make sure all those rivets are tight, and all the flaps still flap..."

"Long legs, tight rivets, flaps... oh how I love it when you talk aviation lingo to me..."

～

Max was flying the plane. Their air route took them over the heel of the boot before they left Italian airspace to cross another ocean, the Ionian Sea, spread out before them. Next landfall, the Greek island of Corfu. Landfall beyond that, mainland Greece. A communication came through their headsets.

"*November Three-Six-Eight Romeo Juliet, do you read? Max Fend, this is Jasem...*"

Jasem was transmitting on the VHF safety channel that the race administrators had set up. Each plane had their own separate channel in case the admin people needed to provide help without giving away information to their competitors.

Renee raised one eyebrow in Max's direction, a "how do you want to play this?" gesture. Max didn't return her glance. The aircraft video would synch with the headset chatter when it was later streamed to the public. He didn't want anyone reading their faces or their body language as judgmental against Jasem, now squarely in their sights as a person of concern. Max smiled for the camera and spoke into the headset. "We read you loud and clear, Jasem. What can we help you with?" Renee got the message, managed a smile for the camera as well.

"*Max. UK plane is in distress. Monitor Corfu air traffic control on VHF. The UK team is diverting for an emergency landing.*"

The Island of Corfu, off the Greek mainland. On a different channel, the UK's Colonel Tuttle chatted in proper English, explaining their dilemma, deadpanning its significance. "*Negative Corfu Tower, fire truck won't be needed. Just request expedited landing clearance...*"

Max switched up to the UK's VHF safety frequency. "Tuttle, it's Fend. You guys all right?"

"Hey, Max. Oil temperature and pressure out of limits. We should be okay. But if we don't make it... keep my ex-wives away from each other at the funeral. They don't get along."

Renee looked at Max. "How can he be joking when he's having an in-flight emergency?"

Max smiled. "He was a career military pilot. He's probably had more than he can remember."

They listened as Greek-accented air traffic controllers gave the British team a priority landing. Renee and Max listened intently until they were safe on deck.

Max switched off the channel. Recording each race team while they were in the air for streaming later had become a nuisance. His cockpit chatter with Renee needed to be for show only. Let each team's concern about the UK plane's drama rear itself and be recorded for playback, allowing for the internet audience to experience the tension the teams were feeling as each potential crisis played out. But the chatter could not be rooted in suspicion and should not hint at concern over foul play. There could be no displaying of one's cards on camera for all to see and hear.

"Renee. Do you feel comfortable taking us in?"

"If you're asking can I land the plane, yes, I can. Do I want to land the plane? No. When we're on the ground I will want some wine, and I will want a massage from you after we're debriefed by our UK friends and the maintenance team on what happened to them up there. Right now..."

She pulled out her laptop and keyed feverishly. "... I want to look more into their engine oil issue—"

She had a screen up, ready to show Max.

"Renee, stop, you're just going to scare yourself."

"This little oil snafu scenario example in particular—the one where the engine has high oil temperature and low oil pressure?—it says here those two readings indicate serious trouble. But the incidence rate on this type of engine is infinitesimal. You aware of all this?"

"Renee, are you calling me an infant?"

"Be serious, Max."

"What are you suggesting, Renee?"

She shook her head. "I don't like it."

"The mechanics will figure it out when the UK team arrives in Athens."

"*If* they get as far as Athens."

"Renee, give it a rest. Someone will address it. Smile for the camera, honey, or you'll be scaring our audience."

A camera reference, to remind themselves to keep their cockpit conversations generic. No loose lips, no covert chatter, stay away from anything controversial. Other keywords and phrases: *keep it clean, let's not bore our audience, do you eat with that same mouth,* others.

He'd already decided on a second addition to his team and Wilkes had agreed, a discussion that was a day old. "*Find me someone who can run interference for us, Caleb. Someone who can handle himself and any resistance we might encounter when we identify our target,*" meaning Nomad. Max had someone in mind, he'd told Wilkes. "*A blood and guts military type. A black ops kind of guy.*" Wilkes knew who Max wanted but he made no promises.

Both additions would need to arrive by tomorrow night in Cyprus, after the race's third leg. Only one of the two, Max's own maintenance person, Lou Dotto, would be visible to Jasem and the air race coordinators and the other teams. Max had more than once entrusted his life to him, his Alfred to Max's Bruce Wayne.

Another Batman reference. Internal, but still...

He needed to reduce his diet of superhero movies.

"*November Three-Six-Eight Romeo Juliet,*" the Greek air controller said, confirming radio contact, "*please ready your plane for your approach. Satellite runway, satellite terminal...*"

"Roger that, Control Tower," Max said. "Runway oh-three-L, twenty-one R."

"*Ochi, chi, no, no, the reverse, runway oh-three-R, repeat, R, and twenty-one L, repeat, L...*"

"Okay, Control, okay, roger that..."

Same issues as with their Rome approach, with air traffic controllers blasting directions in multiple languages to multiple small plane pilots speaking different languages, the planes converging, racing to finish this leg with good times while landing on runways with commercial jets. Max landed the plane, passed the race's pylon finish line, and was directed to a parking space on the tarmac next to one other FW50.

"Look at us, Renee. There's Jasem's plane. We finished second. A distant second maybe, but we still did great."

The maintenance crew went at the engine compartment for Jasem's plane open for service on the tarmac as soon as they exited, the covers off, not waiting to get it into the hangar. "Look at them go, Renee. Damn, they are intense..."

Flashlights, meters, torque drills, torque screwdrivers, grease guns, they all worked like a pit crew at a NASCAR event. There was no sign of Jasem and his co-pilot Camille. Max hustled Renee over with him to talk with the guys servicing Jasem's plane.

"Gentlemen. Good to see you out here already. Any news on the UK plane?"

One hello, two grunts, little other acknowledgment. Men on a mission, not to be distracted.

"Okay then," Max said, amused. "Is the Crown Prince still here, or did he and his co-pilot leave for the hotel?"

The mechanic who said hello thumbed them in the direction of the hangar. "Meeting inside the FBO building. Go through the hangar."

The hangar was adjacent to a private terminal operated by a fixed-base operator, or FBO, a third party providing aeronautical services. Jasem's maintenance crew had taken over the hangar, ready for the arrival of all the contestant planes to begin their service protocols, their jumbo jet at rest two hundred-plus yards from the FBO. Inside the hangar, a surprise: two FW50 aircraft engines, one fully assembled and strapped onto the back of a John Deere Pro Gator utility vehicle, the second one disassembled, its parts on the floor, next to the Gator that brought it into the hangar.

"The luxury of unlimited wealth," Max said. "Full engines for them to diagnose issues. Now Jasem's just showing off."

"You're just pissed you didn't think of it yourself, Max."

"Shhh."

In a conference room inside the FBO, Jasem and Camille were seated at a table with Jasem's assistant Jundiin and his small group of race honchos. "Mister Fend, Mademoiselle LeFrancois," Jundiin said. "Great to see you. Bravo at your strong finish. Please, come join us for some beverages and snacks. We await the arrival of the other teams. We will be conferencing with aircraft mechanics on Corfu shortly, looking for a debriefing. Hopefully all the teams will have arrived in time."

"The UK team is en route?" Max said.

"No, they are not," Jasem said, responding for Jundiin.

"But... does that mean..." Max looked around the table. Jasem, Camille, Jundiin, plus the three arbiters—the race's judges, all UAE men—none of the people in the room had a hint of a smile.

"Yes," Jasem said, "the UK team is gone."

"What? *Gone?* They crashed?"

"No, no, Max, sorry, poor choice of words. They are quite alive," Jasem said, the room of people mirroring his smile, "but they'll be eliminated from the race because they won't finish the leg in one day. I'm sure they will be quite upset when we tell them."

Two more pilots entered the room, the Israelis, with kudos tendered to them by everyone around the table. The telecom equipment in the middle of the table came to life, Jundiin's laptop echoing a similar sound, that of a ringing phone. A whiteboard off the end of the table showed the projected image of a British airman, a social media profile picture that pulsed with the ringtone.

"Your Highness, that's Colonel Tuttle calling," Jundiin said. "Not all the teams are here. Should I let it ring through or—"

"Answer it," Jasem said. "We owe it to our UK friends not to keep them waiting."

The colonel's cheerful, gray face and that of his younger female co-pilot filled the screen, broadcast from an aircraft hangar at Corfu International Airport. Pleasantries aside, the colonel launched into it.

"Let's get through this chinwag so we can get back to the business of flying, Your Highness. The gauges gave us a start, showed high oil temperature combined with low oil pressure..."

The worst combination of oil temperature and pressure readings. It oftentimes preceded a total engine failure. Max met Renee's glance, validating her original concern.

"But let's not let that toss a spanner into the works, Sheikh. Per the mechanic here, the gauges were wonky, producing faulty readings. Hilda, our beloved FW50, is as healthy as a thoroughbred. A new gauge is being airlifted to us as we speak and will arrive this evening. We will be back in the air by midnight. Barring no other issues, we should arrive at Athens International to rejoin the race no later than one a.m."

Jundiin looked to the three pilots serving as judges. They each shook their head.

"Colonel, I am sorry, but that won't work," Jasem said. "Each leg must be completed the day it is started. You will arrive after midnight. Your second leg will officially be a 'Did Not Finish.' So sorry, Colonel, but the UK team is out."

"Cobble together the times, Jasem! Take our landing time in Corfu before the Charlie Foxtrot, then you can add the time from Corfu to Athens. Calling our effort a DNF is grossly unfair..."

Max wanted to argue in favor of the colonel, but he had no standing. The teams had agreed to the rules, and the judges were determined to stand by them. But damn, Tuttle was British intel per Wilkes, and the U.S. could have used having MI-6 onboard throughout the rest of the race.

Renee had her phone out, was texting. Max felt the jolt of an arriving message in his pocket. He read her text.

Per my contacts: European betting parlors had the Brits as 2-to-1 favorites to win this thing.

But the European betting parlors, Max thought, would have had had incomplete knowledge about the Middle Eastern politics at stake with this race, otherwise they wouldn't have taken any bets on it. His curiosity got the better of him. He texted her back.

Odds for us?

Now 19 to 1, she texted.

How about before the race?

Checking... here they are. We were 30 to 1.

Still the underdogs, he texted. *I like it.*

Still dead last, Max. The crawl across the bottom of the parlor screen says U.S. pilot Max Fend will self-destruct.

Max uttered an obscenity and put his phone back in his pocket, done with this conversation. The bettors' assessments were partly his own fault for cultivating this persona over the years, an act that was convenient but necessary for the business he was in. He'd prove those bastard oddsmakers wrong.

Their transportation arrived, one car for each of the six remaining teams, all now present at the FBO. Outside, Jasem motioned for the pilots to gather around him before they headed off to their hotel.

"Here, at your disposal, is transportation for your stay in Greece," Jasem said. "Your drivers are tour guides. Use them to the maximum for the rest of the day and evening. My co-pilot, my team, and I will be dining near the Parthenon. You will receive invitations to join me shortly. If you choose not to join us, perhaps we will see some of you around town later tonight. Enjoy."

"Let's get out of here," Max said, and opened the car door for Renee. Their limo left the curb, Max and Renee keen to a private jet taxiing up to the FBO. The plane shut down. Max recognized the jet's tail number.

Last night. Jasem's uncle.

"What is it, Max?" Renee asked.

"Later, honey," he said, eyeing their driver. "Let's not bore our audience."

The uncle here, again? Was it to help or to hinder? To mentor or to muck things up? And still stuck in Max's craw was the oddsmakers' comment about their prospects in the race. *Dead last*, they had them.

He had a strong dislike for that assessment, and for both words, either together or separately.

9

A jacuzzi. A plastic goblet on the surrounding marble filled with wine, next to the tub. A giddy Renee. She slid her head under the water again, returned topside to blow the mountain of bubbles away from her face. She reached for the goblet and sipped. Max remained fully dressed on the divan in the bathroom, engaged in internet research.

The Abraham Accords, with the standard-bearer being the Israeli-UAE normalization agreement: the U.S. had hoped the peace treaties would start a domino effect, that other countries in the region would formally normalize their relationship with Israel, reducing the hostilities. Remaining on the outside of the treaty were the major players in the region: the Palestinians, Iran, Pakistan, others, but the most notable naysayers were those internal to the UAE. Wilkes said Jasem's uncle was one of them.

"I can help you with that research when I get out," Renee said, the jacuzzi jets fluffing her bubbles. "Remember, I know people."

A silly statement, they both knew people, but some of the other people Renee knew were buried deep inside underground hacking communities. Black hat, white hat, all types. People who had been on both sides of the equation; the hackers and the hacked. Inside players, outside mercenaries, consequential clandestine types who would do anything for a buck. Farther back in her history, Renee had been one of them, and that was why she had the street cred.

"I'm good with that, Renee," Max said. "Get the uncle's name right, grab some online photos of him, and put your friends to work."

"Soon as I finish my beauty bath."

Max snapped his laptop closed and settled his eyes on the visage that was Renee, her shoulders glistening through their stole of white bubbles.

"I know what you're thinking," she said, "and no, you're not welcome in here, Max."

"Fine." He produced his phone. "I just got a text from Jundiin. One place I am welcome is at a restaurant near the Parthenon for dinner. You and I both, as Jasem's guests. Can I text him back and say we'll be there in an hour?"

"Make it an hour and a half, so I can get the word out on needing info on Jasem's uncle Sheikh Shazam."

"Not funny. His name is Sheikh Saeed Bin Rashid Al Abbar."

"Relax, I'll get it right when I give my flying monkeys their orders. Will Camille be at the dinner?"

"He didn't say."

"Let's hope so. She's fun."

⌇

The scent of the sea in the city of Gazi, Athens, was calming and therapeutic. Their limo curled its way through streets lined with steep stairways, gritty yet gleaming, that rose from the alleys to the residences carved into the hillsides. They cruised the flea markets and the cafes, scattering pigeons that lingered in the street until the last second. The driver-slash-tour guide took Max and Renee to the address Jundiin had texted them, at a location known as the Technopolis.

"We are here," the driver announced, and turned off the limo's ignition.

"Where is here?" Max said, peering out the window. They were stopped in what appeared to be a town square full of pedestrians and yellow taxis heading in all directions around their limo. "I see what looks like a music stadium in front of us. I don't see a restaurant."

A hint of a snicker from their driver. "Yes, you are seeing, and hearing" —the driver lowered his window—"our town's wonderful music venue, Mister Fend." An orchestra's strings and woodwinds carried above the small stadium's walls, saturating the square. The smell of corn on the cob and sweet, roasting chestnuts from a vendor's cart wafted inside the limo. "The restaurant will be along any minute."

"It what? Will 'be along?'"

The sun was nearly set above the mountain ridge in front of them, in the distance, its sunbeams glinting off the hood of their car, almost blinding them. It was an arresting, unobstructed, beautiful vision of the end of the day, even if Max was confused by the driver's statement. And then, inch by inch, the sunset disappeared, replaced by a metal and glass structure alighting softly onto the brick pavement like a curtain coming down on a theatrical production. Gleaming windows and roof, the glass box's overstuffed cushiony seats unfolded from a long, gunmetal table, all of it on high-rising suspension wires, the restaurant monopolizing their view as it landed.

"Wow," Renee said, delighted. "Oh, Max. How wonderful is this?"

"It's called Dinner in the Sky," their driver said, his smile broad, the tour guide in him now talking freely about the surprise venue. "The most popular restaurant experience in Athens. A suspension crane takes you, your party guests, and your chefs up a hundred feet, settles you and the chefs in, and gives you views of Athens and the Acropolis hill at their most dramatic, at night, showered by spotlighting. I believe I see your hosts are already seated. They are beckoning for you to join them."

Jundiin extricated himself from his seat facing a table set for fifteen around a center space where the chefs would prepare and serve their dinners. Max and Renee were the last to join the party, although when Max did a head count, he soon realized the Saudi team was missing.

"They preferred eating somewhere other than with the Israelis," Jundiin said. "Maybe someday that will not be the case."

A few of the guests took advantage of their return to terra firma to use the restroom facilities. Jundiin preempted Renee's puzzled look before she could ask the question about bio breaks. "We will return here as often as anyone in the party needs to, Mademoiselle LeFrancois."

"And I'll take advantage of the opportunity as well, Jundiin, before we even get started," Max said, eyeing one other such defector who was straightening his casual clothes for a trip across the square. One of the Israeli pilots. The public restroom awaited them thirty paces away.

"After you, Captain Katz, sir," Max said, and fell in behind the Israeli.

"Thank you, Max Fend." Inside the restroom he spoke to Max while facing the pink bougainvillea that covered the wall, Max waiting in line behind him. Gray-haired, the captain's dark facial hair was also streaked with gray. A distinguished, gentlemanly look. He was shorter than Max by almost a head.

"'Ozzie Katz,' without the 'Captain,' sounds much better nowadays," he said. "I am retired. It's been more than six years since I've carried that rank. The Sheikh Crown Prince—he is quite the host and showman, is he not?"

Max's turn at the urinal, with Ozzie Katz now at the sink.

"'Max,' without the 'Fend,' will do. Indeed, he is. And quite the negotiator. A major player in the normalization agreement between your two countries, as I understand it. I for one am happy to see it."

"I try not to involve myself in the politics, Max. But yes, I'm aware of his role. He is to be commended for stepping up like that. An unpopular agreement for some of his family members, or so I've heard."

Wilkes's debrief about the race participants had included mentions about the two Israeli team personnel, Captain Katz one of them. There'd been no mention, however, of his potential association with Israel's spy agency, Mossad. Now, in this Greek toilet, Max wondered if the CIA had missed it. Ozzie Katz knew of the internal Emirati split on the peace agreement, something that wasn't public knowledge. Was Captain Katz referring to the uncle?

Both men were side by side at the sink, making themselves antiseptic, the restroom otherwise unoccupied. Max went fishing.

"I wouldn't know, Captain... er, Ozzie. The old guard always has trouble with the new guard, doesn't it?"

A slight brush of air whooshed against Max's ankles. His ears perked up, waiting for a squeaky hinge or some other telltale noise validating that the restroom door had opened, the bathroom entry not visible behind a baffle, but he heard or felt nothing after that. Had someone else entered?

"True," Ozzie said. "And jealous that the young have the balls to make things happen."

"Gentlemen." Jundiin's smiling reflection was now in the mirror, standing behind them. Creepy, Max thought. "The rest of the dinner guests are wondering what is keeping you. A sumptuous meal and an incredible view of Athens awaits. The chefs are waiting as well. Shall we go?" he said, gesturing.

"Jundiin—relax, dude," Max said, "just a little pilot locker room talk. Ozzie, after you, sir."

Everyone strapped themselves into their seats. A hundred feet up, the view of the Parthenon was breathtaking. Upswept lights illuminated the ancient Greeks' temple to Athena planted on the hill at the Acropolis. Most but not all its stately columns had survived wars, explosions, pocking, chipping, ransackings, and numerous transitions from paganism to God-fearing religions and back, and the constant drumbeat and march of tourism for over 2,500 years. Tonight's race teams ate, laughed, took hundreds of pictures, and drank their fill of ouzo, the men needing as many trips down to the earth-anchored restrooms as the women did.

Jasem nodded at Jundiin, who tapped his glass so Jasem could speak.

"My esteemed guests," Jasem said, "the bewitching hour approacheth. Was that not an incredible, memorable meal, friends? A round of applause for tonight's chefs, please." The clapping finished, and Jasem began wrapping up. "After two legs and three team eliminations, I am pleased to report that the frontrunners in the race are my UAE team, the U.S. team, and a tie in points for third place between our Israeli friends and our friends from Saudi Arabia. I will have a quick nightcap close by—you are all invited to join me—then for me, it will be off to dreamland to get ready for tomorrow's third leg. For those of you who are calling it an evening, I bid each of you *kalinychta*."

Additional *good nights* echoed around the table as their floating restaurant touched down in the middle of the square now lit up for the Greek nightlife.

"Max." Jasem and one of his bodyguards had gotten the drop on him. Within listening distance but out of the way, Jundiin entertained Renee and

Camille. "I must pick your brain, Max. Please join me for a drink. We won't be long."

Max checked his watch. Nine-thirty. On any other night, this might have been a laughable time for him to call it quits. Not tonight. "It can't be long, Jasem. Fend Aerospace's bottle-to-throttle statute is twelve hours. We need to cork the ouzo by ten."

"And we will."

Inside the nightclub it was one round of ouzo, strong on the anise, then a coffee drink called a freddo, Greece's version of a cold espresso. No alcohol in a freddo, just mucho caffeine. Jasem gestured to his bodyguards to move themselves out of earshot, to a table nearest where Camille and Renee sipped their cordials. Past Jasem's shoulder, Max caught some direct eye contact from three men leaning against the bar amid lingering cigarette smoke, grim looks on them all, each staring at the establishment's two newest male patrons, him and Jasem. In Max's estimation there would be no trouble, considering they could not have missed Jasem's two monstrous bodyguards at the table nearby. Except those were Jasem's bodyguards, not Max's. With no bodyguard of his own, where did that leave *him*?

Max had seen these guys before, but where?

Jasem launched into what it was like being the son of a great man, a monarch, no less, lest Max had forgotten. The expectations, the pressures, and the burden that came with someone anointed to follow in his father's large footsteps. Just how did Max feel about that, his position similar?

An absent nod from a preoccupied Max.

"Max, my friend, what has your attention?" Jasem turned for a look toward the bar. "Ah, I see. My first shift aircraft maintenance men are also here."

Okay, one question resolved. Max's next question: "Why do they look like they want to hurt me?"

Jasem shook his head and stifled a laugh. "Ha! Yes, yes, they do harbor ill intent toward all my racing opponents, Max, and maybe more so toward you, because they see you as a bona fide threat to win this contest. Please don't read anything into it. They are the best of the best, and you must trust that they want each of my opponents to not have any excuses when I beat them in my race. Your plane will be in incredible condition after each layover, for your safety, of course, but also so you can offer no excuses."

Max acknowledged them with a wave. One of them waved back, albeit reluctantly.

"Max," Jasem began. "The world is changing so quickly. I want to be a good leader for Dubai when the time comes. I am sure you have the same aspirations for yourself when you are tasked with leading Fend Aeronautics into the next millennium."

"King," Max said. "King Jasem. I just want to put that title out there. A bit different than becoming president of a company. Or I suppose your title would officially be King Khalil Bin Saeed..."

"... Al Abbar. I know, it doesn't roll off the tongue with quite the same ease as my social media nickname, but I will make it work."

"I expect you will." Max was unable to restrain a smile. He and Jasem were having a moment that did not fit the picture that U.S. intel had of the Crown Prince. "Jasem, I can't pretend to know the pressures you're facing. There's a lot more riding on your title than on me and mine, especially when it comes to dealing with heads of different states around the world. You've made a huge difference in this region already. The Emirati agreement with Israel is a bellwether of the greater good that strengthens the fabric of both countries. If you don't feel proud of that effort, you should."

Jasem's face had a glow, something not there before they began talking, more from an appreciation of Max's words than from the ouzo. Max's perception: this was either an Academy Award performance, or here was a man of genuine conviction in search of peer voices willing to share the same message.

"You embolden me, Max Fend, and validate for me that this great region does have hope for a longer-term peace. Unfortunately, not everyone in my family feels the same way."

Not a surprise, other than the fact that Jasem himself had voiced it. Max knew when to shut up, when to listen, when to absorb. He let Jasem lay it out for him.

"My Uncle Saeed. A fine sheikh, a stellar negotiator, a great family person, but his pride sometimes gets the better of him. He is one who looks to win arguments, and he does so oftentimes ignorant of the costs. He does not support this peace agreement and does not trust the Israelis. He is concerned they will breach their no-new-settlements-in-Palestine promise at the first opportunity. I so hope he stays out of the way so we can move our Middle East peace agenda forward. And now"—he checked his phone—"I must end our chat. It is ten p.m., and I promised to release you by then. Rest up, my friend. I will see you at the airport hangar tomorrow. Good night."

Limo to hotel, twelve minutes, Max and Renee sitting close, tired, overwhelmed by the long day and all the pomp and the pampering. A text arrived on Max's phone. Wilkes. Max ignored it, Renee's head on his shoulder, napping.

He thought twice and thumbed to the message.

Pick you up at your hotel 15 min.

Max mumbled a four-word sentence laced with two expletives.

Renee was fully awake again.

~

Wilkes handed his binoculars to Max. Renee sipped a coffee. They were at a scenic overlook near Athens International, a good spot to see the private airplane hangars, in particular the one where the race's FW50s were being serviced. The spotlights below them revealed hallowed historical ruins and a sprawling plantation of ancient olive trees. Church bells rang through the hills, loud enough to overwhelm the din of a vibrant Athens at night.

"The hatch is opening again," Max said.

The fuselage door for Jasem's uncle's plane got busy as they neared midnight. Max tightened up the focus on the binoculars. "Jasem is out first. I wish I could read lips. He looks pissed."

"Reading lips would work only if you spoke Arabic," Renee said.

"Fine, point taken. But wow, look at him go. He's upset with someone still inside the plane."

"Who?" Wilkes said. He fumbled in a backpack, produced two more pairs of binoculars, handed one pair to Renee, then raised and adjusted his own.

"Not visible," Max said. "Wait. Jasem's admin guy Jundiin just came out. That guy is starting to creep me out."

"So Jasem's yelling at *him*?" Wilkes raised his binoculars, further adjusted them. "We're still building a profile on him..."

"Jundiin's out of the plane, moved past Jasem, is now on the steps. I can't read Jundiin but Jasem, I can, and he's still hot, but it's not at Jundiin. What are we looking for here, Wilkes, and who? Give me a hint..."

Wilkes steadied his spyglasses, swept the scene right to left and back—the airplane, Jasem's vehicle, his two bodyguards on standby, each with one hand tucked inside his jacket.

"We're looking for the prize," he said.

"Nomad? We don't even know what he looks like. And he'd be a day early. If he shows, how would you even know it's him?"

The suspense ended quickly. The object of Jasem's wrath stepped onto the top step and shared it with him: his uncle, alone. There wasn't much room there for two of them on the step together. They were nose to nose.

"Check out Jundiin," Max said. "His phone's in his hand. It looks like he's scrolling through messages."

"Or checking the time," Wilkes said.

"Or videoing them together," Renee said, "and they don't know it."

Jasem did not retreat, instead stayed in his uncle's face. The uncle held his ground, unintimidated, his older age and shorter stature be damned. Jasem slowly shook his head while staring him down—was it condescension, or disappointment, or both?—then he did an about-face, brushing past Jundiin to gallop down the steps, resettling his casual clothes once he was on the tarmac.

His dignity restored, he slipped back into his car, Jundiin hustling in behind him, his phone tucked into a fold in his robe. The car drove off. Not a smoking or screeching tires exit, more like a slow retreat. Then again, Jasem wasn't driving, otherwise it might have been faster, noisier, and more dramatic.

Binoculars down. The great city of Athens spread out below them, an underappreciated view until now, the Parthenon on the Acropolis monopolizing so much of this area of the ancient capital. The airport's twinkling red, white, and neon blue lights refocused them onto what they'd seen here, what had just gone down, whatever it was.

"I don't know, Wilkes. Jasem talked to me about his uncle," Max said, dishing, "and he was plenty personal about him. The uncle's problem—that he's not on board with their new normalization pact with the Israelis—it's consuming Jasem. I have to say he isn't coming across to me as the secret bad guy you've got him pegged to be. I just don't see it. His Uncle Saeed looks more like our guy, not Jasem. Renee, you have input here?"

"Jasem's cool. So is Camille. Is this really much ado about nothing, Wilkes?" she said.

"There can be no debate here," Wilkes said. "Tonight, had Nomad been a part of this rendezvous, things might have been moved up somewhat, but the fact that he wasn't here doesn't change what is on the horizon. Nomad is out there and someone wants to connect with him, wants to hire him for a big hit. He's someone's weapon of choice. We need to know the target, the time, and the place, and intercepting that info is paramount, because the chatter we're still hearing is that the target will be someone we like. Right now, we have nothing other than Jasem and his uncle and our intel, and that this race has attracted other spy agencies. There's something here. We stay the course."

"My guess is," Max said, "after what we saw tonight, these guys need to either stop these secret little meetings or they'll kill each other."

"My guess," Wilkes said, "is they will keep meeting until the person they want to connect with actually makes the connection."

"As in Nomad," Max said.

"Maybe. Hold on a second." Wilkes pulled out his phone to check a text.

"Don't forget about Jundiin," Renee said. "Not sure what that little phone trick was all about, but it looks like he enjoys being the fly on the wall."

10

———

Renee took them up, the second race team airborne for this, the third leg in the race, destination Larnaca International Airport on the island of Cyprus. A six-hundred-air-mile trip, plus or minus. Max gushed into the headgear, teacher to bright student, proud of his co-pilot's performance.

"Beautiful, Renee, just wonderful. Consider that takeoff nailed, honey."

In their headsets: "*Nailed? What is 'nailed,' November Three-Six-Eight Romeo Juliet? We do not copy 'nailed'...*"

It was a female air traffic controller speaking to them. Max hadn't realized he was transmitting externally. "November Three-Six-Eight Romeo Juliet here. So sorry, we were transmitting on the wrong channel. Disregard, Athens Control."

They settled in, Max on Renee's laptop attached to SATCOM, reviewing their route. "I see one possible struggle for us for this leg. Mount Olympus in Cyprus's Troödos Mountain range. Its peak is over six thousand feet. We need to stay away from that on our approach to the airport."

"*One* struggle? That's what you see, only one?" a sarcastic Renee said. "What about, um..."

Her hesitation lingered a few beats. Max glanced outside the plane, then at her, expecting his glance to move her along, to shake loose the rest of her comment.

She instead stuttered into a second "Um…"

The first "um" wasn't an issue, the second was. Max knew she'd caught herself, was regrouping, no loose lips…

Finally, "What about our VFR checkpoints over that terrain?" she said. "They won't be a cakewalk for us, will they?"

A good recovery. A potential slip of the tongue on camera avoided. Nicely done, Renee.

"One checkpoint will be easy to spot," he said, "the other two not so easy, so no, it will not be a cakewalk."

"Okay. Then can you look up a little more on them please, and send it to me? Thanks."

It was a message for them to go silent to avoid the cockpit video, to phone text instead.

Renee's phone buzzed with a text from Max by way of the laptop. She removed her phone from a uniform pocket and pulled the text up.

Whats wrong, Max's text said.

She freed her hands and tapped a response, smiling; this would be a pleasant exchange for their audience regardless of its content, when the video was released.

I almost misspoke on camera. What about us needing to make up 20 min to be in place for when that signal Wilkes told us about starts

Max keyed a return text from the laptop. *We'll figure it out. Lets entertain our viewers, shall we? Follow my lead*

"Here's what's coming up," he said aloud. "The one checkpoint we won't miss is the British radar installation atop Olympus. A large dome. The notes say it dominates the landscape. The other two we need to look for are a set of power lines that ring the mountain's foothills, then a monastery. No worries, Renee, we'll be fine. Now. A different topic. I have a surprise. You'll need one of your AirPods in for it."

It was showtime.

Renee found the wireless AirPod in a pocket, Max did likewise with his own. A twist of one of the headset's earcups exposed an ear for the device. Hiding in plain sight.

"Are you ready?" Max said. He flashed a smile at the camera and winked.

"Go for it, big boy."

Max pressed a laptop button and let 'er rip, the music blasting their ears. Max turned down the volume from the laptop. It eased into a light, bouncy tune heavy on keyboards until a female singer began the vocals.

"What the hell am I listening to?" she said, then, "I… I kind of like it."

"Captain & Tennille. 'Love Can Keep Us Together.' 1970s. And now, so our cockpit audience can hear it…"

The laptop's speakers went live, the song reverberating around the cockpit synched with their earpods and with Max's hands, both moving in rhythm, him hamming it up for the camera.

"Stop it, Max. You'll hurt yourself doing whatever it is you're doing."

"Fine." He turned off the laptop's audio but left the AirPods operational. "I'm in the mood, so more music is on the way."

Because they needed to keep the receivers in place in their ears, waiting on the Nomad signal. He returned to texting, with him spelling out in multiple messages what to expect.

We are receiver operational. Slow beeping means Nomads signal started. Beeping will go from single beeps to intermittent slow to fast the closer we get to the encryption device

The cone concept Wilkes mentioned will kick in when Nomad initiates ground to air contact on this leg

Whatever he uses to communicate to Jasem will send out a signal. The airpods will grab it

We just need to be inside the cone Renee. How about you let me fly

Renee took the cue and put her phone away. "Are you ready to do some flying, Max?"

"I am."

"Your aircraft."

"My aircraft…"

Max accepted the controls and Renee accepted the laptop. Whenever the signal started, they'd need to make up time, to get closer to Jasem's plane. Max was feeling feisty.

"Let's do this. Let me take us up near Rose's maximum ceiling," he said. "And that ceiling for Rose, Renee, would be…?"

Max's smile and lengthening of the question meant this was a pop quiz for his flight student.

"Twenty thousand feet. You know, not every situation is a teachable moment, Max. And let's not get silly. We'd need oxygen up there."

"Humor me, Renee. Correct. I'll take her to a little over nine thousand, no higher for now. The higher the altitude, the less the drag. The less the drag—"

"Yeah, yeah, the faster the speed. But hold on, smart guy, that might be overkill, considering the higher the altitude, the colder I'll be. Give me a few seconds to check something out."

Renee worked the SATCOM connection, keying at her laptop while Max made Rose climb. "I'll look for an optimal altitude..."

A few browser searches later, "Here. This chart says eighty-two hundred feet or so will do the trick. I stay warm and we still pick up some speed."

She texted him more info. Max read it. The chart addressed something completely different.

Radio reception vs altitude. This chart says ideal ceiling for pulling in that signal is around 8200 feet. Over that, more of a chance we'll be too high and miss it

"We can't have Renee be cold," Max said. "Climbing to eighty-two hundred. Let's also recalculate our fuel consumption versus trying to pick up some time. And hopefully less clouds up there."

"'Less clouds, less turbulence.' That's what some pretentious flight instructor I know always says. Stay out of the clouds and maybe you get your wish."

"Damn, that flight instructor sounds smart."

"Shut up and drive."

~

Max frowned. "This looks like a line of storms ahead." Rain began pelting the windscreen, and Max flipped the wiper blade switch to ON, peering through the now-blurry glass. "I don't see any way around it. I think we can stay VFR below... but this might get a little squirrely. You strapped in, Renee? Renee?"

Renee was catnapping, her backrest reclined, her belt on but too loose. The drop lifted her off the seat until the plane went into a negative G descent, which left her arms flailing. Max kept his hands heavy on the controls, feeling them thrash around as they flew through what must have been microbursts—

The vertical speed indicator, the needle that displayed whether they were in a climb or descent, began flicking up and down erratically, up 500 feet per minute, down 1,000, up 500, down 1,500...

Max felt his stomach lurch as the G-force shifted in opposite directions, the rain grew heavier, and then they were completely enveloped in dark clouds.

"On instruments," Max declared. He could see Renee white-knuckling her seat.

"This is not fun," she said. "I think I'm going to be sick..."

Then, suddenly, no clouds, and the VSI leveled out again.

"Owww," Renee said, rubbing her shoulders under the straps. "That's going to leave a mark."

"Sorry. That monster cloud turbulence just cost us"—he checked their altitude—"jeez, now we'll need to pay more attention to that big-honking-ass Mount Olympus coming up, we lost fifteen hundred feet..."

Beeeep. Max's AirPod squawked one time through the music it was delivering. Shortly after, the screen on his phone flashed at him. A text from Renee, to bypass the in-flight camera.

You hear that in your airpod, Max? Was that a nibble? Is the signal in play?

His single, discreet nod in her direction confirmed it.

Olympus was on the horizon, a formidable presence at over six thousand feet, but an equally urgent circumstance was they had to find Jasem. Max moved them to a lower altitude to get more speed and be ready to close the gap when they found his plane.

"C'mon, Rose, show us you care, honey..."

Moments later, Max pointed. "There. That speck. It's Jasem and Camille. Excellent. Rose, you did good, honey."

To the right, Jasem and Camille's FW50 was flying at a higher altitude. Olympus was dead ahead, eye level in Max's sights, their plane now below the peak, pressing their luck, also needing to stay out of the range of Jasem's TCAS.

Radar showed one-point-two miles distance to Jasem's plane, now one-point-one-five miles, now one-point-one...

Good, getting closer.

Beep-beep, beep-beep.

Beep-beep-beep, beep-beep-beep...

Their one-mile-proximity window was within reach, but their course was still dead center into a mountain. Jasem was high enough to fly directly, safely, over the peak, but Max and Renee were not.

Something wasn't right. A spy device generating a signal this close to a British radar installation? No time now to process the implication. "Go, Rosie girl, go..."

... but was the signal coming from the dome?

Beep-beep-beep-beep.

Beep-beep-beep-beep...

The staccato beeping flatlined into a single high pitch. They had to be right on top of its origination point—

Ten seconds passed, the high pitch persisting, their plane within the cone Wilkes described, waiting to pick up the message if it was out there... nothing yet...

C'mon, c'mon, Max internalized. *Can't stay here, too dangerous, this mountain... is Nomad transmitting, is Jasem receiving...?*

The plane's ground proximity warning system kicked in, alerting them to increase their altitude.

A frantic Renee joined the urgent admonition. "Climb, Max!"

Max pushed the throttle forward and pulled the yoke back gently. He banked the aircraft and continued the climb above an empty ski lift and trails on the mountain. The high-pitched beeping in their ears turned weak and intermittent, was starting to retreat...

Renee pointed at the gray geodesic dome just below them, Max needing to lift Rose up to better an antenna near the dome on the mountain's outer edge, clearing it but close enough that Max swore it tickled the fuselage.

The signal went to less intermittent, then to single beeps, then switched off. Their ears were left with the undertone of a soft, romantic seventies lullaby about muskrat love sung by a velvet-tongued songstress.

Max gritted his teeth, resisting a fist pound to the dash... they'd lost the signal...

How much they had cleared the dome and the antenna by, they didn't know, but their height had added another few hundred feet of altitude to what they'd needed to avoid the encounter with their checkpoint. "Guess I forgot about the Brits' radar installation. RAF Troödos. Wow, that was close, wasn't it, Renee? Renee honey?"

Her head was buried in a barf bag. When she came up for air, she punched him hard in the shoulder. "What the hell was that, Max? You almost got us killed. Ugh!"

She went to her laptop and started a keying frenzy. First, she turned off the pop music on the AirPods. Then texts began queuing up on his phone. He ignored them, didn't want to read them.

"You know, Renee honey, we've still got a monastery to find before our approach to the airport."

A grumpy Renee spoke without looking up. "Fine. I'll pay attention to the visuals, you stay with the flying. Didn't I hear some texts come through on your phone?"

He began one-handing his way through them, all from Renee. The first was full of exclamation points and angry emojis, then there were questions.

Did the message transmit

He one-handed an answer. *Don't know. We were probably within a few feet of where we needed to be to intercept it*

How do we find out

Wilkes. Send him a note. We were so close, a few seconds longer

Renee's continued keying accompanied an eye roll. *A few seconds longer Max and splat against that dome*

It was under control honey it's all good

Ugh youre impossible

A new text on his phone. Wilkes. Max checked some instrument readings before pulling it up.

No transmission intercept, Wilkes's text read. *You missed it. Renee said you almost bought the farm*

Max texted him back, said she was exaggerating, room to spare, blah-blah-blah, and at least they knew Nomad made the attempt, so that was good, right, Wilkes?

Yes

What now?

Plan B. We didn't get the message so we're tracking down the messenger

More Wilkes texts, one after another. Max continued reading. Plan B was a CIA-led ground mission prompted by the missed signal, already deployed and overrunning Mount Olympus. If Nomad was out there, they'd find him.

Max read further.

Talking to the Brits cleaning up your mess explaining why one of our assets buzzed their radar station. That was reckless Max

Max responded. *Apologies couldn't be helped.*

An MI-6 location Max

"What?" Max said aloud, confused. Renee, still buried in her laptop, threw him a look at the outburst. He shook it off and keyed a response.

So many questions Wilkes

"Max," Renee said. "What about contacting the airport about our approach? Let's at least get *that* right."

"You do it, please. Larnaca International. Let them know where we are."

Wilkes texted again. *Get to Larnaca I will explain. A surprise for you there too*

~

Twenty minutes later, they cruised between the pylons to touch down at Larnaca International in Cyprus, the UAE plane first, the U.S. plane second, the Israelis a distant third if Max heard the channel chatter correctly, but no sighting of them yet. Max and Renee dragged out their backpacks and overnight bags and headed toward the maintenance hangar on foot. Max put a phone to his ear. "You at Larnaca already, Wilkes?"

"Negatory. It sounds like your daredevil performance might have earned you more points than the UAE team for this leg. Good show."

"I know that's not how Renee spun it to you, but yeah, we closed some of the gap," Max said. A sheepish glance at his girlfriend, a sigh slipping through his lips. Things could have gone better today. "We're walking into the hangar now. The Emirati service guys are here, meeting with Jasem and Camille, gearing up for their maintenance orgy on our planes. Do you know if...?"

"Yes, your maintenance magician Luberto Dotto is there somewhere, in the hangar or the terminal. Already got a report on that."

"Good. Renee, do you see Lou anywhere...?"

Wilkes kept talking. "Let me finish, Max. Someone else is with him. Listen carefully to what he wants you to do. Sorry, but it's necessary. So if we're done here—"

"Hold on, Caleb. Maybe we did fly too close to the sun today, but what the hell were we doing there to begin with, looking for that signal? You guys solution the problem, then discover it's gonna happen that close to an MI-6 installation, and you still leave us in play? I don't understand."

Wilkes laid it out. They expected the contact to be on this leg but didn't know where. Of course they knew the Brit radar was there. They didn't expect it to happen so close to it. While a team was in place searching for a physical manifestation of Nomad in the vicinity, MI-6 was also reviewing its data. They found evidence of the signal but no evidence it connected with a target.

"Confessing here, Max, that we figured no way would it go down like that, right there under MI-6's nose. Nomad was either oblivious and careless, or thinking he's the smartest guy in the room. If it's the latter, so far, he's been right. That's all for now."

They rolled their bags past the first two hangar doors, the hangar's roof ten or more stories tall, the walls and roof braced in aluminum. The floor was spotless, glistening, almost reflective, which it would need to be per Lou, so clean "you can *mangiare* off it," he used to say when readying their Fend aircraft for their races. A maintenance and mechanical genius and mentor. Lou tended to Max, and his toys, on the field and off, in bars, restaurants, resorts, and racing venues. Eight years Max's senior, Lou was a stand-in for the older, more rational brother every reckless playboy, alleged, needed. Loyal, frog-like in stature, Italian, and huggable.

And a sight for sore eyes. Outback hat, open-collared shirt in white, short-sleeved and untucked over a pair of tan gabardine pants. "There," Renee said, smiling broadly and pointing, "his back to us, in front of that workbench."

Hugs, handshakes, and a cheek peck from Renee, Lou's broad smile was infectious, but he quickly turned all business. "First, we are agreed, are we not, Max," Lou said, "that I can extend my stay in Europe after this *competizione*? At Fend Aeronautics' expense?"

"Agreed."

"Second, the new RV—?"

"Lou, you know I'm good for it. You order it, I'll pay for it."

"Third, my ride back to the U.S. is in first class and fixed wing, not what brought me here."

Max scanned outside the hangar's open garage doors up and down the tarmac. "I don't see a helicopter..."

"Fourth, you also pay me double time."

"Lou, you already earn more than two Ferrari mechanics combined, but yes, you're getting double time for this."

Lou's smile returned. "Then I am all yours, Max, you *bastardo*. However, you must humor me please and follow me outside. Your Mister Wilkes had me hitch a ride with your surprise..."

Lou opened a single door and shooed Max and Renee through it. Outside the hangar they found what Wilkes had promised Max: Trent Carpenter, drinking coffee from a thermos. Cargo pants, running shoes, black T-shirt, dark sunglasses, and behind him, a waiting helicopter. The helo was probably part of the CIA's special activities division. Trent was a former U.S. special operator. His bond with Max was by way of a close friend, Trent's brother, a casualty of the brother's inner demons. Trent had been doing contract work for the CIA over the past few years, building up an international black ops resume that included increasingly high-stakes clandestine missions.

"Trent."

"Max."

Renee said nothing, just leaned up to give Trent a huge hug that he reciprocated. Max then drew Trent into him, clapped him on the back, and grunted an off-color appreciative kudo into his neck while the two men rocked and hugged.

"So glad you're here," Max said.

"Back at you, my brother. What do you need?"

Max related his expectation. Trent as a support person would remain invisible to the race's participants for the time being.

"You're on standby for now. I just know we need help."

"Hold on a sec..." Trent retrieved a phone, put it to his ear, walked a few feet away, and began grunting responses into it.

The call over, he was back with Max and Renee. "That was my second in command. No luck on the mountain yet. Still no Nomad."

"That's your team out there?" Renee asked.

"Yes. One gig rolling into another. That's Wilkes for you, showing fiscal restraint. I need to get back out with them, but I'll see you later. If our search doesn't net us Nomad, you and I are going on a mission together. Tonight. Local. Wilkes's orders."

"How local?" Max said. "I'm operating on empty."

"Extremely local. Same hotel you're staying in. We're going to help ourselves to Jasem's personal electronic devices. All of them. Then we'll give them all back. *Mission Impossible* shit."

Trent removed his sunglasses, flashed a smile with his pearly whites at Max and Renee. He walked toward the helicopter and spoke over his shoulder.

"Relax, Max, it'll be fun. See you later."

11

Dinner, drinks, and a soccer match onscreen at a hookah bar within walking distance of their Larnaca hotel. For Max and Renee, it was to be a solo couple night, a welcome respite from the events arranged for them on the first few legs. The restaurant was Max's call: great food per the hotel concierge, well worth the wait, and close by, he said, plus Max was up for watching some soccer. They stood at the restaurant bar a few minutes into an anticipated thirty-minute wait for a table, drinks in their hands.

"Max Fend. We meet again."

An about-face on Max's part. Captain Katz, former Israeli Air Force, one half of the Israeli race team, smiled his pleasure at seeing Max and Renee, then was quick to reintroduce his dinner guest. "You of course know Talia Vaknin, my co-pilot. Ahhh, I see our table is available. Care to join us?"

The concierge was right about the food, all the way through the sumptuous desserts that, for the four, did not include sampling any of the shisha that came with the hookah, although the smoke and its pungent aromas were prevalent around them. After-dinner liqueurs for all. Small talk prevailed, about aviation, the excitement of the race, and even some vagaries about politics in different parts of the globe. Max's peripheral vision found a familiar face across the street at an outdoor bar: Trent, sipping a beer, dressed casual in an open-collared American bowling shirt and shorts, invoking his tourist persona. His glances up and down the street and occasional eye contact with Max had him in full intel mode, keeping a safe distance. A lion watching the prairie from the bush.

Mr. Ozzie Katz returned from the restroom. The conversation moved from vague talk to the more specific, Ozzie initiating it. "Our government was uneasy about an Israeli team participating in this race."

Max bit at the comment while Renee and Ms. Vaknin paused their conversation. "The reason being?"

"Concerns about security. A bit too early for this type of camaraderie with the host country, according to a security brief we received. They could not guarantee our safety."

A *brief*. Intel language. Max went all in, feigning surprise at hearing someone speaking "spy" in a casual environment. "That sounds so... cold war-ish. Who gave you 'the brief?'" he said, smiling with the air quotes.

Ozzie shrugged. "My superiors. But between us, the brief mentioned other groups. Intel agencies, the Pakistanis, maybe even the Brits. And when the first U.S. team was taken out with food poisoning at the last minute, that might have been preemptive. What your country calls a red flag."

In for a penny, in for a pound. What more did Ozzie know? "A red flag? About what? Wait. Old guard versus new guard. UAE royalty? Jasem versus his uncle?"

"Again, I don't know, I flew fighter jets for my country. I was not an intelligence officer. Now I fly only for pleasure and sport."

Max's phone buzzed, something everyone at the table heard. "Sorry." He excused himself to glance at the text. "Unimportant. What is important, now, for me, is a restroom visit. Excuse me."

Max took the time on the way back to sign for the entire bill for their table. The text was from Wilkes. *Call me from someplace secure.*

Maybe they got Nomad. Either way, it was time for him and Renee to leave.

"Ozzie, Talia." Max stayed standing when he returned, segueing into offering his regrets. "Perhaps we can get together again before this is over. Please accept this evening as my treat. Right now, I want to call it a night."

Outside, a lazy night greeted them, the car and foot traffic light, the fog light, too. Trent had come and gone. Max and Renee held hands, Renee's head against his shoulder as they walked a block on the quiet street. One block became two...

"We need to make a call as soon as we get back."

"Sure, Max, but..."

Renee patted his butt, a gesture that appeared playful but turned into a message when she pressed her hand against the weapon back there under his sports jacket. "Do you see what I see?" she said.

He did now. A storefront reflection; someone was following them. Max cast a lover's smile at Renee, then pulled her in close, speaking to her as best he could through a kiss.

"I recognize him. Security for the uncle. I'm glad he's not good at this..."

They resumed their walk but quickened the pace, Max's head swiveling, looking for an alleyway, an alcove, a dark space where they could disappear so their stalker could step up his stalk and overshoot the mark. But there were too many storefronts with too much reflective glass and no good places for hiding. They would need to run.

"All right, Renee honey, get ready, you'll need to get rid of your heels—"

They were off on a sprint, their arms pumping, Renee's fisted hands filled with spiked heels ready for gouging. Max's Sig remained in its holster, undrawn. He would count on it if necessary, but for now, eluding their tail was the call. The sidewalks on the next street led to dark alcoves and alleys that had no light at their end, then ones that did. Max selected one and pulled Renee with him, Max's footfalls the only ones echoing while they rushed through rain puddles gathering from poor drainage, the two of them scrambling to the alley's end where Renee tripped and spilled shoulder-first against a curb. Max wheeled, footfalls in their wake, shoe leather slapping against blacktop, their unseen pursuer closing in. Renee popped up on the strength of one arm and grimaced, and with one look behind Max, her eyes got bigger. A man casting a large shadow clambered up the alley toward them, finally slowing down, his prey in his sights again. Max pulled Renee by her good arm around the corner where he flattened her against the wall with a forearm across her chest, out of sight of their pursuer. He squeezed between her and the street corner and pushed himself flat there too. He unholstered his Sig.

"We make our stand here," he whispered. Renee nodded, her spiked heels raised. The slapping footsteps following them returned to a trot, then slowed down in caution as their pursuer approached the corner.

A speeding car pulled up to the curb next to them, screeched to a stop in full view of the alley they just left. Max saw well enough into the interior to notice the handgun raised at the end of the stiff arm of one Trent Carpenter, the gun pointing up the alley, where their pursuer was no doubt now having second thoughts about taking even one more step. Trent goosed the gas, and the car lurched another twenty feet onto the curb to where they stood against the wall. His toothy mug called at them through an open car window.

"Get in."

Renee and Max piled into the back seat. Trent caught rubber as he fishtailed down the wet alley and forced his way into traffic. He made the first turn he could off the main road.

Max shouted to better the accelerating engine. "Not the hotel, Trent, that guy knows where we're staying…"

"Strap in, you're coming with me. A safe house near the airport."

"Renee," Max said, "your shoulder, honey—"

"Hurts, but I hope not separated."

"Trent," Max refocused, "I like your timing. A safe house sounds fine. Any luck on finding Nomad out there?"

"We combed the mountain. Three hostels and one cabin on its face. No Nomad."

Renee, still shaken, put her hand inside her evening clutch and rested it there, not unnoticed by Max.

"Is what I think is in there, in there, Renee?"

"Don't be a dumbass. Yes."

"You have your handgun, but you went with your spiked heels as weapons instead?" Max squinted his puzzlement. "Because…?"

"With these heels in my hands there was no room for the gun. Besides, you have yours, so no problem, right?"

For Max, Renee getting hurt made this too real. He was afraid for her life despite her cavalier comments. "Renee, sure, of course, I won't let anything—"

"What? Anything what? Let anything happen to this pair of twelve-hundred-dollar heels that I adore? Well, me neither. Now, why the hell was he following us? Who does he, or they, think we are?"

"I'm hoping," Max said, "regardless of who they think we are, they don't consider us a real threat. I do wonder what might have happened..." Max eyed Renee's purse, was again aware of his own gun, nestled back inside its holster. "If we hadn't run."

Trent spoke without looking up. "I can take care of that for you, so it doesn't, you know, happen again."

"That would pretty much blow our cover. We need to keep a low profile so we can stay in the race, to see this mission through. Wilkes wants me to call him. How soon to the safe house?"

"Five minutes."

"Max?" Renee said.

"Yes?"

"That guy following us. How do you know him?"

"The uncle's security guy. He stands out. Massive, but with a face like a young Omar Sharif. What, you don't agree?"

"Um..."

"You don't know who Omar Sharif is, do you? Egyptian actor. *Lawrence of Arabia*? *Doctor Zhivago*? Trent, help me out here."

"Sorry, amigo, but no can do. I don't much follow the movies, bud."

"You guys are killing me."

Renee had her phone out, was keying. "I'll know all I need to know about your Omar Sharif in point-eight-nine seconds, but I'd rather know that guy's real name..."

Max was on the phone with Wilkes, on speaker, with Renee and Trent listening. They were inside the safe house, a shuttered veterinary care hospital close to the airport. Trent made a call and had a local physician assistant there within ten minutes of their arrival. Renee's shoulder was only bruised, not separated. When the PA was gone, Wilkes went into his feedback.

"Here we go. The elder sheikh, Jasem's uncle—Saeed Bin Rashid Al Abbar—has been supporting anti-Israeli causes using Dubai-based shell companies, and Langley is upset big time about it."

"Anti-Israeli causes like what?" Max said.

"Hamas, for one," Wilkes said.

"How can he support the peace agreement if he's funding terrorist groups?"

"Short answer is, this is the confirmation we were expecting to see, that he's not supporting the agreement. Langley believes he wants it to fail, that he had Jasem set up the air race so he—the uncle—could disrupt it. The idea per Langley is your race promoters do expect some faction of the Israelis to do something in poor taste, but rather than take a chance that that doesn't happen, they'll make it happen themselves and blame it on them anyway. Poor sportsmanship or aircraft sabotage or an international incident, but the biggest concern is it will be all the above. Something the uncle and Jasem would pin on the Israelis after the dust settled. They do think Jasem's a party to this, but the uncle is also working at odds with him. He looks to throw Jasem under the bus for his personal gain."

"Wilkes, this comes across as a hot mess," Max said, "and I'm not buying the Jasem part of it. He was just telling me how proud he was of that peace agreement. Either he's a gifted liar, or he isn't working with his uncle on anything nefarious."

Renee had broken off from the call and was aggressively keying at her phone while sitting on a dented chrome examining table left over from the building's prior business. "Pardon the interruption, gentlemen, but how about we reshuffle the deck a little. I've got feedback from my crack team of misfit keyboard jockeys. They just loaded up a ton of stuff while you and I were shaking loose that tail, Max."

"Flying monkeys and keyboards," Max said. "There's got to be a bad meme about that somewhere out there."

"Hey, *I* get to call them flying monkeys, not you. Here's what they got—"

She summarized it. When she could get at her laptop, she'd have access to tons of private communications among the Emiratis, encrypted but not well enough, including obscure info on digital currency transactions floating in the ethernet. The royal family's dirty laundry hanging out in the darknet, the deep web, and all over social media. But one item stood out as enough of a showstopper that a hacker thought it merited a separate text.

"This one, right here, this private email—it was something the uncle sent to an email address my hackers don't have details on. The uncle was furious when Jasem was named the Crown Prince. Spitting-fire, Arabic-epithets furious. He thought the king was going to hand the monarchy baton to him, not Jasem."

"Send it all to me, Renee," Wilkes said, "and send a bushel of bananas to your monkey friends."

"Stop it, the both of you," she said. "I'll scrape together internet gift cards and some treats and things and send them off. And it will all go on my expense report, Wilkes."

"I rest my case," Max said. "It doesn't sound to me like Uncle is lined up with Jasem. How the hell does Nomad fit in here?"

"Which brings us to the other reason we're talking, Max. We made some progress on our dead agent in France. Ever hear of a smart rifle?"

Trent raised his hand and walked closer to the phone. "I have."

"Forgot you were there, Carpenter. Yes, you would know about it. Or at least about the American version of it. It's a precision-guided firearm. Here's what the higher-tech version of this gun can do, not the one developed in the States. It's something the Israelis built with origins in the same technology, but more advanced, and they put this thing on steroids. Israel's Mossad Intel shared it with us. Listen up."

Wilkes rattled off the most important aspects of the gun.

It could fire armor-piercing bullets. Pinpoint accuracy based on satellite-guided radar. The rifle scope had an onboard computer. It was able to navigate a bullet through any weather conditions, any wind speed up to 150 miles per hour, any barometric pressure, any rifle "cant," even when the shooter and his target were traveling at different speeds. And the one aspect that made the technology extremely coveted: it could turn a novice gun owner into a sharpshooter from up to two miles away from a target.

"... which was every bit the distance the bullet traveled when it took out our agent at the Dune du Pilat in France, fired from an offshore cabin cruiser. It is extremely precise if it's fed good targeting information. It just does not miss."

Max went directly at the obvious. "So how is it that Nomad has it? This thing sounds like it's a million-dollar project—a *billion*-dollar project. Wouldn't the Israelis be really pissed off if they somehow lost it?"

"And there, Max, is the ultimate subterfuge," Wilkes said. "The Israeli gun, or guns, are all accounted for, at an Israeli research facility at a top-secret location. What they can't locate— and this is the classified info I couldn't give you earlier—is one of the prototypes. One of their engineers stole it."

"So now tie it to Nomad for me," Max said.

Wilkes sighed. "We can't. We don't know for sure if Nomad has it. Deductive reasoning only. What we do have is proof that the gun killed our agent, and that our agent had implicated Nomad as a contractor of interest to the Dubai royal family. Israel is combing the black market, the deep web —all the arms dealers anywhere in the region. It's the reason Langley thought the transmission would come before the race reached the Middle East, where Israel is saturating the area in its effort to find it. This gun, in the hands of an assassin like Nomad, is unstoppable."

Max mentioned the time, after eleven p.m. It was really a plea for them to not do what Wilkes wanted them to do tonight, which was break into Jasem's suite at the hotel. "Can't that wait?"

"Max, this circus moves from city to city every day. If the message we wanted to intercept on that mountain got through to him, it's buried in one of his electronic devices. You need to borrow them to see if they give us any leads on Nomad's target. Then you need to give them back. Trent, are you ready?"

Trent held up a black duffle bag.

"Let the record show," Max said for Wilkes's non-visual benefit, "that Trent is holding a bulky duffle bag and he's giving you a thumbs up. But hold on, Wilkes, I almost forgot. Renee. Darling..."

"I am at that," she said, her look smug. "Took you long enough to remember me. Yes, Max?"

"This won't work, right? You'll need more time than we're going to have to, you know..."

"For most forensics needs using over-the-counter software, it would take a prohibitive amount of time to break the passwords and download the data. For me, I'll say I can name that tune in two hours. Just don't get greedy with the number of devices you bring back."

"Meaning?"

"Don't come back with ten phones and four laptops, okay? A couple of laptops, maybe three or four phones, we can handle those in a two-hour window. We know we're looking for phone messages, so I can do some targeted data acquisitions, I'll root the phones if I have to, or I'll jailbreak them—"

"Renee..."

"... maybe do some sideloading—"

"Renee, please, in English."

"We'll push everything through multiple laptops simultaneously—mine, yours, Trent's—after I share some highly proprietary software. If everyone in that suite can stay incapacitated for two or more hours, we should be able to download everything. Then it becomes Langley's challenge. But about the sleeping agent, Wilkes—can it handle that much time?"

"Two to three hours is the top end for the slumber party, so yes, that should work. Max, you guys good? Max?"

A commercial jet rumbled over the building, its takeoff reminding them of the safe house's proximity to the airport. Max waited for the jet's roar to doppler past, his last excuse for delaying his response and the inevitable outcome of it. "Then I suppose we're really going to do this. Fine. We're good, Wilkes."

"Excellent. Break a leg, people," Wilkes said.

1:35 a.m. Renee held the binoculars to her eyes, watching Max at a distance of four hundred forty-two feet according to the optics projected onto the lenses. The hotel mid-rise was a half-circle that curled around a ground-level mall area, she on one end, the target room on the other. Her phone in her pocket, her AirPods on, she stood on the balcony of their suite, lights out behind her to give her anonymity. Her focus was ten rooms over, one floor up: the penthouse, which took up a quarter of the hotel's top floor, a long balcony connecting the penthouse rooms. Hers was a good vantage point to see all movement in the target space, as long as the drapes for the rooms were open, and they were, except for one, the Crown Prince's bedroom quarters for the night, where the lights were off. Lights were on everywhere else in the suite. While Jasem slept, his bodyguards didn't, one sitting on a chair on the balcony, one in the living room watching TV.

Renee spoke into the phone. "You read me, Max?"

"Copy," Max whispered. In cat-burglar black head to toe and on the roof directly above the penthouse, Max gave her a thumbs up from behind the suicide fence.

"Door to the roof secured?" she asked.

Max eyed the steel spike behind him, hammered into the roofing material and jammed against the bottom of the door to prevent it from opening out. "Door secured."

"You read me, Trent?" Renee said.

"Copy." Trent stepped into a leather body harness attached to a rope wrapped securely around the base of the hotel flagpole. A spotlight illuminated the mast, Cyprus's colors the topmost flag, the hotel's pennant below it, but the rest of the pole was in the dark. Elsewhere on the roof the lighting was limited, at foot level only, a twilight effect.

"The balcony guard is thumbing at his cell. If you lower the sleeping aid behind him, Max, he won't see it."

"Copy. One can of temporary incapacitation, on its way over the fence and down."

"A little to the left, Max. That's it, it needs to be right behind him or it won't work."

A can of sleeping gas in an open-air balcony. Industrial strength, its particles of sleeping agent bordering on surgical anesthesia per Wilkes, so yes, it would work as prescribed. Max settled it onto the balcony without a sound, behind the preoccupied guard. No hiss, no muss, no fuss, the guard slumped back into his chair, unconscious, would stay that way for two hours at a minimum. Max pulled the can back up.

"Trent?"

"Copy, Renee."

"Go."

Trent climbed up the fence and vaulted it, rappelled down the side of the hotel, silently lowering himself in a controlled descent onto the balcony. The bodyguard outside was asleep, the bodyguard in the living room was not. Trent reached the glass slider adjacent to the living room area, the slider ajar, so he didn't need to pick the lock. He inserted an aerosol can nozzle between the separation and let the sleeping agent do its job. In seconds, bodyguard number two went limp. Trent walked the length of the balcony.

"Good to enter, Renee?" he whispered.

Renee repositioned the binoculars to the darkened bedroom, refocusing them. "Go for it."

Trent tugged on the slider to Jasem's room. Locked. "I'll need to go through the living room."

"Copy," Renee said. "Max, you still good up there?"

"A starry, starry night, Renee. I'm good."

Trent slowly wheeled the glass slider open and slipped into the living room. He found the bedroom door, checked the clearance underneath it. He sprayed the sleeping gas agent between door and floor, waited, then jiggled the doorknob. Locked. He produced two needle-like tools and picked the lock open.

"He has female company," Trent reported from the inside.

"Copy," Renee said.

They were both in bed, both unconscious. He snapped some pictures, retrieved two laptops, three cell phones, and one small electronic device of unknown capabilities. He stuffed the equipment into his backpack.

Retracing his steps to the balcony and back up the rope, two minutes later he was standing on the roof again with Max. Five minutes past that, they were back with Renee at the end of the hall one floor down, in their suite.

"Okay, what we have here is," Renee said, keying away, "all three of our laptops are doing somersaults after our software gave them rogue root access to get at some of the data areas. Nothing out of the ordinary on these devices regarding operating systems or apps so far. We're making excellent progress. With a few handy-dandy wires we'll uplink everything to Langley, fellas, then the agency can do the heavy lifting offline." She eyed Trent's phone, next in line. "Pictures, too, Trent? Good for you. Was Camille with him?"

"A leggy, curly-haired blonde. You tell me."

"That doesn't sound like Camille. You guys were stellar up there. Wilkes will be proud."

"We still need to return all this," Max said, "so no celebrating yet. How much longer?"

Renee looked at the clock. "Downloads are still in progress. The last cellphone will finish shortly."

Renee now picked up one other item Trent brought back with him, an egg-shaped non-phone, non-laptop device in white, meant to look like something other than an encryption device, as in something personal. She wanded it to see if there was a signal. Nope, no signal, but as if on cue, the egg started twitching. She gave Trent a wry look.

"'Take all communication devices,'" Trent said, stone-faced, "or anything that looked like one. A clever use, maybe too clever, but those were the orders."

"Fine. Just return it to where you found it," Renee said.

"Roger."

Renee, back on task: "Get back up there, guys, and wait for my all-clear signal, then do what you need to do. I'll hear back from Langley soon, or at least from Wilkes. It's now…" She checked the time. "3:20, Max. Don't dally. We're nearing the upper limits of the sleeping gas window."

Max, on the roof, was there to protect Trent's rope lifeline. Like a cave spelunker, Trent rappelled over again, Max listening to Renee give the play-by-play: onto the balcony, through the living room, inside the bedroom. When Trent returned to the living room, he froze.

"Trent," Renee said, "what is it?"

"Someone's at the door, knocking. Now he's raising his voice. Now he's using a card key…"

"Get out now," Max said.

"Working on it."

Five seconds later Trent was on the balcony, pulling himself hand-over-hand back up the rope. Fifteen seconds after that, he climbed up and over the fence and dropped down onto the roof.

"I'll pack up, Max," Trent said, out of breath. "Change out of that outfit in case whoever that was ends up in the hall. FYI it didn't sound like security. I'll do the same, then join you downstairs."

"Copy." Max started undressing, changing into gym trunks, a wrinkled Nike top, and Crocs. "How do I look?"

"Like a sleepwalker," Trent said.

Dark clothes packed away, Max left the roof and found the stairs that emptied him onto the hotel's top floor. One more hurdle, to pass the door to Jasem's suite. He peeked into the hallway. Food trays, carts, no people. He stepped it up, was tempted to whistle while he passed the door to the prince's room but did not.

Bad timing. The door to the penthouse opened and Jundiin backed out in front of him, his voice raised, scolding a bodyguard. "… you idiots! No one answered the door!"

For Max, nowhere to run, nowhere to hide.

His backpack, damn it, was in his hand, an oversight. He eased it to the floor.

Jundiin raised his hand and his voice, his back to the hall, delivering a crisp tongue-lashing at someone inside the room. "You were asleep!" His pointer finger moved into chest-jamming mode. "That is unprofessional. I will have you replaced!" Then, noticing his audience, "Oh. Max Fend. Hello. Why are you on this floor?"

Max slid his foot away from the alcove, having discreetly pushed his backpack there. He slurred his words like a person who'd awakened from a sound sleep, his eyes half-lidded.

"Jundiin. Hi. Don't mind me, I'm on an ice run, no ice bucket on my floor. Renee wants something cold." Max began walking away, feeling Jundiin's narrowed eyes on him as he found the ice machine.

One floor down, Max swiped his card key through the reader and entered their room with a bucket of ice and the overstuffed backpack he'd circled back for.

The ice bucket went to a counter. "My cover," he said to Renee. "Jundiin saw me." He dropped hard onto the sofa.

"Did he buy it?"

"Don't know. Wait and see. I think so. I'm exhausted. Sleep."

Trent pushed into the room in shorts and a football jersey and wasted no time repacking his gear from the roof. "Any feedback yet?"

He and Max held expectant looks until Renee spilled.

"Good news is Langley got through everything, encryptions, passwords, even damaged sectors on the hard drives. Jasem's documents, notes, contacts, social media posts, all of it. Whatever was in any of those devices, we now have it. Bad news is, so far they've found no communication with anyone looking or sounding even remotely like Nomad. They did find a ping from an outside source directed at one of his phones. The time of the comm attempt matches our record of it, when we flew near Mount Olympus, but the phone didn't answer."

"Where does this leave us?" Max said.

"Langley's looking to pinpoint the origin of the ping. No promises, they said."

Max leaned his head back into a comfy cushion. "I can't deal with this right now. We'll hook up with Wilkes in the morning."

"Good idea, sport," Trent said, thumbing Max off the sofa. "Now get off my bed."

12

Reveille for Trent was 0600 to meet his unit at 0800 for their copter lift out of Cyprus International. Max was awake to see him off and take care of his half of a guy hug.

"See you in Cairo later, Speed Racer," Trent said, and was gone.

Room service breakfast. Washed, fed, but still tired, Max and Renee were ready to move by nine a.m. for their limo trip back to the airport.

At the hangar, five aircraft and five teams readied themselves for takeoff: UAE, the U.S., the Pakistanis, the Qatari team, and the Israeli team. Smiles all around, the teams pushed together for yet another round of official pictures by the race committee photographer under Jundiin's direction. Jasem and Camille would be first in the air again at ten a.m. sharp, again with Camille piloting.

"You notice anything about Jasem, Max?" Renee said after they broke from their photo lineup. "Any hangover?"

"Nope. He seems no worse for the wear from last night's visit. Langley will love hearing that. An incapacitating agent with no noticeable side effects. More of that stuff, please," would be Max's message.

Still no word from Wilkes even after Max called him, so there were no new insights on their mission yet. They'd missed the Nomad window in Cyprus, had to do some B&E, got in, got lucky while getting out. Some part of their intel had to have been wrong. Yes, there was a signal. Yes, being close to the UAE plane gave them access to it. Yes, it was directed at Jasem's plane. All good info, but it didn't net them what they wanted: info on Nomad's target, or better yet, Nomad.

In the air and traveling south, they cruised at five thousand feet over the Mediterranean, blue water below, blue sky above, seamless horizon, seventy-eight minutes into the leg to Cairo International. A new voice came through their headset. "*November three-six-eight Romeo Juliet, come in November three-six-eight Romeo Juliet.*"

Max looked at Renee, who answered. "November three-six-eight Romeo Juliet copies. Who is this?"

"*Pilot Nazir Zaman. I co-pilot the Pakistani plane with Bibi Mizka. I am patching you into the air race channel with everyone else. Hello, all my racing friends. I am sorry to report that we have not left Cyprus yet. There is an issue with bad fuel...*"

The last-place Pakistani plane would need to wait hours before they could get into the air. The culprit, contaminants from the jet fuel delivery system.

Max texted Renee while they listened.

Former ISI spy Bibi is probably gone. Bother you?

His phone chirped, Renee responding.

Nope

In the air at that moment, per today's staggered takeoffs, were the Emirati, U.S., Qatar, and Israeli teams. Each team reported on the performance of their engines, none with any observable issues, so Jasem encouraged all teams to stay their course unless or until they saw trouble, confirming his maintenance team would get to the bottom of the issue at the next stop. The teams signaled they'd be signing off the frequency. "*Safe trip,*" "*See you tonight,*" "*Shalom...*"

As soon as the radio reports ended, Max and Renee heard a loud bang. Gray smoke and yellow flame burst out of the engine air intake. An eerie silence filled the cockpit. The engine noise gone, all Max could hear was the air rushing over the plane's exterior.

"My God. Max! What—"

"My aircraft!" Max yelled, then took control of the plane. His eyes fixed on the smoke spewing from the intake and past the cockpit. "Shut off the fuel—"

Renee's hands searched for the proper lever and pulled. "Fuel off."

His gaze darted to his airspeed indicator—"Setting max glide airspeed" —then back outside the cockpit as he made his call on the radio. "Mayday, mayday, mayday, November three-six-eight Romeo Juliet is a few miles east of the airport at four thousand feet, declaring an emergency. Engine failure. We're... uh... landing on the beach."

Max could see Renee's shocked expression. "We are?"

On the right, the wide-open Mediterranean Sea, on their left horizon, a distant landfall. The race teams heard it all, but everyone knew to stay quiet on the radios now. Air traffic control was saying something but Max blocked it out, focusing as his heart beat faster, GPWS barking at them, the ground getting closer. In his head he ran through an emergency procedure checklist, one he barely knew for this aircraft, but hey, how different could it be versus his Cirrus? Airspeed was around sixty knots. Landing gear up, no flaps, controls trimmed, and zero engine noise... just an eerie wind sound outside as he banked the plane into a wide, shallow arc. Renee began counting down the altitude, her voice an octave higher than normal.

"Rose honey," Max said, "now's a good time to tell you I'd like us to have a long and healthy relationship. *Please*, girl..."

Max adjusted the angle of his bank to begin a slow corkscrew pattern that would hopefully allow him to level out at a section of shore below. If he didn't time it right, they would end up touching down a half mile offshore, or in the unfavorable terrain onshore. This engineless landing had to be perfect. It was the kind of thing pilots trained for all the time. But there was no way to train for the final part of the landing... that part couldn't be simulated.

The sunbathers on the sandy beach below raised their heads to look curiously at a silent airplane circling lower and lower above the surf, with Max expecting to land on top of the seaweed and their sandcastles and their umbrellas, hoping for the best for him and Renee and anyone at beach level.

"Damn it, too many people. Too dangerous, honey."

"What are you doing?"

"Water landing, Renee, get ready, love you—"

Renee pointed, then shouted, "Max, there, parallel to the beach...!"

A flat, paved road with wind-driven sand on the surface. She was right. He checked his altitude. Six hundred feet and falling. They could just make it if he went now.

Max carefully banked the plane, being sure to keep the nose pointed down enough that he kept the max range airspeed. When he was lined up on the gravel road, he moved the stick right, to roll wings level.

"Come on, Rose, c'mon, sweetie..."

"Wires, Max, I see wires, right side..."

Max saw the set of power wires just in front of them and instinctively pulled back on the stick. They gained another one hundred feet of altitude, but not without a cost.

"Airspeed, Max!" Renee said, pointing at the panel.

To his horror, he heard the stall warning. The power wires passed a few dozen feet below them.

Max pushed the yoke forward to keep from stalling. A stall at this altitude would kill them both. The impact would surely ignite the fuel in their tanks.

"One hundred feet!"

Max said, "Gear down!"

Renee, eyes wide, flipped the switch and they could hear the gear opening into place. The ground was rising to meet them, closer and closer...

They touched down with a jolt, the gear fully in place, rubber to blacktop, and Max controlled their direction and slowed them down with the foot pedals. They came to a halt with one wheel on the sandy shoulder.

The cockpit was now completely silent.

"Rose has landed," Max said. The cheering that came through their headsets was deafening, the other race pilots screaming kudos, one of them crying.

Renee leaned over and kissed Max on the lips, looked him in the eyes, hers moist, and said, "Nice landing."

Moments later they were out of the cockpit. Max wrapped his arms around Renee. They circled their aircraft dumbfounded, feeling lucky to be alive.

People from the beach arrived and surrounded them, comforted them, with Max checking to make sure they hadn't pulled a Dorothy Gale by landing on anybody. No one under the wheels or the fuselage, check, no bodies in their wake, check…

"Now to find out what the hell happened," he said, then got on the phone with Jasem and Camille to confirm Rose's safe landing for the other teams. His next call would be to Wilkes.

"Where are we, Renee?"

Renee pointed at a sign planted in the sand. "Drummers Beach. My phone says that's in Tel Aviv. Welcome to Israel, Max."

13

A CH-47 Chinook helicopter, airlift capacity twenty-four thousand pounds, had deployed from Ben Gurian Airport within an hour of their landing after the right people knew Max and Renee were next to an Israeli beach due to an emergency landing. Trent Carpenter called in the request and Wilkes had Langley cut through the red tape. But there was no way Max would be able to sidestep the questioning he'd get from Jasem about having friends in high places.

A symphony of precision execution commenced, including help from Israel's civilian police handling car traffic control. The Chinook's U.S. Army techs landed on the road and assessed their mission: airlift a four-thousand-pound small plane and haul it to Ben Gurian International.

The copter returned to the air and hovered, jostling the plane. Army Rangers attached cabling to four chainmail slings, one fore, one aft, and one for each wing. With the plane secure in the slings, the Rangers pulled themselves up into the Chinook, joining Max and Renee strapped into the helo's jump seats. The copter bucked then leveled off and the plane rose, the cabling snapping taut, secure.

Max was on the phone with Wilkes: "Get Trent and Lou Dotto to Ben Gurian asap. ETA for us is ten minutes."

"Max, they're already at an FBO hangar waiting for you."

Max switched gears, moving into assessment mode and thinking ahead. "News on the Pakistani team?"

"Never left Cyprus. They're out."

"Okay. Wow. Which means we've got one pissed-off Pakistani female ex-spy out there. Does that concern you?"

"You worry about yourselves. Now you're racing against time to stay in the race."

They had a midnight deadline to complete this race leg otherwise they'd be out, too. Broken plane, no answers as to why, no idea if they'd even be able to take the plane back up. Things were looking bleak.

"Roger that. Thanks, Wilkes."

Max sidled up next to Lou as he unscrewed the fuel cap on the left wing and lifted it to his nose. "It's contaminated, boss," he said. "Here, check it out..."

"You can smell contamination?"

"*Si*, yes, sometimes. Smells like *ammuffitto* socks. That is not the case here."

"Ammu-what?"

"Um, ah—"

Renee chimed in, her phone giving her the translation. "Mildewy."

"*Si*, mildewy. Fuel smells okay, but..."

He pointed at the tiniest of specks on the inside of the cap, a red flake. "An important find. Before I say more, I want to check the other fuel tank."

Lou unscrewed the cap on the other wing, looked at the cap's underside. "No red flakes, but we are not out of the forest yet—"

He stuck a finger inside the fuel pipe, circled the pipe interior with it, then pulled his finger out. "Ah. See? More flakes. I believe the problem started with the hose from the FBO fuel truck, the one used to fuel the plane. It's *degradare*."

"Degraded?"

"*Si*. Degraded. Bad. Those red specks look like hose lining. If those specks get into your fuel tanks, it can be a problem. The engine will run long enough to get you airborne. After that, those flakes can plug up your fuel screen."

"When will you know for sure?"

"When I take the fuel delivery system apart. I will do that before I install the new engine."

Max looked left and right, bewildered. "What new engine?"

"You have some influential friends, Max. A replacement Continental CD-300 is in the helicopter."

Max shook his head, amazed. "Wow. I have to hand it to Wilkes, coming through for us. A miracle-worker."

"Ahem. What about the U.S. Army?" Trent said. "Last I checked, you need parts *and* labor, amigo. These Chinook guys have the tools and the equipment, and they can provide all the manpower. Mister Dotto, we are at your service."

Two p.m. No need to throw in the towel and drop out yet. Not, Max boasted to Renee, if he had Lou Dotto on the case.

Lou had the fuel system apart, was pointing. "Our culprit, Max, right here. I was right. These little red floaters from the hose lining choked off the fuel, the engine overheated, and the fire shut it down. But you are lucky, boss."

"Lucky how?"

"It will be, how does my young nephew put it, a 'plug and play?' Three new parts from the spare CD-300 will fix it. No need to replace the entire engine. Let me get to work."

Inside the hangar, Max was on a SATCOM video call with Wilkes on Renee's laptop. "You blew me off after the hotel room search was a bust, Wilkes. What was that all about?"

"Langley was regrouping, and I knew where to find you. There's no change to the mission, Max, sorry. Drumbeats still say something's up, and there may be more players than we realized. And that one pesky little piece out there about Memona Qureshi, the Pakistani female pilot who's an ISI reject not going by her real name—she's no longer tethered to anyone, far as we know, and Pakistan as a country isn't thrilled with the normalization agreement. She might have a problem with the treaty, too."

Max rubbed his temple, not happy with the answer. "We're back to square one. Any recommendations? If we're able to stay in the race, should we?"

Max saw the hesitation onscreen, the stare, an involuntary signal that Wilkes was also second-guessing whether they should maintain their role, would they still be useful, could they still be effective? Would their safety be further compromised?

Wilkes came back with a blunt question: "Was it sabotage?"

"Lou confirmed what caused the flameout: contaminants in the jet fuel. We don't know how it happened. Different FBO fuel tanks? A gasoline hose mistaken for a jet fuel hose? He felt he was on top of the refueling while it was in progress and hadn't seen any sleight of hand. All the team refills came from the same FBO fuel tank, as in as far as he could tell, there was no switching of the hoses. What we don't know is whether someone went back later and siphoned out some of the fuel, then topped it off with fuel from a different tank with a different hose. Or cannibalized an old gasoline hose for some lining detritus and dropped it into the tanks. Or did the jet fuel have the contaminant in it to start with? The particles can be explained away as having come from the hose, just not how they got there."

"Short answer is you don't know," Wilkes said. "A question for you, then. What do you tell the other teams? Was this sabotage, or was it just bad luck?"

As soon as Wilkes said it, he caught himself. "Full stop," Wilkes said. "Forget I said that. Sabotage or not, you can't say that's what it was. The Crown Prince will shut the race down. If he does that, then Nomad runs free, an unidentified asset will still be in danger, and a delicate peace treaty will be jeopardized. We want Nomad, and we don't want to have to lose an asset to get him."

"All well and good that we stay quiet," Max said, "but Jasem and the rest of the teams aren't stupid. If we're still able to compete, we'll have to explain a few things, like how I got a thirty-million-dollar military helicopter on short notice to bail our civilian asses out."

Wilkes's tactical SATCOM image on the laptop froze, the connectivity compromised. This gave all parties a moment to reflect on the problems, real and perceived, that the fuel issue had created. There was a larger global game afoot. Indications were that other intel agencies also thought something was there. Max and Renee would need to keep quiet and pay attention. But they might now have a bona fide bullseye painted on them.

The laptop screen unjammed, Wilkes piping up. "Max, do this: remind Jasem you are a wealthy contractor who does favors for his country when his country asks him. Tell him the U.S. government wants you to stay in this race to help Jasem any way you can, because we see the goodwill the race is providing and its value in maintaining the peace that his Middle East diplomacy has fostered. You need to sell this."

"'And by the way, Jasem, my friend,'" Max said, trying out his response for Wilkes's benefit, and answering a question he knew Jasem would ask, "'do you realize that I am not covert?'"

"Correct. You are not covert," Wilkes said, parroting him. "Get your airship back up there, get to Cairo, talk yourself back into this race, and see how Jasem and his uncle play things going forward."

"Easier said than done."

"A person less talented than you might find it diffic—"

Max ended the transmission while Wilkes was still talking.

14

Bad Israeli coffee inside the FBO hangar. Max, Renee, and Trent drank it up, but after Lou smelled how burned it was, he had Max go inside the airport terminal for three espressos from Starbucks. Lou slammed each of them down as he worked on Rose's engine. It was nearing eight p.m. Aircraft parts littered the hangar floor.

"Lou?" Max said, looking for an update.

"*Sta 'zitto, tu,*" Lou said.

"That's no way to talk to your boss."

Lou doubled down, threw in some Italian obscenities to emphasize what he would do to Max if he didn't shut up, which was what Lou had told him to do. Then, moments later, "*Venti minuti,* we start her back up."

True to his word, twenty minutes later they started the rebuilt engine. He attached every diagnostic instrument the FBO hangar had available, watched the scopes, listened with his keen ears, stayed smiling through it all. He wiped his hands on a rag. "She is ready, boss."

Max wrote up a flight plan. He gave it to Lou, Trent, Wilkes, and transmitted it to the airport control tower. He would also have Renee email it to the race committee. They'd need one practice flight to assess Lou's repair, Max flying solo: take off, circle the airfield, land, then report the results to Lou.

Done, no issues. At 10:20 p.m. he and Renee took Rose back up, their destination still Cairo International, stop number four in the race, 244 miles, estimated flight time one and a half hours give or take. On paper, it was enough time to make the midnight deadline.

Eight minutes into their flight southwest over land, a call came over their frequency, garbled. "You understand any of that, Renee?"

"No. Sounded like Hebrew…"

With the desert below them and darkness above, two aircraft dropped out of nowhere and settled in next to Rose's wings, bookending them. Their headphones crackled to life again, this time louder, this time in English.

"*November three-six-eight Romeo Juliet. Captain Haddad, Israeli Air Force, come in, November three-six-eight Romeo Juliet…*"

Max gritted his teeth, swiveling his head; fighter jet on the left, fighter jet on the right.

"I'm not going to respond," he said to Renee, feeling the pressure. "Get our attaché on the line right now."

One SATCOM call and forty seconds later Renee had a second someone on the phone after a call in between. Her first contact had been the U.S. diplomat's attaché's office in Israel, but a patch went through to Wilkes, whom she identified for the race's eventual video audience as simply *Attaché*. The ruse of needing to speak in code, working around the decision to capture the race's cockpit chatter, was wearing on them all.

"They are Israeli F-16s…" Renee relayed to their attaché. "Your superiors complained to Israel, Israel is pushing back. We see now the Israeli Air Force is just trying to be nice. We'll communicate with them unless someone thinks we shouldn't. Copy?"

"Roger," Wilkes said as attaché number two. "Does that resolve it?" he said to Renee.

"Yes, resolved."

"Good. Have a safe trip the rest of the way, Ms. LeFrancois," Wilkes said, then signed off.

More pilot chatter. "*Sorry to have scared you like that. We will speak in English. We are here to say hello to our American friends and to shadow you. We will help escort you out of our airspace and on your way. You may follow behind me if you can handle the heat, maybe get some faster speed because of it…*"

Cleared to respond, Max started a friendly two-way. The chatter with the pilots on their frequency accompanied them south and west, back out over the Mediterranean, past the Gaza Strip, and crossing into Egypt's Sinai, destination Cairo. There the F-16s lowered a wing in a goodbye salute and peeled off.

Max kept their intrepid Rose out over the water, the Sinai coastline on their left, staying close enough to terra firma in case they had engine trouble again. A text popped up on his phone.

"It's from Jasem. It's a few hours old. He wished us luck, said he hoped we'd arrive by the midnight deadline, and says the race will take a one-day respite, more days if necessary, to better understand what happened to our plane. Tomorrow in Cairo will be downtime for all the teams. He closed with 'Stay safe, looking forward to your safe arrival.'"

"A day off," Renee said. "I like it."

"Renee?"

"Yes?"

"Please send that diplomatic attaché a note on your laptop, or a text, telling him we appreciated his assistance."

"Sure, Max."

"And ask him, in your best voice, meaning no potty mouth"—this was Max being cautious, aware their chatter would air later to Jasem's wide internet audience—"if he has any suggestions for places to go and things to do during our day off in Cairo."

"Will do, but you're forgetting the pyramids, Max. Now we have time to see them. And don't forget, my friends will have suggestions, too. I'm waiting on their reviews on the best sights to see. And stop projecting, Max. You're the one with the potty mouth."

"Am not."

"Are too."

Potty mouth. Playful banter, but also code for her to question Wilkes about new developments or suggested courses of action for them to take now that they had a full non-flying day to spend in one place. A little sight-seeing, sure, but running down intel might be more important.

Renee's "friends"—her maverick hacker corps, who also had all the data from Trent's late-night trespass into Jasem's hotel room—had already responded. More fodder that she would research more closely after they landed.

"We okay on time, Max?"

"ETA nineteen minutes. It's 2320 hundred hours. We're doing great. Get a hold of Cairo airport control tower for clearance. We're about to drop in on them."

"Copy that. Max, a favor."

"Yes?"

"Do we have time to buzz the pyramids before landing? The Giza complex is lit up at night. Can we get an aerial view of them before we see them at ground level?"

Max did some quick calculations. "We can make it work. Let's do it."

They banked right, and Max took them down. "We probably need permission to do a flyover. Ha-ha. Oh well," he said, hamming it up for the social media audience who would hear this chatter tomorrow when it was released. "Folks, don't try this at home. Easier to ask for forgiveness than it is to get permission. Here we go."

Max took them full circle around the complex's circumference. Three pyramids lit by spotlights on all four sides, plus spotlights illuminating the face of the Great Sphinx. A positive outcome of today's near-death experience: their late arrival was giving them a more dramatic view of the site than if they had arrived in the daytime.

Renee's eyes spilled over a little. She swiped at them with the back of each hand.

Max didn't miss the tears. "What's that about?" he said. "Are you okay? Renee?"

"That permission comment: 'easier to ask for forgiveness.' You, uh, quoted one of my most favorite people." She spoke, her eyes still taking in the amazing view that this detour was providing, and still wet.

"And that would be?"

"Grace Hopper, Rear Admiral, U.S. Navy. Early computer science geek. Grandma COBOL. Stop looking at me like that, I can have a U.S. hero or two. And Max?"

"Yes?"

"It's so lovely up here. I am really having a great time. I just want you to know that."

"Copy that, Renee."

15

———

Max and Renee, tired, haggard, entered the airport hangar. The reception was unexpected, Jasem and co-pilot Camille first to greet them followed by the four other teams still in the race, all clapping their arrival. Jasem's maintenance men, working on the other planes, paused to clap as well. It was moments past midnight, but they'd passed through the pylons just under the wire. The celebration was uplifting and didn't last long, didn't need to, with time enough for each of the race contestants to pay their respects then retreat. So late, and so long a day behind them, yet...

Max felt a camaraderie, a fostered kinship, with these people. Respect among rivals, with him feeling a little ornery, knowing the contest could be decided by serendipity, or by attrition from tragedy, or worst of all, by sabotage. His words to Jasem in the hangar included an account of what they'd experienced in the air, and a slightly longer explanation of how his ace mechanic Lou Dotto had come through for them to keep them in the race. And about the Israeli F-16s...

Jasem couldn't hide his enthusiasm.

"You had an Israeli Air Force escort. That pleases me to no end, Max, seeing the Israelis support our race like this. Tomorrow, you will tell me more about it and the rest of your miracle turnaround."

Encouraging words, but they were coming from someone identified as plotting with a family member against his own landmark peace agreement, with that private jet for this disreputable family member seemingly tethered like a kite to him. Yet for Max, so much of the intel on the relationship between uncle and nephew just did not fit.

On the flip side, there was Renee with Camille. An acquaintance that was becoming a friendship, their concerns for each other's wellbeing visible on their faces. This was comforting for Renee, was Max's assessment, and comforting for Max to see it happening. Something good had come from these difficult last twenty-four hours.

They all settled into seats on the limo bus. Max took a moment to text their arrival status, separately, to Wilkes, Lou, and Trent. No talk of nightcaps among the passengers, either at the hotel bar or anywhere else. The limo ferried them to a beautiful location on the Nile, the moon aglow, so overpowering an image, and haunting, serving as the dot to the "i" that was their hotel beneath it, the Four Seasons Hotel Cairo at the Nile Plaza, which was too tall for Max or Renee to count all the floors in the dark.

Max and Renee fell onto their turned-down bed in their suite. "Nice hotel," Max said into his pillow.

"So tired, Max. I'll take your word for it."

They fell asleep in each other's arms, exhausted.

Bells and rings and beeps went off in unison at nine a.m. from laptop alarms, iPhone alarms, and an automated wakeup call on the hotel room phone. Max grunted, didn't move. Renee slipped out of bed, silenced all their devices, and wrapped herself in a hotel robe. She went to work on her laptop on the terrace outside their bedroom, the River Nile snaking past the hotel and into the distance, already teeming with sailboats. They were expected back at the hangar in an hour for a debriefing by Jasem's service team, and to get feedback on the fuel contamination, something that now involved two planes, theirs and the Pakistanis'.

She reviewed content from her army of hackers. "What do any of you have that is new about Nomad, people?" she said to herself. "Anything?"

Most of it qualified as speculation only, coming from published news stories around the globe. The ricin poisoning of a Chinese diplomat at a Vietnam shopping mall. The alleged perpetrator was caught on a mall camera, the facial recognition software excellent. The Interpol case was still open; it was only a matter of time before they'd have leads on that one. "Too sloppy," she said aloud. "Not him."

A bus terminal in Tokyo, where an industrialist was found murdered in a public toilet, the case also still open. Again, many cameras in the terminal. Persons of interest had been identified and were being sought. Too public, too much abandon on the part of the assassin. "Nope."

She'd worn herself out paging through the possibilities, none appealing as Nomad's M.O., and would need to wake Max in a moment. Plus, they needed a car.

An email to the concierge prompted a quick response. Limo and tour guide acquired. It would be waiting for them outside the lobby.

One last piece of input, from a South African hacker friend sending messages through a darknet protocol about a Cannes, France, incident. An open case with the Cannes police department, gleaned from deep web chatter about large-scale sales of illegal assault weapons.

April 2018. International gambler attached to gun trafficking in Sweden was found dead on the deck of a yacht in Vieux Port du Cannes from an exploding package he'd opened. Dead also as collateral damage was the bicycle messenger who delivered the package, a nail bomb. In the heart of Cannes, at a dock...

Cannes. The coincidence was tantalizing. So too was the nail bomb package. Also unsettling: there was collateral damage. Of all the kills labeled as Nomad hits, only one other involved a nail bomb that had taken unintended victims: Renee's godparents, murdered in Acapulco.

"2007," she said absently to herself. That year would always haunt her, and for that reason. Two wonderful, elderly French Canadians. A great loss for her family, the couple living their retirement dream in Mexico.

Puzzle pieces, niggling leads, but no clear picture.

Time to roust Max.

"Max. Get up. Jasem just sent a reminder text to all the pilots. Our debrief is in less than an hour. We've got a rental car for later. I'm getting in the shower."

Max grunted into his pillow, mumbled an okay, and put his feet on the floor. Renee moved to the bathroom. Another ping on her phone. She stopped brushing her teeth to read it. A surprise text, in French:

Can we talk after breakfast, just you and I, before you start your day? Thank you so much. Camille Gagneux

A catered breakfast awaited them in the air hangar, variations of falafel and egg and cheese dishes and locally harvested dates and nuts.

"The short answer," Jasem said to the assembled teams, "is that we don't yet know what happened. The security cameras in the hangar—there were only three—show the mechanics working on the planes. No noticeable sleight of hand on the part of any of my mechanics, or anyone else. My country's intel group was dispatched to Cyprus and is now looking over the FBO's jet fuel records, plus they are taking apart the fuel tanks' delivery systems. If there's a bad hose or other failing equipment in the mix, they will find it. In the meantime, I have offered to install a new video security system with thirty cameras here in this hangar, and the hangars at each of our remaining two stops in Saudi Arabia and Qatar, before our Dubai terminus. The FBO operators have graciously accepted my offer. Our race officials are poring over the records of the fuel suppliers at these next two locations as well. My friends, I've chosen so far to accept that there was no foul play in Cyprus, only poor service, and I hope you accept that as an explanation for now. We will analyze additional feedback and decide on further action if necessary."

Jasem wound up his summary and wished them a good day of sightseeing around Cairo, the second day for the other teams, the first for Max and Renee. Dinner would be in a rooftop cabana overlooking a bevy of swimming pools in the early evening hours, reserved for them for the night.

"Max, a word before you leave," Jasem said, and motioned him to exit the hangar. "Your lovely co-pilot does not need to be a part of this. Please, follow me."

Here was where Max expected the interrogation about their miracle recovery in Cyprus, something more than a cosmetic discussion. Outside the hangar, another stretch limo awaited. Seeing the car with its deep tinted windows and a large bodyguard opening a door for him, Max's tension escalated... maybe this would turn into a lot more than a light talk.

A discussion, or a beat-down?

"Let me text Renee, to give her a heads-up."

"As you wish."

Max keyed his phone and hit send.

Jasem asked me to take a ride Ill be fine but tell Trent and Wilkes

"I hope this will not take long, Max," Jasem said, folding his hands in his lap. "So, please tell me how you did it."

"Did what?" Max feigned surprise at the question, then his surprise turned into a 'fessin' up smile. "Sorry. You want to know how I managed to pull off what came across as a tactical military response assembled for the benefit of our tiny aircraft, to get us back into the air."

"Yes. That."

Max used lines like wealthy government contractor, the benefit of a civilian doing favors for his country when asked, staying in this race to help you, his government sees the goodwill, the value of your Middle East diplomacy...

"Plus I think you know I hate to lose as much as you do." This earned an appreciative nod from his host.

Max's turn now. "You brought in your Emirati intel folks. I might wonder the same thing about you, Jasem."

Jasem was smiling now. "I will be king of my country someday, Max. My intel agencies will not let me forget what that means, that my country entrusts its future to me. There can be no separation going forward, sorry to say. I am now forever tethered to my national security people."

Jasem studied his folded hands. A pensive moment, Max not missing that the weight of the responsibility resting squarely on Jasem's shoulders was substantial, maybe even overwhelming for him.

"My days of fun and games as a social creature are almost behind me. I accept this new mantle with pride, and I am proud of the first steps I have taken while wearing it."

Max nodded. His glance outside the limo caught a different discussion in progress: Renee with the shorter Camille, the two walking arm in arm away from the hangar. Jasem addressed it, the women together, Max not getting a chance to bring it up.

"I swear to you, Max, that this was not an attempt to divide and conquer. Camille Gagneux is her own person. Whatever they're talking about, it was not at my prompting. Strong women both, representing their gender well."

Camille hailed a baggage cart, empty save for a driver. They headed off in the direction of one of the two airport terminals.

"Truth be told, Camille does enjoy your company, Max, but she's more concerned about your co-pilot than she is about you." He and Max watched the cart turn into a speck in the distance. "I expect she's grilling Renee right now on how well you guys handled the crisis. She's not a wallflower, and she's not one to be denied her say. Maybe Renee will learn something."

"That works for me," Max said, hoping for the same, but for different reasons. "Our plans for the day can wait. Are we done here, Jasem? I've got a few calls to make..."

Their meeting over, Max made those calls, then ate more falafel, drank more mud trying to pass for coffee, played with his phone, and greeted Lou on his arrival at the hangar, his transportation from Tel Aviv by way of air shuttle. Lou went to work immediately, shadowing the maintenance crew. Max re-buried his head into his phone, read some mail while checking the horizon infrequently for any mirages shimmering on the tarmac that might turn into baggage carts, anticipating one would contain the returning Renee. He texted her twice, but she hadn't responded. Back to his company emails...

Renee materialized next to him at the table, startling him.

"A little jumpy, aren't we? Let's go," she said, not bothering to sit. "Get up, now. I hired a limo and a tour guide. We're going to see the pyramids."

"Camille and you, what did you—?"

"I'll tell you in the car."

In the limo, Renee raised the privacy screen between the front and back seats. She got down to business.

"Camille's worried about me. We had a nice chat in French over fruit smoothies made with dates. Really good. Here's what was on her mind, in no particular order..."

How had Max handled the crisis?

What was his checkdown protocol?

Jasem and I aren't sleeping together.

I like your loose-fitting top...

"No context for that clothing comment, her just being friendly, but hell, I said I liked her loose top, too, something we had in common. I also asked her how many air race teams had she been hired to pilot? 'Every aerobatic yoke I could get my hands on,' she said. That one gave us the giggles."

In Camille's words, the Pakistani team had ended their participation because of the fuel contamination. Captain Zaman had left immediately. "Bibi" Mizka a.k.a. Qureshi did not, wanting to shadow the race the rest of the way.

"... and the one question I should have anticipated that Camille would ask but I hadn't: are you guys spies? She asked it, air-quoting the word."

Max gulped, stayed silent. Renee kept him hanging. Then she punched his arm.

"I said no, and I was convincing. 'Max is a mild-mannered, passionate U.S. citizen with access to many wealthy, worldwide industrialists. He's maybe a little immature, but he means well. He shares aircraft technologies with these world-beaters, nothing more, because he knows nothing more.' Camille was relieved. Then she gave me a hug, wished me luck, and said with a wink, '*Que les meilleurs pilotes gagnent.*' May the best pilots win."

Max studied her, waiting for her to mention something else, Renee returning the scrutiny, staying silent. She blinked first.

"Fine." She opened her backpack, removed her phone, placed it in her lap. "Yes, per our 'always be prepared' discussion, I recorded the entire conversation. You can decide for yourself how it went. But there's nothing *there* there, Max, and Wilkes will agree."

Max nodded. "Good work." He patted his shorts pocket where his phone was. "Likewise, I recorded my conversation with Jasem. We'll compare notes. He says he's been working with his security folks. He asked me similar questions. This could have been a coordinated effort, him and Camille talking to us separately intending to compare notes later, but I don't think it was. Wilkes will hear all of it. I believe we're still in good stead with everyone. We just don't know much more than we did before."

"That's why we go out to the pyramids early, we get our fill of Egyptology, get back here for dinner, then regroup."

Renee sipped a bottle of water from the limo bar. She helped herself to a bag of nuts, poured a handful of them into Max's hand, the two of them chilling. She watched the desert scenery zip by outside the limo window. She munched.

"You think they'll try again soon?" she asked. "Jasem and the uncle?"

"What, connect with Nomad? Or Nomad with them? Wouldn't that be nice. Maybe."

They left their limo and transferred onto their next mode of transport, mules, their tour guide in the lead. Sunscreen, bottled water, hats and sunglasses. This view of the Giza complex at ground level was nearly as dramatic as last night's aerial view, the two of them plus their guide wandering the grand expanse of desert, sidestepping rocks and boulders that had been hewn into blocks as extras for the pyramids, having sat now for millennia.

"Last of the seven wonders of the world," their guide droned in excellent English, "... pharaohs... builders not mummified... buried in mudbrick tombs with beer and bread for the afterlife. Ten thousand laborers working in shifts three months at a time... it took more than thirty years to build a pyramid..."

Max's mind wandered.

Chasing a nomad in the desert... the Nomad, maybe nothing more than a whisper among the intel agencies... a zephyr... does he even exist...

The tour guide raised his voice. "... and one pharaoh named Steve Martin. He and his hired help were reincarnated as King Tut and the Toot Uncommons in 1978... and here is the grandaddy of the pyramids, the Pyramid of Cheops..."

Max shook off his trance. "Wait. What did he say, Renee?"

She chuckled. "He's making sure you're still paying attention, Max. Thank you, sahib," she said to the guide, "that was cute."

The tour ended. They returned to their plush seats and air conditioning, the limo's creature comforts and pampering never feeling so good for their ride back to the hotel.

A cabana dinner on the top of the hotel. Private, with the hotel's rooftop and pools closed to other guests for the evening at the last minute. This had to have been at a hefty price, but what the hell, Max thought, this was the wealthy Crown Prince. Eight diners only, the four co-piloting teams who were still in the race, Max and Renee included. Each team's support folks were relegated to eating at other culinary locations inside the hotel or out.

Steamed and wok-fried Dim Sum, glass noodles, chicken, beef, and seafood dishes all cooked to order by a chef assigned to each couple. With their dinner orders placed, Jasem spoke from his seat at the head of the open-air table, a soft wind ruffling the table's settings and the tall palms nestled among the four pools a relief from the heat of the day.

"My admin Jundiin organized this dinner for us tonight, then he promptly banished himself," Jasem said, chuckling. "Tonight, we eat from the hotel's Cantonese menu, but it will all be prepared right here for us, anything on the menu that you'd like. The significance? We number eight diners at this table. Eight is the luckiest number in the Chinese culture, and the hotel's Cantonese restaurant carries the same name, *Eight*, for the same reason, so why not grab some of this luck while we can, I said to Jundiin. Enjoy your meals, my friends."

Light conversation, the adventurers shared experiences about their time together on the ground and separately while airborne since the start of the race in Cannes. A camaraderie among competitors, with country politics off the table. Then Jasem tapped his glass to get everyone's attention.

"My friends." His smile remained wide, a signature that conveyed the genuine thrill that his manicured, sheltered life had been affording him, but his eyes betrayed this persona. He was suffering a bit, tempering his enthusiasm. "This contest was my brainchild, birthed as a fanciful lark to foster goodwill among our nations, and meant to showcase our similarities while downplaying our differences. In so many ways, it has achieved this. But there are concerns that have emerged from levels above our individual stations, and that all of us are feeling. We have no more information, yet, about the recent misfortunes regarding the aircraft fuel, but regardless, I have decided that our next stop, originally scheduled in Sinai as a refueling dine and dash, should now be an overnight stay."

The particulars had been decided. Overnight accommodations were already booked and there would be no elimination of contestants for that leg. Jasem added an extra day for the race committee and the contestants to analyze the charged atmosphere surrounding the race, to finish the fuel contamination discussion, and to provide more relief of the tension. Tomorrow's departure would go as planned, with the staggered starts picking up again at ten a.m.

Renee spent more time with the other women co-pilots comparing notes about their days in Cairo, then she and Max paid their respects for the night. She grabbed his arm and held it as they entered the elevator. The door closed.

"You showed restraint tonight, Max," she said.

"Good to know, but how so?"

"You're here with me now, on the way to our room, not back there doing shots then cannonballs into the pool."

He opened his sport jacket, removed a bottle of beer from a vest pocket, and popped the cap. "I see," he said, smirking.

"I'm not taking it back," she said. "I still think you're making progress. One more thing. A serious comment."

"Okay. Go."

"Camille's talk with me earlier today was all about my safety, but I worry about hers."

16

Two hundred thirty-four miles from Cairo International to Sharm El Sheikh International, Sinai Peninsula, Egypt, for a planned refuel that was now scheduled for an overnight stop. Staggered starts again, with Max and Renee the last team in the air at eleven a.m. Desert, then cross the Gulf of Suez, then desert all the way to Sinai. Approximate time in the air, one hour twenty minutes.

At the end of the leg, Renee's call to the tower cleared them for their approach to the Sinai airport. Then a return call from the tower said now they were no longer cleared. Max responded.

"Sinai Tower, November three-six-eight Romeo Juliet," he said. "Interrogative. What's the problem?"

"November three-six-eight Romeo Juliet, Tower, a priority aircraft is on final. Please enter holding two miles west of the airport at one thousand feet. You will be next."

Max snorted. "Priority aircraft? Hmph."

Renee's phone lit up and jitterbugged around the console between them. Not a call, texts.

She read them in silence. Then, staying in character for the benefit of their streaming audience: "From our diplomatic attaché again. A message from them, which included a message from your father, Max."

Max hoped his double-take didn't look too sudden on the camera stream. He gathered himself. "Really? What's up?"

"He said don't be surprised if we get a visit from your uncle in Sinai looking to catch up with everyone. He'll be landing at 1230 hundred hours." She cast an expectant look Max's way. "I'd say there's a good chance he's on that larger private jet that just bumped us out of the landing queue."

"Ha. Super." Max managed a smile for the camera. "It will be good to see what my good ol' uncle is up to."

Max had no living uncles. Jasem's uncle, however, was very much alive. The messages were from Wilkes. This was to alert them that Jasem's uncle was back for another visit.

Land the plane, limo to the hotel, unpack, showers. The Four Seasons Resort Hotel Sharm El Sheikh was an incredible oasis. Renee pulled up an email note from the hotel concierge to all the teams that contained sight-seeing suggestions. Sharm El Sheikh's tourist trap attractions for the day might include a promenade around Naama Bay; an ocean dive to see a WWII British cargo shipwreck, SS *Thislegorm*; a trip to "the Colored Canyon"; snorkeling the coral reefs; quad biking in the desert; or a visit to St. Catherine's Monastery at the foot of Mt. Sinai, where Moses received the Ten Commandments.

Renee spoke to herself, the wind whistling across their terrace. "Saint Catherine's sounds interesting." Then it was back to thinking aloud while reviewing the content she'd received from her army of hacker misfits. "Okay, so what do any of you have that is new about Nomad, people?"

A weary Max sat beside her on the covered terrace in full appreciation of the incredible view their vantage point gave of the Red Sea. "Anything of merit from your internet hooligans?"

"Nope. I suggest we do some religion today, Max. We can ride out to Saint Catherine's Monastery on Mount Sinai. For a Catholic girl like me, even though it's Old Testament, I need to see it. I'll hire another limo."

"It's a Greek Orthodox monastery, not Catholic."

"What difference does it make who tends to it? It's the delivery of the Ten Commandments. Moses at his finest."

Max agreed to the trip. In fifteen minutes, Renee's dancing fingers got their arrangements done.

She grabbed his hand, led him down a hotel corridor. "You ever ride a camel, Max?"

"You've got to be kidding. We just did mules…"

"Me neither. I booked two of them with guides, for a trek up the mountain. But first, the monastery. We won't have time to go all the way up the mountain, but damn, to be in Sinai and not take a closer look at it, or not see icons like the Burning Bush and where God spoke the Commandments to Moses—for me, it would be like going to the Vatican and not seeing the Pope."

"Happy for your enthusiasm," Max said. "But camels?"

"Camels."

Jeans, short sleeves, sunglasses, backpack, and cans of flea spray that were only partly effective. Cash, in Egyptian pounds, for the camel tenders. Patience. The complete trip to the monastery and the ascent to Mount Sinai was a seven-hour trek, but it gave them a view of the same mountains Moses purportedly visited over three thousand years ago, plus a monastery dedicated to a namesake, St. Catherine of Alexandria, yet another martyr beheaded for her faith. Renee felt exhausted but fulfilled, Max simply exhausted. His fulfillment came from multiple phone conversations with Wilkes while they bounced up and down on the camels.

One of them: "You say you have something?" Max said, bettering his camel's grunts and the camel tender's admonitions to his complaining animal.

"We intercepted a comm Jasem received on his phone. From the uncle. They meet again tonight."

"But Jasem planned a tent dinner for us on the beach. Where and when will he and the uncle meet?"

"Both are TBD. The uncle's text said a third party will be there."

"Fine. When you get more info, we'll make it happen. Can you get Trent to make an appearance?"

"He's on standby. Once the particulars are ironed out, we'll get him there."

Music accompanied their tent dinner on Naama Bay. A jazz trio, no vocalist, a Bedouin sword and fire performer, and belly dancers. An open bar. A bit of the old Jasem playboy bravado was rearing itself, Jasem inviting groups of giddy nightlife female tourists wandering past the tent to join his dinner party. Another night where things could get out of hand. Max now wondered if this was Jasem's M.O. for when he'd planned to get extracurricular with his clandestine wanderings, as in a diversion that kept his guests from paying too close attention to him and perhaps a planned exit.

The pilot teams partook of the indulgences, shots and nightcaps arriving in full force, Renee chumming it up with Camille when the dinner ended, Max making their discussion a trio. Tomorrow was a flight day, the next stop, Buraydah International in Saudi Arabia, another long leg. Best to show restraint, Max knew, and best to keep an eye on Jasem while he worked the tent, visiting with his party guests old and new. Max convinced himself his frequent glances Jasem's way were warding off his exit from the party.

"Max? *Max?*" Camille leaned into his line of vision. "Why so serious, *mon ami*? We are sorry, aren't we, Renee, for all the French? We will speak English now, so you can join our discussion, *oui*?"

They clinked glasses, Max smiled, accepted the apology, and squeezed Renee's hand. He glanced back at Jasem on the other side of the tent, or at least where Jasem had been, but he was gone.

"Excuse me, Camille, Renee," Max said, "I just remembered something. I need to go."

He hustled out of the tent. At 9:45 p.m. the streets of Naama Bay were lit up for tourists as bright as an urban college campus at midnight, but they were no help, because there was no Jasem in sight. Car, limo, cab? Was Jasem walking, or maybe running? Wherever he'd planned to go tonight,

Max had planned to follow him to find out, except Jasem had already disappeared.

Max's phone rang. Renee. He slowed to a fast walk and put the phone to his ear. "Damn it, I lost him."

"No worries. I know where he's going," Renee said.

Max stopped, did an about-face, started jogging back toward the dinner tent. "How? Did Wilkes call?"

"No. I asked Camille."

Huh. Imagine that. "Okay. Great. You ready?"

"Paying my respects."

I'm sleepy from the alcohol, I need a good night's sleep, I'll see you in the morning, Camille, etcetera, etcetera, then she and Camille hugged their goodbyes. Renee met Max at a street corner. They started jogging back to their hotel.

"Spill it, where's Jasem going?" Max said, catching breaths as they ran.

"Camille said the airport. Royal family stuff, a special guest and, surprise, Jasem's Uncle Saeed again. I texted Wilkes already."

A special guest? Nomad?

The rental car GPS said twenty minutes to the airport, but Max was determined to do it in ten or less, could visualize himself speeding down one of the service drives to the hangars. Renee had her binoculars in her lap. As they closed in, she raised them, scanning the area.

"The uncle's plane is still here. It seems all buttoned up. There, I see a car, a limo, right there, behind a hangar, not the hangar with our plane in it. The car's engine is running, there are other cars in the lot..."

"Jasem's?"

"Don't know..."

Max slowed down near the hangar housing the race planes and drove past the entrance. Inside was well lit and busy, the service guys hard at work on all the planes. He stopped short along the side of the building, Max and Renee out of the car quickly, backpacks, black bag, binoculars. Max eyed their surroundings as they walked the length of the exterior hangar wall. Cars, vans, baggage carts, food scooters, a motorcycle. At the building's corner they raised their binoculars for a view at the hangar next door. Same idling car, no people in the parking lot, no other activity. A sweep of the tarmac: the uncle's plane, close but not very, had its hatch closed.

"The uncle's jet is a hundred yards away, Max. If he's here to meet him, why isn't Jasem closer?"

"Right. Might not be Jasem?"

A limo door opened. The suited driver got out, a big man. He scanned the parking lot, then opened the back door.

Jasem stepped out. He checked his phone, began poking at it, his bodyguard still vigilant.

"Max... look. Out there..." Renee pointed at the edges of the parking lot.

Parked cars came to life with gunning engines and screeching, smoking tires, all bearing down on Jasem's limo, right, left, rear. The bodyguard unholstered his weapon, turned to shove Jasem back into the limo but missed the open door because the limo had been rammed from behind and pushed sideways, where it picked up a second hit from another car. The bodyguard sidestepped a third ramming, raised his weapon at the windshield, but was taken down from behind by a taser before he got off a shot. He began twitching like a flounder.

Max shoved Renee back into their rental. "Go back to the hotel, call Wilkes, Jundiin, Camille, all of them. Get his other security guys out here...!"

"But what if it's Nomad?"

Max checked his options for impromptu vehicle transport to commandeer. Car, van, cart, motorcycle.

"This would be our lucky day, then. Track me on my phone GPS. Go. Now."

Renee and the rental car fishtailed out of the lot. Max tried car doors, van doors, then hopped on the motorcycle, a high-end Suzuki. If he got it running, he'd catch them within seconds. He fished in his black bag for his keyless ignition override, pressed button after button, got nothing. Another scan of the lot. Putt-putting in idle at a hangar side door was a pizza delivery scooter.

Max turned the corner of the hangar on the Vespa scooter in time to see Jasem shoved into a BMW at gunpoint and watch it speed off. He scanned the scooter's instruments, looked for speed indications, knew some Vespas could reach eighty miles per hour, but not ones that delivered food, and definitely not this one. He topped out at forty-five, lost one of the pizzas, swiped at bugs, and followed the speeding sedan back onto El-Salam, the road they'd taken to get to the airport, reversing their direction. Not a busy road, he saw the car's red lights ahead as it opened the distance, one vehicle between them. The red lights brightened when its brakes engaged. The sedan turned left off the highway.

Max made the turn. *Maritim Jolie Golf Course and Resort*, the sign said. A busy place with traffic and stoplights... he could close the gap—

Max barked admonitions that no one heard. "Don't go in the resort... Don't, I'll lose you, you bastards. Go left, not right..."

The sedan complied, turned left, followed a sandy road that ended at what looked like a banquet hall under construction, lights strung low inside an incomplete interior. The BMW stopped hard, its doors opening. Three men manhandled their hostage out of the car, each of them heavily tattooed, each with bling around their necks and wrists. Gangsters or gangster wannabes. Max's first impression was these were boys looking to become men, wanting to be players, might not have even known what the hell they'd signed up for. Not professionals, and not ready for what would happen to them when someone found them, and with Renee assembling the cavalry, someone would. In the meantime, they hustled Jasem out of the car and into the building job site, cracking jokes while manhandling him. Did they even have guns...?

Yes, one did for sure because it was out and pointed at the back of Jasem's head. The thug and his gun shoved him inside the building.

Max checked their car as he tiptoed past. No one else inside. He was at the doorway now, peeking in.

"Ransom money, you royal piece of shit," one young thug said in English. "Make some calls, get our recruiter some money. You've got a lot of it, and he wants some."

"Okay," Jasem said, "that can be arranged. How much does he want? Better yet, how much is your cut? Maybe we can..."

"Ha, don't try that shit, Sheikh. Not interested. He wants five hundred million in digital currency. You know, Bitcoin and all that other goofy computer money floating around out there."

"Okay, but that's a lot. I can't get someone to pull together that much and transfer it so quickly—"

"You have an hour, Sheikh. That's it. We've already been paid. One hour"—their spokesman pointed his gun at Jasem's temple—"before we turn you over, and it doesn't matter in what condition, either."

Delivering a ransom that high in any capacity would never happen, Max knew. Not enough time. The call Jasem would make would turn the kidnapping into a bloodbath, with Jasem a potential casualty.

Only three of them, and Max saw only one gun. The time would need to be now.

A pizza box skittered along the floor, ended its skid against a tall stack of palleted drywall. Four pair of eyes followed it, but before they could find its origin Max emptied a can of Mace into the gun guy's face. A punch to the head separated him from his piece, which Max kicked to Jasem. The two other men went to their jacket pockets, but Max already had his Sig out and leveled between them.

"Go ahead, take out your guns and put them on the floor. The sheikh might not shoot you, but I sure as hell will."

Behind Max a new voice startled the group, one that sounded a lot older than the three gangster kidnappers. "*You*, fool, put *your* gun on the floor. If one of us begins shooting, you all go down. Slow turns now, please, so we can see your faces... There. Thank you."

Max and Jasem faced four men armed with assault-style weapons. Max assessed the room—more thugs, more firepower than he'd anticipated. He looked for the cover they'd need when the place got busier, because it would, and soon.

"Drywall," he whispered to Jasem, and glanced furtively at the pallet of stacked wallboard that had stopped the sliding pizza box, less than ten feet from them.

Max's phone beeped, heard by all in the large room. Not a call, a text. One beep became two, two became four, then came the series of beeps, text after text after text.

The older thug, the speaker, had more to say to Max. "We'll be leaving with His Royal Highness now. I'll give you a chance to look at your phone. You can text them back to let them know where to pick up your body."

More beeps on Max's phone, text after text arriving, beeping, ticking the time away. Undeterred, even a bit underwhelmed, Max went fishing. "Where you taking him?"

"Ha. So this is where you think you'll keep me talking and I'll tell you all about our diabolical secret plan instead of just killing you. You watch too many American movies. Sorry to disappoint you, but no. Go ahead, text them back, that beeping is killing me."

Max shook his head. "I don't need to text them back, tough guy. These beeps tell me they already know where I am. What you need to worry about," he said, "is when the beeping stops. That... will kill you, for real."

With that, his phone went silent. Warned, the three thugs went on alert, squaring themselves, readying for an assault or some other interruption. One second passed, two seconds, three became four... The older thug sneered at Max. "Ha-ha, you had me for a moment, you pathetic American dog. And now—"

The room erupted in automatic gunfire, overhead and at floor level. Max dragged Jasem behind the drywall where they both lay low, Max keeping his gun drawn, Jasem doing likewise with the piece he held. Short bullet bursts cut deep into the stacked drywall, sending chunks of gray gypsum flying in all directions, a white cloud of dust enveloping them. After thirty or so seconds that felt like an hour, the gunfire stopped.

A face painted in camo green and black turned the corner of their protective pile of drywall: Trent, in head-to-toe tactical gear. He dead-panned a comment.

"What, you don't answer my texts anymore?" He pulled Max to his feet, then Max did the same with Jasem. Some chest bumps, handshakes, and then came the confirmation from Trent that Renee was safe. She was outside the building in an SUV.

"She's waiting for you to show your face, hopefully no uglier than it already was, or she'll be coming after me," Trent said.

Max assessed the group assembled for the assault; he was majorly impressed. Trent ticked off the members' affiliations. "Jasem's security team, the Egyptian police, my guys..."

Max scanned the bloody scene. "How many hit?"

"None of the good guys. One kidnapper wounded." He turned to hover over some bodies, eyed the carnage. "And these three wasted."

The dead were the ones who'd had the speaking parts, the older guy and the younger one Max had Maced.

Max clicked some phone photos of the dead men. He delayed the march of the other captives to a waiting van outside the building so he could get additional pictures. He sent everything to Wilkes.

He had reassuring words for Renee in their SUV after he received an emotional hug and kiss from her. "Far as I'm concerned, this was a setup. We'll need to debrief Jasem, and I for sure want him to debrief us."

"Any of them Nomad?" she asked.

"I doubt it. But on the receiving end, had they gotten Jasem, I'm thinking it would have been yes not too far down the line."

Trent helped the Crown Prince into the vehicle with Max and Renee. Max offered him some bottled water, then started in with the questions.

"Jasem. These guys—what in the world do these Egyptians have against you that they would pull something like this?"

Jasem gulped at the bottle, swallowed, then took another pull. He spoke after a long sigh, still shaken. "They're not Egyptians, Max. They're Israelis."

17

———

"You need to tell me what just happened in there," Jasem said. On one side of the SUV, Trent stood conversing with his teammates. On the other side, two of Jasem's bodyguards stood like guard dogs waiting for their master's commands.

"I saved your ass is what happened," Max said. "We need to hear from you first. Who were those guys?"

"I... I don't know. The ones who took me fashioned themselves as players in the Israeli underworld, but they weren't more than, what do you call them, punks?"

Max knew the type. Young, unprofessional gangs with no morals and no moral compass, looking for street cred. Unpredictable and trigger happy. Never the brains in the job, the tools only. Highly volatile. Which made their kidnap gig completely suspect. Anything could have gone wrong for them, and a lot of anything had. From the start, chances of successfully handing Jasem over to the pros were iffy at best. This was not feeling like a Nomad gig.

"They made the trek from Israel all the way here, to go after you?"

"Sounds odd, but yes. Boasted about it while I was in the car. They earned a large payday. But just as important to them was their performance. Building their resume. I meant little to them other than the completion of a task that would get them noticed."

"But who were you supposed to meet at the airport? The reason you were there?" Renee said, speaking up.

"Sheikh Saeed Bin Rashid Al Abbar, my uncle, whom you've both met. He and I... I hoped we could patch things up between us. We are on different pages regarding our country's diplomatic efforts."

"Regarding Israel," Max said.

"Yes. He has little faith in the peace agreement. I am starting to wonder myself if I have overestimated the strength of this normalization treaty, and the wills of our respective countries to honor it."

The agreement was important, to the region and to the world. Jasem second-guessing his efforts was not a good thing. Max could offer only simple, biased counsel. "You are right to protect the treaty. Your uncle is wrong. The U.S. believes the Israelis are acting in good faith, Jasem. Who arranged your meeting?"

"My uncle texted me the date and time."

"Anyone else know about it?" Renee again.

"Jundiin, my admin. My uncle included him on the text. And I mentioned it to my co-pilot Camille."

Renee got bold. "Your Highness—Jasem—can I see the text from your uncle?"

"I will send it to you and Max."

"Sure. Thanks. But I want to see it on your phone, if you wouldn't mind, please."

A puzzled look at her, then a look at Max. "No. I would rather not. I'm sure you understand. Don't forget, I have questions for you as well. I... wonder about your roles in this."

Max, in a placating mode: "Sure. But one more thing I'd like you to consider, then I'm all yours." Deep breath, pending a confrontational question.

"Who else, aside from your uncle, could have something to gain from eliminating you? If this was not your uncle's doing, then whose was it?"

"Max, stop. I do not know, but it's not my uncle. We have our differences, but we are still aligned as part of our family, and we have the country's best interests at heart. I repeat, Uncle Saeed might try to discredit me, but he would not harm me."

Max had hit a nerve. This drew Renee back in: "Jasem, please, we're trying to be on the same team here. Who do you think set this up?"

He gazed out the window beyond his bodyguards, into the dark night, into the desert. "I am a UAE Royal. I am visible. I have enemies I don't even know about. I... fine, I agree, maybe I should not rule anyone out, not even my uncle. So"—he'd made a decision—"here is what I am going to do..."

The Crown Prince of UAE, a man of action, a leader, puffed his chest a little. He would increase his security team, have his country's intel groups scope out the remaining race stops for anything out of the ordinary, and tweak the race agenda, especially the ceremony at the end in Dubai. He would debrief his father the king now, tonight, then have a more intimate discussion with him about his apprehensions when he returned home. In the meantime, he would have no further contact with his uncle, just in case.

"Now, Max Fend, as the world-beaters that you and your father are in your private sector," Jasem said, his confidence restored, "please tell me again how it is that the U.S. government seems to respond to your beck and call."

Max would tell him a bit more about his relationship with his government, except there would be no mention of intel agencies, and no mention of Wilkes. He began his curated boast.

Trent Carpenter, a good friend with extraordinary talents gleaned in his country's special forces units, was his bodyguard on call, his black bag guy. Trent's significant access to similarly trained personnel around the world could be activated at the hint of a crisis.

Max, and his father Charles, had direct lines of communication to U.S. ambassadors with substantial reach inside American bureaucratic units. Back scratchers and back slappers all, the lot of them.

"What about Mademoiselle LeFrancois, Max? How does this lovely lady fit in?" Jasem demurred a glance in Renee's direction, then refocused on Max.

"Aside from our personal relationship, you mean? Well—"

"Mister Royal Highness," she said, her tone sharp, "speak directly to me, please. Max, a Fend Aerospace executive, can't program his TV cable box without my help, so I provide tech support for his household devices and equipment when he needs it."

Max raised his eyebrows in agreement. "What she said. So why don't we call it a night and—"

"One more thing, Jasem," Renee said. "The first set of gangster-types who rammed your car then abducted you—you said they told you they were 'completing a task that would get them noticed.' Completing a task for whom? Did you ask?"

Jasem glanced Max's way. Max's nod said *good question*.

"They were going to hold me for a short while, then hand me off. Not sure if it was to the men with the assault rifles at the construction site or someone after them, but it was supposed to be to someone who would pay a ransom."

"Did that someone have a name?" Max asked.

"None I can recall. Wait. Maybe. Yes, they did mention someone. Someone they called their recruiter. But the final handoff was to be to a group of nomads, I think they said. Yes. To nomads."

18

———

"*... to nomads.*" They made no attempt to correct him. They let Jasem think that's what he'd heard. This was what Max told Wilkes on the phone during their ride back to their hotel, on speaker, Trent driving, Max and Renee strapped into the SUV.

Max turned analytical now that the adrenaline had worn off. "We left a big mess back there, Wilkes. Trust me, after fighting our way out of that, it doesn't look like Jasem is leading this effort."

"ETA to the hotel seven minutes," Trent said.

They could hear Wilkes fumble with something on his end. "Found it," he said. "Your itinerary. Your next race stop is Prince Naif bin Abdulaziz International Airport, Buraydah, Saudi Arabia. Five hundred eighty-eight miles." More fumbling. "After that, Qatar. Then the race ends in Dubai. Fine, Max. I'm starting to think we're being played. Maybe the whole idea behind the info fed to our intel was to let the race run its course. Let its logistics collapse on itself. Plenty of places where its audience would get to see the fragile political relationships in the region, plus witness the naiveté of our young idealist, the Crown Prince. It seems to be working. Jasem looks like he's in over his head."

Max spoke. "The region needs idealists, Wilkes. We'll talk tomorrow while we're in the air. We need to address the whole video streaming of the race, too, but it's too late to turn off the cameras now. It would be like all of this had failed—the race, the relationships, the treaty. Plus, the evening uploads of the cockpit chatter are too popular. Tomorrow, in the air, we'll regroup. Signing off."

Trent announced their arrival and volunteered his agenda for their remaining hours in Sinai. "My team will sweep your plane for any electronic eavesdropping equipment. Once tonight and again tomorrow morning, after the maintenance jockeys and your buddy Lou release it."

"Hadn't thought of that," Max said. "Whose idea—?"

"Wilkes's. Better late than never. Cut him some slack, Max. The intel's not always perfect, but it's second to none out there. Get some rest. Anything comes up, we'll debrief you guys in the morning. One other thing: a suggestion about the cockpit streaming."

"Okay, let's hear it."

"Turn it the hell off, talk however you want, about whatever you want, then turn it back on. Just say it malfunctioned; a temporary blackout. As long as there's some footage for the day, that should keep the Crown Prince's audience happy. You're welcome."

With Max and Renee's plane the last to cross the pylon threshold in Cairo, it again made them the last plane airborne the next morning. Four teams remained: UAE, Qatar, Israel, the U.S. The plane engine on, Renee was flying, ready to taxi them into position to await tower clearance for takeoff.

"Look at those two," she said. Lou Dotto waved at them from outside the hangar, tired, Trent beside him, delivering a subdued thumbs up. No listening devices had been found inside the plane or on its exterior, no faulty mechanical equipment, no bad jet fuel. The plane was in tiptop shape, all systems go, thanks to these guys.

"Trent looks worse than Lou."

"He should. Getting zero sleep after neutralizing those kidnappers last night would do that to a person. Lou was up all night, too. They'll rest today on their ride to our next stop."

Max checked their flight route for hints at where they could make up time, altitude, air currents, and the like. With only four teams left, it now paid to take a closer look at their competitors' routes as well as their own. Max and Renee didn't need to finish with a better time or more points than all the other teams on this leg, they just needed to finish better than one of them.

He stretched his arms and legs like he'd just awakened from the best sleep of his life and made cooing noises to that effect. The stretch was a test, a ruse to gauge his head, arm, and leg room inside the aircraft cabin, to see how much space he had before bumping any part of his extended body into anything electronic. In the middle of a second stretch, he whacked the mounted video camera centered above them. A light on the camera went from green to red.

"Oops..." he deadpanned.

The camera was now offline, the video and audio feeds suspended from recording. Max rubbed his wrist—"Ouch, that might leave a mark"—but now they no longer had to be on their best behavior and could converse freely with no need to text each other. "Okay then, a lot to do. I decided on which team we should track. A no-brainer. The Qatar team. I drive, you snoop."

"Your airplane," Renee said.

"My airplane."

Renee retrieved her laptop. Her fingers blazed the keys and began browsing. "The task is we want to know how the Qatari team planned to fly this route."

"Correct. Their planned altitude and speed and whatever other flight markers they intended to use. Then we'll take our beloved Rose to a better altitude, which will help us fly..."

"*Faster*. See, I am paying attention."

The leg was a little less than six hundred miles. At 175 knots, about a three-hour trip. But if they increased their altitude by a few thousand feet, the winds become much more favorable, making them fly ten knots faster over ground than the Qatar team.

There was also this. "Lou had a suggestion," Max said. "He wanted to juice our engine up with a few modifications so we could get more horses out of it."

"And?"

"I said no. Too much of a chance Jasem's maintenance guys would notice a modification and blow the whistle. How are you doing?"

"The password on the air race website for the Qatar team's flight plan is—drum roll—*QatarTeam1*. That's how I'm doing."

"At least they made you work for it."

"Took a whole one-point-nine seconds to solve. Whew, I'm bushed. Here's what we have..."

Renee opened the Qatar flight plan file, which included their intended altitudes on each leg of the flight. For some of the legs, they were flying lower, probably to make out the navigational checkpoints on the ground.

"Okay. We'll fly twenty-five hundred feet higher than them. Our checkpoints are easier to see on this route, so we should be fine to do so. With the predicted winds aloft, we should arrive ten to twenty minutes earlier than them, give or take. You'll need to check the topography. To make sure we stay away from any sand dunes that are nine thousand feet high."

"That a joke, Max?"

"Maybe it was, maybe it wasn't. You tell me."

The tallest Saudi mountain elevations exceeded ten thousand feet and were to the south and west. They'd need to take a diagonal, southeast route across the country, to fly around the higher elevations rather than over them to make best use of the higher altitude, all the way to Buraydah International, their destination.

"I looked at it," she said. "It's doable."

"Good. That's the spirit. Now let's get hold of Wilkes. I've got a few more questions for him."

"I gather you neutralized the online streaming," Wilkes said to Max.

"Yep. Shit happens. We'll get back online after we're done talking here."

"Okay then. Let me catch you up..."

They talked onscreen via Renee's laptop. She fed the voice through to their headsets, Wilkes dishing to them an update. "Langley's been busy. First, they got through to the Doughnut..."

The Doughnut: headquarters for Britain's intel group known as Government Communications, or GCHQ, in Cheltenham, England.

"It seems Colonel Tuttle confirmed for GCHQ they'd discovered a puzzle piece that no one else had."

"Wait. Air race Colonel Tuttle?" Max asked.

"That's the one. GCHQ has been monitoring Jasem's uncle for a lot longer than this race. They won't give details, but they now believe strongly that the uncle, not Jasem, was trying to connect with Nomad."

Renee pulled up different files, revisiting the spoils of Trent's sleeping-gas visit to the Crown Prince's room. "Wait a minute," she said, reading, "let me catch up here..."

She found what she wanted and sent it off to Wilkes. "Check out the file I just sent you. There, right there, on Jasem's phone—we see him reaching out to multiple phone numbers in quick succession. It looks a lot like a daisy chain, like a..."

"Like a caller being sent from phone booth to phone booth to confuse the cops while trying to deliver a ransom," Wilkes said.

"Yes. In this case, trying to make the connection that we've been chasing, to Nomad. Then the calls stopped. All from Jasem's phone number."

"Did any of them connect?"

"Yes, each of them did. To a burner. All the calls were to burners. But calls from Jasem's number," she said, "don't necessarily mean they were from Jasem."

Max spoke. "Copy that, Renee. Look, I'm going with GCHQ's assessment. My instincts say everything we're seeing indicates Jasem's not the guy. Hell, Jasem even gave his admin guy Jundiin permission to act on his behalf on occasion. Too easy for a guy like Jundiin, or the uncle, to be doing this and make it look like it's someone else."

"So, your instinct tells you that," Wilkes said. "That's interesting, coming from a guy who believed a spy wasn't a spy because the spy told him he wasn't."

"Hey—"

"Wilkes, what about motive?" Renee said. "We're really struggling with why the Crown Prince would sabotage his own agenda. If we put Jasem's uncle in the mix... What does he want more than anything? For things to stay the way they were; the way they *are*. Sameness. He hates that his brother the king went along with Jasem's progressive peace deal with Israel. He doesn't think it's right to make peace with his enemy."

"Yeah," Max said. "It insults him, and he thinks they're screwing over the Palestinians. But what insults him more is that Jasem was named Crown Prince."

"Enough," Wilkes said. "I get it. Jundiin needs a closer look. The uncle does, too. We all get it—"

Max's gaze wandered, eyeing the panoramic view from the cockpit, the heavens surrounding them. The higher-level clouds, the calming, endless, foreboding desert below, and next to him, his angelic co-pilot. But Renee was more than that to him. She was partner, and friend, and lover to the nth power.

"Copy this, then, Wilkes," Max said. "Who stands to gain more with Jasem's elimination? On a micro level, his Uncle Saeed. On the macro level —hell, further destabilization of a region means a few countries win, like Iran, but the region, the continent, the globe all continue to lose. The uncle's totally jealous of Jasem. He wants him out of the way. Wants more influence. Wants to be king, something I'm not even sure Jasem wants. The question is, does he want Jasem *dead*? It's clear someone does. And to you, Renee..."

She didn't respond, stayed keying at her laptop, waiting for him to continue.

"Honey..."

This quieted her fingers, earning him a surprised look from her.

"Much as I would miss you, Renee, I wish you were back in the States, sitting this mess out. You'd miss all this excitement, but—"

They'd seen the social media explosion brought on by the nightly downloads, leg after airborne leg of the contestants' cockpit chatter and drama, the exotic destinations, country-by-country bipartisanship, the silly memes making the rounds. But what the audience hadn't appreciated was the risk.

"... this shit scares me," Max said. "At least you'd be safe."

Renee swiped at her eye to remove a tear. She could manage only a contented smile.

"So that brings us back to you, Wilkes. We're on the world stage here. This race has gone viral. Only four teams left, and frankly, we're all in danger, during this leg and through one more stop, then the final leg to Dubai. It's suddenly a death-watch race. I'm tempted to quit this thing right now"—he eyed Renee again—"so the people who depend on me, and the people who I care about, get to go on with their lives with me still in them."

"Max, let me get a word in," Wilkes said.

"... As to Nomad, or the uncle, or anyone else—it can all go away in an instant for all of us. So maybe my friends and I just go home, and we let the chips fall where they may on someone else's watch."

Wilkes finally spoke over him. "Quiet, Max, please, just... stop. I don't do maudlin well, and I sure as hell hate hearing someone else do it, especially one of my agents. I'll meet you tonight in Saudi Arabia. We'll get more intel when we're there, from multiple agencies. In the meantime, if you call it quits and decide to put down somewhere in the middle of the desert—spoiler alert, I'm worried things could go south on you guys out there very quickly." Wilkes ended the call with Renee's laptop screen freezing on his serious face.

"Max, tell me I heard wrong. Tell me he didn't just threaten us with abandonment if we had to leave the assignment."

"There are protocols in place to disengage the U.S. government from an asset if it becomes necessary. Disengagement, disavowing knowledge, whatever form it would take... it's a decision based on the agency's assessment, not the asset's."

"You're not helping here."

"Shorter answer is no worries, they'd extract us, but they would deny any involvement. And we're not quitting, so let that go. But know this, Renee. I meant what I said. Your safety is more important to me than protecting obscure, unidentified U.S. assets." He swallowed hard. "Let's get back to work."

Airspeed at 175 knots had them cruising comfortably, their FW50 Rose performing well. Max goosed her up a bit, hit 180, just short of redline. Now for some further misdirection on their part.

When the online streaming app stuttered back to life, with the green light on the camera blazing, it caught Max sipping from a juice box and Renee peeling a banana. He'd tell the race officials later that they hadn't even noticed the camera had been turned off.

19

Neither Max nor Renee let up on Rose's throttle until they passed the race pylons on the tarmac, the fuel gauge bordering on empty. By Renee's calibration of their start and end time, they could not have navigated the route any better than they had, altitude-wise, speed-wise, and fuel-wise. A few quick texts to Wilkes and Trent let them know they'd landed. All four air race teams were now on the ground at Buraydah International, Saudi Arabia.

An embarrassment of riches filled the airport hangar, the host Saudis celebrating Jasem's diplomatic brainchild, the air race showcasing his diplomatic efforts. They had a crush on him and his larger-than-life personality, Jasem fast becoming the younger, progressive face of the entire Arabian Peninsula. Hot celebrities, sports figures from Saudi football, cricket, basketball, and horse breeding, plus the royal family from the House of Saud itself, all had turned out to greet Jasem and his air race teams in the flesh.

"We appear to be underdressed, Max," Renee said. "*Mon Dieu.* Over there. Is that who I think it is?"

"Sure is. His Majesty, the Saudi king. Nearest him on his right, his successor, the Saudi Crown Prince. He and Jasem have a lot in common—royal lineages, crazy wealth, huge fan bases, plus jealous relatives still jonesing for the title they now own. Plenty for them to talk about. I see there's a receiving line. Be prepared for a pat-down, Renee. Do you see Trent anywhere?"

"No. But I'm not getting in that line. The Saudis are so far off my moral compass, so against my politics, so against women's rights—they kill journalists who exercise their right to free speech. I'm sitting this out."

"Renee—"

"Enjoy yourself, cowboy. I'm going to hook up with Camille and hang with her. Maybe we can sew each other burkas."

A bevy of Saudi admin people arrived alongside and gently separated them from their overnight bags and their backpacks, spiriting their baggage away to "a waiting limo on the other side of that exit door, Mister Fend and Mademoiselle LeFrancois," one tall Saudi attaché said. "Please be advised that, per your American attaché, we will take very good care of your belongings, and we will reunite you with them after you have enjoyed the king's hospitality."

Their escorts pointed them to restrooms "to freshen up, so you are best prepared to greet His Majesty," and handed them bags emblazoned with the Royal Standard of Saudi Arabia and filled with toiletries for their use inside. Renee didn't push back and accepted the gift before entering the women's restroom. Max, while indisposed next door in the men's room, received a long text from Trent.

I know where you are. Take care of business, exit the restroom, look for me on the far right in a bullpen area surrounded by cordons. Im with the journalists doing my best to look touristy and journalistic. No more than a nod when you notice me. Current update is no new issues to report. I'll reach out to you later. FYI Wilkes is on the ground.

A nod from Max on his way out. Trent reciprocated.

Mouth-washed, tooth-brushed, and underarm-deodorized, they were fed back into the receiving line by their escorts, the line now conveniently cleared of all other guests. They'd be the last of Jasem's revered party of race participants to gain an audience. "Enjoy your meet-and-greet, Max," Renee said. "Don't forget to curtsey."

"I might fist bump the old guy," he whispered as they approached the Saudi royal family. "It'll be a crowd-pleaser."

"You do that." Renee peeled off at the last minute, begging the indulgence of the attaché, and blended into the crowd.

Max reached the royal family and waited until he was cued into a handshake. The salutations from the king and the Saudi prince included greetings and wrapped gifts that they wanted Max to take back to his father, Charles Fend, a good partner in their aeronautical advancement programs for many years. The introduction was smooth, with no hitches or hiccups even though Renee was absent.

After the introduction, Max spent fifteen minutes with Jasem, and Renee spent those same fifteen minutes separately with Camille. Max, after citing fatigue from the long, anxious flight, left Jasem and collected Renee.

A driver opened the door to their stretch limo. Inside, chilling with alcoholic beverages in tumblers with ice, the Israeli team's Ozzie Katz and co-pilot Talia Vaknin greeted them. Max and Renee dropped into the seats across from them and released tired sighs.

"Being in this limo with you," Max said to Ozzie, "does that mean Jasem and his pilot Camille are double-dating with the Qatar team?"

"No putting anything past you, Max Fend, my friend," Ozzie said, smiling and sipping. "Yes. We are the fortunate ones, paired together for the ride to the hotel, because the Qatar team will need to wait for Jasem's audience with the king to end. That could be a while. Plus, we must congratulate you."

"For what? Did we win something?" Max said, his smile sarcastic.

The Israeli captain flashed a sudden, toothy grin, then pressed a button on his armrest. The privacy screen behind Max and Renee rose and locked in tight to the ceiling, separating them from the driver and a bodyguard riding shotgun.

"Why yes you did, Max," Ozzie said. "You finished this race leg with a time that was fifty-four seconds faster than Qatar, who finished last."

"Wait. The results… they've been released?"

"Goodness no, that won't be until after dinner tonight with Jasem. Ha. I guess something *did* get past American intel, Talia. The results aren't released yet, Max, but they've been tabulated. You've made it into the next leg. We're in, UAE is in, Qatar is out. Here. Have some scotch."

They toasted their respective finishes, four tumblers each, then settled into their ride to the hotel. Max addressed what he'd heard. "Let's revisit what just happened, Captain. You say you have access to the unvalidated, unreleased race results?"

"You are correct. They have not been released, but they have been validated. And yes, I have access."

"How?"

"You surprise me, Max Fend." Ozzie Katz eyed Renee, whose backpack was tight against her side on the seat, not in the trunk with her overnight bag. Max had neither of his bags in here with him. Nor did Ozzie. But Renee and Talia, the Israeli co-pilot, both had theirs.

"What is in your co-pilot's bag, Max?"

"That's irrelevant. Just tell me—"

"What is in your co-pilot's bag, held closely to her person, is the same equipment that is in the bag my co-pilot holds closely to her person, and for the same reason. Laptops, for information gathering and data collection."

Co-pilot Talia Vaknin waved to Max, then patted the leather briefcase on her lap. She and Renee traded stares.

"In other words, my American friends, we work for similar organizations. Which thrills me to no end, mind you, because we can work together if necessary. Plus, I have to say it also thrills me knowing that we beat the Americans to a piece of intel, trivial though it is. Like your *Dirty Harry* film hero, it is making my day."

Max shook his head, doing the math then chiding himself. *They are Mossad.*

"You told me you weren't affiliated with any intel when we spoke before," Max said. "I believed you."

"That I did. Imagine that, Max Fend," Katz said, shrugging, "an intelligence officer who was not totally truthful. Let's wrap this up before we get to the hotel, shall we? Our lips are sealed, Max, as long as everyone stays within their lanes. And we won't share any intel unless our government clears it first. What we are all doing here, acknowledging each other's covert existence—none of this conversation happened."

"I haven't acknowledged anything," Max said. "It's... it's not true..."

"Okay. Play it that way. This discussion is the only one we'll ever have regarding our respective monitoring of whatever the hell is going on with Dubai's new Crown Prince. Which apparently is formidable, because this race has intelligence people of all colors and stripes up in arms. Ah, I see we have arrived. We will see you tonight, Max and Renee, at Jasem's dinner, I hope?"

~

Max double-checked the suite number. Eleventh floor, 1104 on the door, also the number of the reservation per the text from Jundiin, and the number the desk clerk gave them. Except the door's safety bar was between the door and jamb, which kept it from closing. Did the hotel screw up? Was the suite occupied?

Or was someone in here, waiting for them?

He removed the Sig from its holster and entered on light feet, did not call out, Renee staying back at the threshold holding the door wide open for a quick exit if necessary. Quiet footsteps down the room's short hall, the sliding glass door straight ahead, mid-afternoon shadows slanting through it, a sun-drenched terrace, the air conditioning humming, no other noise. He'd need to peek around a wall.

His phone beeped, startling him...

Damn it, the beep, the surprise is gone...

He needed to move now. His arms raised, he spun around the corner—

"Wilkes?"

Wilkes was settled into an armchair, his legs crossed, his eyebrows tenting when he looked up from his phone into the barrel of Max's gun. "Max. Hi. There's a good chance the text that just arrived on your phone is from me, six or seven minutes late. It's letting you know I'm in your room."

"Goddamn it, Wilkes, why do you sneak around like this?"

"You really need me to answer that?" he deadpanned. "I let myself in. Where's Renee?"

"Here," she said, pushing past Max. They moved their bags inside, dropped everything in the bedroom, and rejoined Wilkes in the sitting area.

Max spoke. "I've got some news for you. First, what do you have for us?"

"No, you first."

"We finished this leg ahead of the Qatar team. Less than a minute difference in our times. They're out. UAE was first, the Israelis second, us third. We were welcomed by the Saudi king and his crown prince. Big shindig at the hangar honoring Jasem and the race participants, a receiving line and everything. I met the Saudi royals, Renee opted out, wouldn't get within ten feet of them." He looked Renee's way.

"They're pigs," she said.

"Anyway, they like my father. Not much else to report," he said, shrugging, "unless you count that the Israeli pilots came out as Mossad, and they outed us as CIA. You know, normal shit. Okay, your turn."

Wilkes double-clutched his gaping mouth. "What? How...?"

"It was the Mossad stuff, wasn't it? Yeah, surprised me, too," he said. "They didn't say 'Mossad' or mention the CIA, but they inferred both. What're you gonna do, right?"

Wilkes stood and paced, hurling a few F-bombs around the room.

"How many intel agencies does that make now?" Max said. "Five? Yes, including us, that's five, not counting the second UK group, and not including whatever the hell Jasem is doing with his own people. Everyone's interested in a certain contract assassin, and whoever might be trying to engage that assassin, and for whatever reason."

Wilkes sat, leaned forward, his brow furrowed, hands folded. "Explain 'outted.'"

CIA, Mossad, MI-6, the Pakistanis. *Our cup of spy agencies runneth over,* Max thought. "No details, just their perception. I told the Israeli pilot he was wrong about us. He almost laughed. Ours will be a shared silence. The impression I have is, he accepts that we're in this together."

"We all want Nomad," Wilkes said.

Wilkes keyed some notes into his phone, or maybe sent a text, Max couldn't tell which, so he asked. "What was that?"

"Change of approach. I was on with a military contact. You guys now have a bodyguard."

"Can I assume—"

"And you would be right. It's Trent Carpenter. Good luck to the three of you. Other intel I have is, you can add the GID to the other five agencies."

"The General Intelligence Directorate?" Max said. "The Saudi spy agency?"

"I've been introduced to them. I'm having a closed-door sit-down with a Saudi intelligence officer tonight. I want you guys to come."

"Nope," Renee said. "He probably wouldn't let me in the room without me wearing an abayah. I'm not going through that humiliation." She added some French, no doubt off color.

Max cleared his throat. "You don't want her to translate that, Wilkes. Tonight, it'll be you and me only. When and where?"

"And Trent. I'll let you know."

"On the outside of the hotel you will find camel trading posts and the world's largest dates market," Jasem said, their splendid dinners eaten, "but they are all closed now. After we announce today's race results, I suggest we have our nightcaps here, in this magnificent hotel ballroom. Perhaps each of you can get a massage and retire totally relaxed. That is my plan, so I can wake up refreshed. And then"—he winked in Max and Renee's direction—"as our bold Americans might say, my co-pilot and I will kick your asses all over the place on tomorrow's leg. That is, assuming I am still a part of the race."

Chuckles and laughter rose from around all the tables, mostly from Jasem's hangers-on, Jundiin included, more invested in Jasem's wit than everyone else. Polite laughter came from Max and Renee, the Israelis, and the Qatar team, Camille appearing skeptical of their sincerity as well. The rigors of the race, its diplomatic significance, was wearing them all down.

"Jundiin, please read the results from today's long and grueling flight."

The smallish man summoned a carnival barker voice. The announcement was anti-climactic, Max positive that the Qatar pilots were the only contestants unaware of the race results beforehand. The congratulations, attaboys, and condolences worked their way around the dinner guests, a tough pill to swallow for the Qatar team. So close to the U.S. team's time, they were eliminated one stop short of their home country.

"Max." Renee cast a look over her raised coffee cup at the well-lit terrace visible outside the hotel's ballroom. "He's here."

"He" was Trent, dressed casually at a table by himself. A bottle of beer in hand, he surveyed the distant, dark desert that reached hundreds of miles, thousands in some directions, beyond the hotel. Trent checked his phone, read the screen, then raised his head to catch Max staring at him. Max's phone beeped with a text from Trent.

Be ready in 15. I'm driving

Jasem had been correct, this late at night the camel trader pens were closed. But they weren't off limits. Trent stopped the Jeep next to a cinderblock shack, one of many in the open space that spread out in front of them. The air was foul and still oppressively hot, even at this hour.

"Wilkes's phone GPS says he's here," Trent said. "He should be waiting for us."

"Where is 'here?'" Max said. They'd driven around closed shacks and open pens and pickup trucks before stopping, the cloudless sky heavy with humidity, making the stink worse and the darkness darker.

"Where some camels come to die," Trent said. "I've been around these places before. These animals are one step away from the slaughterhouse. I swear the camels know it." Trent checked his phone, looked ahead of where they walked, and pointed at a faint light in an open passageway, the way into a long, single-story building with a corrugated half-roof. "This way."

Inside, the camel barn's open stalls were filled with dromedaries, the one-hump camels staple to the Middle East. Lanterns lit their way. "Sixth stall down, Wilkes says. He also says don't be surprised by the non-reception. The intel officer is here with no visible support other than his camels, but his camels are really big, and according to Wilkes, ornery. The key word in his text is, whatever support is here, it's not 'visible.' Then again, it could just be him bluffing his way past being here on his own."

Max read the room. The grunts and growling that the camels made when he and Trent entered stall number six said the camels didn't like them.

"No introductions," the Saudi intel guy said, his Islamic wear covering him from head to toe. He pointed at empty stools around a washtub with a fire in it. "I know enough about who you are, so I do not need to know your names. Sit." Wilkes was already sitting. "Let us begin now so we can finish soon. But first, you must have something to eat." He spooned some stew out of a pot hung over a robust fire.

The setup, Trent had told Max on the ride over: "*Saudi intel guy has a grudge against his country. The recent slaughter of a certain Saudi Arabian journalist working for a U.S. newspaper put him over the top. If you recall—*"

Max did recall. The world did. Murder and dismemberment of the journalist lured to the Saudis' Turkish Consulate. Denial by the Saudis. They fessed up when confronted, but not to any connection to the Saudi royals.

More from Trent. "*... this intel officer didn't know about it until after it happened, then saw his colleagues get executed as scapegoats for following orders. He's feeling betrayed. He doesn't want to end up like them.*"

The Saudis' official ambivalence toward the Israeli-UAE deal had been overtly public and overly dramatic. Their Saudi intel guy said that, internally, his country condemned the deal and did not want it to work. Externally, their opinion remained benign, nowhere near the actual disgust they harbored for it. And yet, they were keen on celebrating Jasem's air race.

Trent, on a roll. "*They knew of Nomad, Max, had used Nomad in the past, and they will use Nomad again. Our Saudi intel guy's assessment, corroborated by his own GID: it was the uncle's call to involve Nomad this time around, not Jasem's. Target's still not determined.*"

The fire in the pit crackled, its updrafts spiraling like fireflies ascending to the heavens. After the full meal Max had consumed at the hotel, he declined the stew. Wilkes partook, as did Trent.

"Eat it," the Saudi said to Max, "or this meeting will look suspicious."

Suspicious to whom, Max couldn't surmise, considering the barn was empty except for them and the penned camels. Max complied, nibbled on the meat, nibbled more until its camel gaminess became too much for him.

The intel officer summed up his info. "There have been multiple contacts. Not with Nomad. With a Nomad associate. I can open your eyes regarding these movements. But before I do, I am interested in what you might have in the way of potential movements for me."

Wilkes handed the officer a folded scrap of paper. "Open it. There is a name on the inside. Read it to yourself, do not speak it here."

The camel broker did as asked, lingered a moment, then folded the paper back up and found a pocket for it. "I must verify this later. I cannot do it now."

"I know," Wilkes said. "The best we can do."

The Saudi retrieved a single-page readout from a fold in his tunic and handed it to Wilkes. "Here, here, and here," he said, pointing.

"His recruiter," Wilkes said, analyzing the data. The readout showed texts from the uncle's phone number, likely sent to a burner phone. "This is excellent work, sir."

A flicker of light reflected against the fire's rising ashes, creating a yellow aurora, a suspended glow above them. Not a nighttime trick of a sunset long gone, it was the reflection of a vehicle's headlights, the vehicle stopping short outside the barn, its tires crunching the asphalt, its doors opening then slamming shut.

Trent liberated one semi-automatic handgun from behind his back, then two. Max drew his Sig. Wilkes stared down his Saudi counterpart, whose head shook vigorously, his hands up, pushing back, signifying denial, no, this isn't what you think...

Wilkes drew his gun, stuck it in the intel officer's face, now the fourth gun pointed with bad intentions at their contact. "You will die before we do," Wilkes said, affirming the obvious.

The camels in nearby stalls bleated their disapproval and bucked their restraints, pushing against their stall doors, stomping hard, kicking up dust. The ground beneath them shook from their outbursts.

The Saudi pleaded his case. "Put your guns away, my friends, now, or this will turn into an unnecessary bloodbath. These are my men coming to fetch me from what they believe is a meeting about my side business. They are not my enemies or yours. Do it, before they see you this way..."

Wilkes, last in to liberate his gun, became first out: he lifted his suit coat and reholstered his weapon. Max followed. Trent hesitated, then relented. Three Saudi men pushed through the barn entrance into the interior, not being especially quiet, talking trash to the feisty camels in the first stalls, the camels now even noisier, or what sounded like trash talk to Max because of the voice inflections.

A momentary standoff, the tension not fully released, four men around a campfire, hands empty and in full view of the three new guests, all Saudis. On a nearby table sat bowls of partially eaten stew; their cover. The tension ended with their Saudi host grabbing one of the camels by the neck to give him a pat, then a hug, the camel squealing in delight.

Their smiling host addressed his arriving posse. "Wonderful! My Uber, right on time." His associates chuckled at the joke and retreated to the animal pens, occupying themselves.

The intel officer wrapped up their meeting with commentary consistent with his cover. "I am glad, my American friends, that you enjoyed the stew. If you do decide to bring the flesh of our beasts of burden, or other nomadic creatures, to your American cities, I would be happy to assist you in that endeavor. Good night, gentlemen."

20

A formal breakfast at the hangar, again hosted by the Saudi royal family. Music by the Saudi orchestra, a newly formed group of world class musicians. A martial arts exhibition in progress on gym mats spread in front of a long, covered table set for the royals, other country dignitaries, and the three remaining air race teams. The orchestra and the martial arts displays were recent cultural advancements, both pet projects of Saudi's crown prince.

Max stood flatfooted in the wings with Renee, ready to escort her to their seats at the table. She hesitated; he coaxed.

"Jasem explodes on the world stage, gets feted for his recent wins, takes the world by storm," Max said. "Another Arabian crown prince decides he, too, must show off his own accomplishments. We eat, we watch, we listen a bit, then we fly. No harm, no foul. How about it, Renee?"

She didn't budge. "You've called it for what it is, Max, one-upmanship on steroids. But adding to that, in my mind, the Saudi Crown Prince will always be a monster. I'll take my coffee out to our plane. See you out there."

Max dined at his assigned seat and listened to Jundiin's speech representing the race committee, him ticking off a long list of kudos to every Saudi involved, down to the camel herders. Max paid his respects and dashed.

Renee, Trent, and Lou stood shoulder to shoulder on the tarmac admiring their trusted aircraft Rose when Max joined them.

"Tell Max what you told me, Lou," Renee said.

"Clean bill of health, Max," Lou said. "She looks and sounds good. She will work her tail off for you the rest of the way."

"But?" Max said, watching each of them while waiting for a shoe to drop, anticipating something other than the news he was just told. "C'mon, what's the issue?"

"The plane is fine," Renee said. "The forecast for the weather, not so much. Lou?"

"Conditions here and in Qatar, for the next six hours," Lou said, "are crazy winds and a low-hanging sandstorm. Things could get rough down here and up there. I could not prepare Rose for it any better than she was already."

Max's first reaction was to look for the other two planes. He shielded his eyes and scanned the tarmac, could find only one.

"Jasem and Camille are airborne already," Renee said. "I spoke with Camille. She was aware of the forecast and expected to avoid the turbulence, told me *J'y suis allé, c'est fait.*"

"Meaning?"

"*Been there, done that.* Her military experience. Jasem has confidence in her piloting as well."

"The Israelis?" Max said, eyeing the other FW50 close by.

"Not sure…"

The propeller on the other plane started up.

"That answers that," Max said. His phone buzzed. He checked the name: *Unrecognized.* He answered anyway. "Fend here. Is that you, Captain Ozzie?"

"Indeed it is. Ozzie and Talia here on speaker. I see you eyeing my stallion as we prepare for takeoff. We have been cleared and are going up. Storms are coming through…"

Jundiin arrived alongside Max and his posse, the rest of the race committee in his wake, Jundiin looking to interrupt. Max held up his finger to keep him quiet so Ozzie could have his say.

"I suggest that you not stagger your takeoff," Ozzie said. "Tell Jundiin you need to get in the air as soon as possible to avoid what is coming through Buraydah. That is my advice even though I recognize that you are now my direct competition. But I am a good sport. Heed my word, Max Fend. We will see you in Qatar."

Max turned to Jundiin. "What is coming through Buraydah?"

"Per our meteorologist"—Jundiin presented the man next to him—"a sandstorm."

"Okay. How tall and wide?"

"Two-to-three miles wide," the weather guy said, "and around four thousand feet in height."

"Give me some space, gentlemen, I need to discuss with my co-pilot."

Max, speaking with Renee away from Jundiin and the race committee: "Honey, we have a decision to make. Take our plane up and fly over the turbulence, or we can call it quits. What do you say?"

"We can also fly around it."

"That, too."

"We go up," she said, without hesitation. "As long as I'm with you, I'm good." She caught herself. "Lose that cocky smirk, Max, that sounded more romantic than I intended it."

Her disclaimer couldn't stop their hug and cheek-peck of a kiss. Max disengaged, ready for his audience with the race committee. "We're going up, gentlemen."

"As you wish, Mister Fend," Jundiin said. "Do not dally. As soon as the control tower clears you, you should go."

Bags loaded, their handshakes and hugs with Trent and Lou behind them, they could board now. Renee belted herself in. Max climbed onto the wing. Jundiin moved in for another message.

"His Royal Highness just texted me. They have seen what is ahead of you. He says stay right of the center of it by going south and east. Climb quickly, and you will be fine. Good luck."

They closed the cockpit glass. Max turned the ignition on, then awaited instructions from the tower, their eyes on the horizon.

"*November three-six-eight Romeo Juliet, Tower, runway two-three, winds two-seven-five at seven knots, clear for takeoff.*"

Taxi, increase speed, a throttle pull, nose up, lift, and they were flying.

Max continued their climb, no challenging conditions so far. One thousand feet, twelve hundred, sixteen hundred. "Looking good. This could be much ado about..."

"There," Renee said. "I see it. Eleven o'clock."

A visual on the sandstorm that was headed their way, askew of them to the left of their direct route, but only by a few degrees, and spreading very wide right.

"Hell, flying right of its center puts us into the middle of it. It looks big. Worse than that, it looks tall," Max said.

"How high can these things reach?"

"I don't know."

Renee keyed at her phone, which had no signal.

She unloaded her laptop quickly and keyed in the SATCOM protocols. She did a search and clicked on one of the responses, then pulled back from the laptop. A serious look at Max.

"Oh my." Her face showed a wide-eyed, newfound respect for what was in their way.

"What is it?" he said.

"This says a dust storm can reach as high as twenty thousand feet."

"Stop. You're scaring yourself. The race's weather guy couldn't have been that far off. Our altitude now is..."

He did a double-take at the altimeter. Forty-four hundred feet. And they still couldn't see over the top. Or past the right side of it, either.

The last-minute instructions from Jasem via Jundiin—"*stay right of center by heading southeast*"—seemed way off.

Particulates of sand and dust swept into them, soft at first, buffeting, but soon the storm was slamming the underside of the fuselage with an incessant rat-a-tat-tatting like strafing bullets from a jet fighter. They were fighting a wall of dirt and sand and dust kicked up from the surface by crazy air pressure changes that could whip desert winds into a fifty to sixty miles per hour frenzy. Max was able to make Rose climb at enough of a slant to keep the sand particulates from hitting the cockpit glass.

"Where are we, Max?" Renee shouted into the comm mouthpiece.

"Forty-nine hundred feet. She's doing great, holding steady, she'll need a new paintjob though... fifty-one hundred... Where the hell is the right-side edge...?"

Intrusion on their frequency, another voice, male, persistent, the voice raised, almost screaming.

"NOVEMBER THREE-SIX-EIGHT ROMEO JULIET, NOVEMBER THREE-SIX-EIGHT ROMEO JULIET, NOVEMBER THREE-SIX-EIGHT ROMEO JULIET, come in, Max, come in, Renee..."

"That's Ozzie Katz. Ozzie! Come in, Ozzie..."

"Max," Renee chided, "stay on the throttle, don't give any of it back..."

Crackling noises as intrusive as thunder diminished the communication, their headsets picking up only every few words—

"... made it over the rainbow... cruising... bounced us around... six thou... storm ceiling sixty-five... how are you..."

The transmission cut out. Max released the breath he didn't know he was holding. "Renee. We're at..." He checked the altimeter. "Six thousand and change. Do you feel it? Do you feel the shift? We're not getting slammed as much. We're topping out above the storm..."

"And there's the right-side edge of it," she said, pointing at the sunlight glistening off the right wing.

Max leveled them off at a little over sixty-five hundred feet, the altitude Ozzie said was the storm ceiling. He patted the dash. "Nicely done, Rose. You did really, really good, young lady."

Renee pushed. "Take us to seven thousand, maybe? We might not be out of it."

Max nodded. "We'll go to eight thousand. We can ride out any straggling storm issues at that altitude. We'll pick up some time on the competition depending on how long the Israelis spent at that lower altitude. I'll give it ten minutes at eight thousand, then we're taking her back down."

True to his word, after ten minutes he took Rose down to six thousand feet, low enough that they could see camel convoys in the sand, emerging from the storm. A splendid sight, some camels driven lazily by their tenders, others saddled with riders. Renee had her phone out to zoom-shoot the caravans and the people traveling in them as their plane flew over. A much-needed release of tension, some calm after their race to the top of the storm and over it.

With Max still piloting, Renee tidied up the mess in the cockpit. She focused on the horizon, then returned her gaze earthward, watching the endless swales of dunes and troughs of soft tan and orange sand rise and fall as they cruised above them.

"We flew directly at that storm," she said, thinking aloud, "because someone's last-minute directions took us that way."

An innocent comment, but maybe too inflammatory for their streaming audience when it would air. Max defused it. "Yeah, well, what are you gonna do, right?"

Renee retreated to her laptop. A text hit Max's phone, then another. Max engaged the autopilot to free his hands and read them.

Per Jundiin that was what Jasem's text said

Max nodded.

But she persisted, still texting. *That suggestion turned us into the storm.* Her mouth hung open while she continued keying. *I never liked Jundiin. Im texting Jasem about it*

Max's crinkled nose said don't do that. "How about some peace and quiet for a bit, hmm, honey?"

"Okay," she said, but her fingers worked to the contrary.

Fine no contacting Jasem. How about I text Camille to see how they're doing

No mention of texts from Jasem just a hi how are you we're fine we made it through the storm where are you, ok?

Max hesitated, thinking, then, "Okee-dokee. Disengaging autopilot, Renee."

Renee keyed her text to Camille, waited, sipped water from a bottle, waited longer.

"You look disappointed," Max said.

"Camille didn't answer my *hello, how are you* text."

"She's probably piloting the plane, not doing Google searches or gaming with her iPhone, like someone I know."

"Hey. Our best shot at surviving that storm was with you piloting. Give me credit for understanding. And I wasn't playing games on my phone either, buster."

"Then what were you doing?"

"My job." More keying. His phone again pinged. Max glanced at the text.

Im messaging my hacker army. We need more info on Jundiin

Renee was in her element, doing what she loved most, deep dives into the crazy world of hacking freakdom, Max staying out of the way. Her eyes betrayed this obsession, drilling into the laptop screen. Her mouth soon turned upward. Something on her screen made her happy.

"Excellent. Camille answered my text. She's piloting. She says they're a little over an hour from landing in Qatar."

"Then we're tracking well against them," Max said, checking their navigation computer. "Super."

"She's... huh, she says the storm didn't faze her. Says she dodged all the sand particles, ha-ha, so they wouldn't damage her new plane. Added a smiley face with a French beret. Cute."

Max visually checked their aircraft's wings, nose, and cockpit glass. Rose's glossy white and orange paint looked bruised and dulled in spots, speckled in others, but he saw no issues with the glass. Camille's comment reminded him that these expensive toys were now owned by each contestant, something that would mean more to Camille than to him.

Renee droned on about Camille's texts. "... Says she went through this twice before... a dust storm near Las Vegas the day before a Red Bull race... avoided a surprise dust storm when she competed in Acapulco, too. I'll close out our chat so I can do some flying and you can get some rest."

Max answered texts and emails on Renee's laptop plus he heard from Trent, who had hitched a ride with a Navy fighter jet to Qatar and would arrive before Max and Renee would. Now to address an email from Wilkes labeled "Top Secret."

"Okay, what do we have here..." he said, then read to himself.

More detail on the theft of the Israeli-developed smart rifle, Wilkes catching him up on Interpol updates. The Israeli engineer who stole it was found executed in Nazareth, Israel. And the broker who put it for sale on the dark web was found in a Paris hotel dead of a drug overdose, but it was staged. The gun's whereabouts were still unknown, but deemed somewhere in the EU or the Middle East. The cryptocurrency transactions in the bowels of the darknet were almost indecipherable, but—

... the trail is there, inside the crypto's blockchain code. When someone finds the gun, Wilkes's email said, *someone finds Nomad. I'm already in Qatar. See you when you get here.*

Max drifted off again, then jerked awake, his hands still on the keyboard but the laptop inactive. "Where are we?"

"Twenty minutes out of Qatar. That was some catnap, tiger. Here, it's your turn to drive."

Five minutes later they experienced a change in atmospheric conditions. Cruising at eighty-two hundred feet, the temperature outside rose to one hundred eight, the humidity ninety-three, the visibility in the hot, steamy, foggy air less than a quarter mile. An air traffic controller at Qatar's Hamad International jolted them to attention, speaking hard and fast in Arabic, then repeating himself in English.

"Cleared to land, cleared to land, November Three-six-eight Romeo Juliet. Steady speed, do not come in fast, one plane ahead of you, small like you, same runway, forty second difference..."

"Holy shit, Renee." Max could make out the small plane's wing lights, then its landing lights. "We're closer to them than that, damn it—"

"I see them, I see them..."

He eased their speed down, thankful they could follow the other aircraft in, concerned they were so close. "Easy, Rose... easy..."

At four hundred feet the controller's transmission cut out. When it returned, he was in the middle of an exclamation in panicky Arabic that he translated at the last minute: *"... er, dust devil out of nowhere! Big!"*

A whirlwind more than four hundred feet wide spun onto the runway, engulfing its entire width, a funnel of hot air wide and deep, swirling upward like it was getting sucked out of a chimney, heading to a height unknown. It rose between them and the plane ahead of them. Missing the whirlwind was impossible, slamming it unavoidable. Their propeller cut a hole into the spinning wall of sand and dirt, the plane's wings waffling, the dust devil lifting them into a port-side lean that threatened to tip them over into a cartwheel. Max gripped the yoke with both hands, rammed it starboard, fought to re-level them, needed to over-correct—

They leveled off, wings bucking the spin, then fully level again. They were through the dust devil, their altitude now under a hundred feet. The air controller finished with "... *watch pylons!*"

Ahead of them but too late, Max saw through the steamy fog one of the race's two air-filled, illuminated pylons, eighty feet high, that bookended the runway like yellow dunce caps and looking as big as floats in the Macy's parade.

A brief flash sparked at the tip of their port wing, the runway wide enough to handle the jumbos but now not wide enough to handle their off-course drift. Max jumped. "What the hell..."

"A pylon—that was the pylon!" Renee said. "We sheared off the top..."

Max steered starboard, found the middle of the runway, eighty feet, seventy, fifty... a kiss of the tarmac, then a bounce, then a return for a solid grab where he was finally able to ease into a smooth taxi. Evidence of the sheared pylon hung from the tip of their port wing like a deflated Mylar. A fluorescent-vested ground crewperson directed them to their parking space next to the Israeli team's plane. Max powered their plane down, his adrenalin still coursing. He released a deep breath.

Renee found a barf bag and hyperventilated into it, taking restorative breaths until her head cleared and her stomach settled.

Max held out a hand, reaching for her. "Renee honey, I am so sorry..."

She tossed the bag, unstrapped herself, and jumped onto Max in his seat, wrapping her arms around him. "You saved our lives again, Max Fend, no need to apologize..."

On them quickly through the steamy fog at tarmac level were Ozzie Katz and his co-pilot Talia, waiting for them to step onto the ground. The four shared a heartfelt relief, genuine on all their parts, even as competitors.

"Well, Max Fend of the U.S., let me be the first to congratulate you two, my friends, for the expert flying. I'll add that it is with mixed emotions that we, as intel operatives, have bested our U.S. competition in—my goodness, I feel we should have a drum roll here—"

Max looked from face to face at the Israeli piloting team, then at Renee, wary and unsure where he was going with this.

"... once again, we have learned the top-secret results of the race before they will be released, and certainly before you could know them."

"We've been on the ground for less than ten minutes," Max said. "How could you possibly already know—"

Talia, his co-pilot, patted the bag hanging from her shoulder and shrugged through a sheepish smile.

"Electronic data readouts from the pylons. We again win the spy stakes, Max Fend of the U.S., but alas, the results of those readouts show that we have lost this leg. Max and Renee, you finished fourteen seconds ahead of our time, net of your pylon penalty. It is done. You've earned you way into the final showdown with the Crown Prince and Mademoiselle Gagneux. Let us be the first to congratulate you, not only on so outstanding a performance for this leg, but on the race overall. Come, let's get inside the hangar. And please, no mention that you know what you now know. Let Jasem have his moment, and we will bask silently in our moment as well."

The two piloting teams hustled into the hangar. First to greet them were Jundiin and the other race officials, all with broad, relieved smiles. The group parted when Jasem and the diminutive Camille arrived for the celebration. Jasem pulled Max into a hug, Camille doing likewise with Renee.

"Max Fend, I am in awe," Jasem said, clapping his back, then squeezing his shoulder. "You and Renee are heroes for your performances today. Allah, in his infinite wisdom, could not have chosen worthier pilots to test their mettle. You were equal to the tasks. And I could not have scripted the three-plus hours of footage to be any more dramatic. It will take our social media followers by storm when it is released..."

Camille had a different message for Renee, spoken in French while Jasem fawned over Max. Its translation: "I am beyond thrilled that you have survived today's freakish weather, but I need to talk to you again in private. No details now. After dinner tonight."

21

"Two of us left, Max. To be honest, I'm not sure how I feel about that," Jasem said.

"Meaning?"

Another Four Seasons hotel, The Corniche in Doha, Qatar, a tan and pink-sand-colored high rise with a beach only footsteps from the Arabian Gulf's shoreline. Dinner prepared by the hotel's incredible Japanese chef in residence. Max enjoyed the cuisine, was cleaning his palate of the sushi with a post-dinner bottle of beer, he and Jasem tucked into a corner of their reserved half of the restaurant. Four other men, their protection, were within a few steps of them and each other, Max's muscle, Trent, included.

"I had a secret wish that the Israelis would be our opponent for the final leg," Jasem said. "It would have been a perfect end to my race, showcasing the region and the new regional peace deal with our newest friends."

"Interesting," Max said, a sly smile forming. "Why no mention of how thankful you are that you, too, have earned your way into the final two?"

"If you're inferring that I gave myself an unfair advantage of some kind, or that there might be some monkey business involved, you are wrong, Max Fend. The only unfair advantage I gave myself is sitting over there with your Renee. Camille Gagneux is an amazing pilot."

He gestured at a café table on the near side of the restaurant where Camille and Renee were in close conversation.

"She's an ace, Max, in every sense of the term. I have never seen anything like her. Her instincts in the air are uncanny, her reflexes better than a pro-video gamer. I just had to have her as my pilot, and as we can both attest, it has paid off tremendously."

Their discussion drifted to tomorrow's final leg, designed as a potentially dramatic finish at Dubai's Al Maktoum International Airport, the shortest route of the race, a 225-mile sprint. The two aircraft would jackrabbit forward head-to-head at the sound of a starter's pistol, no staggering, from starting lines on separate but parallel runways within sight of each other.

"Such great theater, Max. You should take a lesson from me with your new aerobatic race program. Expose yourself more on social media. Give your program an identity. Be more open like Richard Branson, less reclusive like Howard Hughes. And if you want to give the Fend Aerospace racing team a better chance at winning some of its own racing exhibitions," he said, chuckling, "do not invite Camille to participate as a contestant."

Across the room, their co-pilots were deep in conversation, again in French.

"I will share what I know," Camille said, leaning closer to Renee. "People speaking around me overlook my presence. Being a woman, in these countries, can be an asset that way. Two things. First, Jasem's admin person—"

"Jundiin," Renee said.

"Yes. Some troublesome news from him. He said our Pakistani pilot friend Bibi Mizka is missing. She followed our flights after quitting the race, taking commercial air from Cyprus to Cairo and from Cairo to Sinai, but she never checked out of the Sinai hotel. There is no record of her on any flights leaving Sinai, per Jundiin, and there is no record of her returning to her residence in Pakistan. Second, Jasem is aware that his uncle is working against him..."

Per Camille, someone with a protected identity would arrive tonight at this hotel, to close a deal with the uncle. "This person is paid to eliminate problems at the highest levels, and for the most notorious of people, and he is here to help the uncle. That is what Jasem is hearing."

Renee stayed stone-faced, offered none of her insights regarding this information or this person, betraying no confidences.

"For now, Renee, cleanse yourself of today's travails and celebrate. You stared death in the face, and you have won this round. Shelter in place and let Jasem's people handle things. That's what I plan to do."

"Understood, Camille," Renee said. "But I have to ask. How do you know these things?"

Camille's smile was furtive, but her eyes synched with her lips. She reached into a jeans pocket and gave Renee a quick glimpse of a phone, then put it back. Her glance in Jasem's direction said the phone was his.

"He's had me carry it occasionally. I see things."

~

Max, still talking with Jasem, felt a text jolt the phone in his pocket. Renee was still at their table, her phone in her hand, her thumbs a blur; Camille was gone. Max wasn't the only recipient of a text from her; she'd copied Wilkes.

"It's from Renee," Max said to Jasem, flashing his best sheepish, nothing-to-see-here smile. "Please accept my apology, Jasem, but we do want so much to kick your butts tomorrow on the final leg, so we're heading upstairs to get some sleep. Good night."

In their room, Renee opened her laptop quickly and dialed up Wilkes. Suit, tie, no nonsense government ID picture, but no video came up, only a static image. "Okay, this will be without live streaming," she said to Max. "He must be using his AirPods only. He's on his way up here."

Wilkes spoke through breaths that came from a person on the move, short audio bursts only, his footsteps echoing in a stairwell. "The contract... has apparently... been moved up. It's now in play." Vague speak, with no naming of names. "Our efforts will now be focused... on stopping him."

"Excuse me, but stop him from doing what?" Max said. "And how the hell is it that we know something's going down now?"

"Renee?" Wilkes said, which was a request for help.

"It's all here, Max, from Langley," she said. "An attempt on a do-over of the Dubai monarchy by assassinating Jasem and his father, the king. Tomorrow, in Dubai. Evidence gathered by the analysts. Plus, my group of crazies have been out there scouring everything from children's piggy banks to accounts for international crypto lenders. They've secured amounts and the dates that our target expected payment. Jasem's uncle has been busy. He has digital accounts all over the place on the dark web. Multiple cryptocurrencies. The key was to learn when it was supposed to happen, and now we know. They meet tonight. Tomorrow, the assassinations."

"Another installment payment was made today," Wilkes said, "on the way to totaling twenty-five million in cash and digital equivalents when the job is done. The most recent transfer came from another of the uncle's dark money accounts."

Renee's face turned grim, her mouth now a slit. "This is not a drill, Max. He's coming, or he's here already. Camille said so, and these transfers say so. Tonight is a big night. I want in."

Wilkes stayed serious, his tone direct but bordering on breathless. "I have a team thirty minutes away that I've mobilized, but I don't want to wait. We might not get this opportunity again. Where's our other partner?"

"Already here," Trent said, projecting his voice, leaning against the room's minibar. A beer in hand, he had on a loose-fitting Hawaiian shirt over tan pants. He joined Max and Renee in front of the laptop screen. Wilkes's unsmiling face was still no more than a static screensaver. "What do we have, boss?"

"A room number and a Qatari car license plate," Wilkes said. "No pictures, text messages only, from the uncle's phone, plus cell phone tower triangulation. The target and the uncle are somewhere in the building, so we'll hit the hotel room where we think this little rendezvous is going down."

"Hold on, gentlemen," Renee said, then she moved Wilkes's laptop image out of the way on screen, replacing it with a floor plan. "Max, Trent, the hotel's website shows the layout of that suite right here."

"Whose room is that?" Max asked, studying the diagram.

"The target's. A *Mr. M. Dayan* per the reservation."

"That sounds familiar. Where...?"

"Moshe Dayan was a famous Israeli general," Trent said. "Maybe our target thinks he's a funny guy."

"Or maybe it's a message implying Israeli military involvement. Either way," Wilkes said, "we need to stop him."

"Just to confirm," Max said, wanting to spell out the goal of their operation, "we're going for his capture plus proof that this is who we think it is."

"Capture?" Wilkes said, fighting for breaths. "Sure, Max. As loosely defined as we need that word to be. He needs to be neutralized before he can complete his assignment, and the uncle needs to be arrested. I'll meet you at the top of the south stairwell. Hold on, I need to rest a minute..."

"Ease up, old man," Trent said. He lifted his loose shirt to show off a military-issue fanny pack attached to his waistband, in camo black and green. "Good stuff in here, but no defibrillator. If you need one, you're S-O-L."

"Roger that. Fourteen floors on foot, gentlemen, so we can surprise our person of interest in one of the hotel's ambassador suites at the top. Sorry, Renee, but this can't include you. Sit tight where you are. We need you to follow department protocols if this doesn't work out."

"Damn it, Wilkes, why do you keep—"

"Not now, Renee. Max?"

"We're on the move."

Max and Trent ascended the stairwell steps at floor nine, huffed and puffed until they reached the top floor. Wilkes met them on the landing, was doubled over, catching his breath. No exchange of words, nods only, the three of them listening for additional footfalls in the stairwell, hearing nothing close. Wilkes pointed at the card key device for the hotel hallway entrance; Max swiped his card. They entered one at a time.

The hallway stretched the length of a football field, was wide enough for people to pass each other in either direction with no interference. They walked, Trent in the lead, with Max and Wilkes trailing. They passed a few doors, the hotel's top-of-the-line accommodations on this floor, all large, luxurious suites. Trent stopped them with a palm up at their destination. A look up and down the quiet hallway gave them a count of five suites. Their weapons stayed hidden.

Trent duck-walked to the front of the suite's door, staying below the peephole. Max moved to the left side of the entry, made himself flat against the wall; Wilkes did likewise behind him. Trent reached up, pressed a thumb-sized piece of plastic explosive against the card reader, then ran a worm-thin sliver of it north a foot to address the latch. He inserted a wire in the putty that led to a plastic button the size of an M&M between his thumb and forefinger. He stayed low, moved to the right of the door, book-ending Max and Wilkes. With his free hand, he drew his weapon. They did likewise.

Trent nodded and said in a low voice, "Fire in the hole."

His press of the button rocked the door off its hinge with a soft blast that pushed it inward. Trent streamed inside first, Max and Wilkes following, their guns raised. They marched down the short hallway to a sitting room, the dining area right, the kitchen adjacent, which brought Trent face to face with a man, an apple in his hand with a bite gone. The man halted, eyed Trent's weapon, also eyed the handgun on the table.

"Don't," Trent said to him. "You won't make it."

The man threw the apple at Trent, quick-drew a concealed handgun from his waist, and raised it. Trent dotted him with two silent shots at the man's face. Blood splattered the kitchen wall and the refrigerator behind him, the body thrown backward, bouncing against the appliance's doors and sliding down, reaching the floor where it sat twitching, then the twitching stopped. The wound bled out from both his eye socket and the back of his head.

"Man down. Not the uncle," Trent called.

Max and Wilkes filled in behind him and gawked. "You need any help, Trent?" Max asked, eyeing the gun next to the dead man's hand.

"Nope."

Max and Wilkes left so they could sweep the suite's other spaces, their guns raised. Bedrooms, bathrooms, closets, the terrace. No uncle, and no other occupants.

Trent went through everything in the man's pockets, shoving the contents into a zippered pouch that rode above the small of Trent's back. Wilkes and Max watched him conduct the search.

"Nomad?" Max said, releasing a breath.

"Don't know," Wilkes said. "I'm disappointed there's no one else here."

Quick phone pictures of the deceased went to Langley and Renee. Facial recognition software might reveal an identity. The problem was, associating a name to the photo didn't mean enough, Nomad forever an enigma, no good facial photos of him anywhere. Maybe it was Nomad, maybe it wasn't. They'd need to toss the suite to look for anything else that might label him. Wilkes picked up the room's battered entry door with its huge hole and propped it up against what was left of the jamb, then moved an armchair into place behind it to block the entry.

Wilkes focused them. "Let's have a look around, gentlemen."

They didn't have to look far. A backpack on the coffee table gave up plane ticket info and hotel reservations that shadowed their air race stops, diagrams of airport hangars, and routes to and from airports and hotels. There were handwritten suggestions for sabotaging the racing team planes during their overnight maintenance. Notes on the fuel contamination angle, specifically IDing rubber hose fragments as foreign substances that would ruin aircraft engine parts. Food poisonings info. References implicating two complicit aircraft mechanics with ties to the uncle. And the coup de grace, a handful of computer thumb drives.

"We have a name," Wilkes said, looking at a plane ticket printout. "Gilles Khalifa."

"Never heard of him," Max said.

"Yes, that would be the point, wouldn't it, Max? We'll have our analysts piece together Mr. Khalifa's movements where possible."

"Copy Renee," Max said. "The more the merrier."

Wilkes inserted one hard drive stick into a drive he plugged onto his phone. "Password-protected. Trent, do you have that software, that... what's it called again?"

"*Hulk Smash*. Give the stick to me."

Trent removed a green drive reader from his pouch. He attached it to his phone, popped the thumb drive in, and pulled up a password decryption program.

"No known settings or configurations, no clues about the password, no problem," he said. "And with the agency's *Warp Drive* upgrade, virtually no waiting. The brute force approach. It will rearrange the guts of a thumb drive, but what do we care what happens to it as long as you can read it. Here." He handed Wilkes his phone, the drive reader and thumb drive attached. "Knock yourself out."

Wilkes registered small smiles with each drive he inserted, transactions appearing one line at a time as he thumbed through them. Specific crypto wallet payments, where to find them, and cash transfers to offshore banks that Wilkes recognized. "These drives will go to Langley."

Trent called from another bedroom. "Wilkes, get in here."

Hiding almost in plain sight standing upright in an armoire was what might well have been their Holy Grail. Trent eased out a tall black trunk and laid it on the floor. He examined the trunk's electronic lock. A three-number combination.

The three of them ogled the closed case. Brass corners, latches, stenciled writing on the top. Inside the trunk could be anything from a trombone to a short-range bazooka. It could also be booby-trapped.

"I don't suppose either of you reads Arabic," Trent said.

"It's Hebrew," Wilkes said.

"Whatever." Trent removed a digital lock scanning device from his fanny pack. "Take pictures of it and send them off. I'll bypass the lock. If this scanner doesn't work..." He patted the fanny pack where he kept his stash of plastic explosives.

"Bypassing the lock is highly preferable to exploding it, Trent," Wilkes said in between taking photos and forwarding them. "Wait a minute. A message from Renee."

Wilkes had a response to the photographs. "Huh. She translated the Hebrew."

A pleased Max smiled, happy she'd remained fully engaged after being rebuffed. "Quicker than Langley, mind you," Max said. "And the answer is?"

"She says the words read 'Modified XS1, property IDF, top secret.'"

"What the hell does that mean?" Max said.

Trent answered quickly. "IDF is Israel Defense Forces. XS1 is the original name for the American version of a personal precision-guided firearm."

"A steroid version of a smart rifle," Wilkes said. "Maybe it's the Israeli smart rifle everyone's looking for. Let's hope our smoking gun is inside. Can you pick the lock, Trent?"

"We'll find out. Get as far away from me as possible, gentlemen."

Wilkes and Max went into the kitchen, sidestepped the body, waited. Five minutes, six, seven, no noise from the other rooms, explosions or otherwise, eight, nine...

"All clear," Trent called.

They rejoined him in the bedroom, the hinged lid to the trunk open. Inside, cradled in cushiony foam padding, was a long, black rifle with multiple accessories that all screamed space-age technology. Maybe a winner.

Trent put on nitrile gloves. He lifted each piece out of its cushion interior and examined it, talking all the way. "Gunstock. Barrel. Powder smell. Lower and upper receivers. Your common bipod stand. Magazine with ammo. More ammo. Hell, these are armor-piercing bullets. And here's what looks like a radar-guided precision rifle scope. This is really nifty..."

Wilkes put out his hand, wagged his fingers. Trent dropped the rifle's scope into it.

"This... is where the action is," Wilkes said, checking the heft. He found a toggle switch on the scope, pushed it. A green light came on. He raised the scope to his eyes. "Fully active optical HUD."

"Speak civilian for me," Max said.

"It's a Heads-up Display," Trent said, looking over Wilkes's shoulder. "The digital screen shows the field of view. It identifies your target, locks on it, and gives you the vital info you need to obliterate it when you pull the trigger. Wait, what's that on the HUD screen, Wilkes? There. Lower right corner," he said, pointing.

"That indicator... is where it accesses an internet app," Wilkes said, "that streams real-time video. The optics the shooter is seeing... the app lets someone else see it on a tablet, a phone, a laptop. Inside this scope, an onboard computer uses satellite data to adjust for barometric pressure, severe weather, even hurricanes. A boatload of variables. It won't let you pull the trigger until all systems are go, and it broadcasts what the shooter sees in real time. Wow."

"Yeah, but what's the effective range?" Trent said.

"Two miles," Wilkes said, "according to the Israelis."

"You skeptical, Trent?" Max asked.

"Damn straight. When I was in sniper school, they told us about the longest-range confirmed kills. Those were in the two- to three-thousand-meter range, and these shots were taken by some of the best trained special ops guys on the planet. Two miles? What's that in meters? Thirty-two hundred meters maybe?" Trent said. "So yeah, it looks good on paper, but... hard to believe until I see it in person."

"Looked good in the tests, too, according to Langley. This might be the real thing, gentlemen." Wilkes checked out his buzzing phone. "Okay, let's pack it back up. Our guys are in the hallway. We'll leave it for them to analyze."

"Our guys?" Max said.

"My CIA team arrived. This gun is leaving with them."

"What about the body?"

"Their lucky day. They get him, too."

With the armchair out of the way, six business-suited men with suit-cases and backpacks entered the suite, grunted greetings to Wilkes, then went to work. First out of the bedroom, the small trunk with the gun. Second to go was the body, bent and folded as required to make it fit into the large piece of luggage the agents brought with them. The remaining two men stepped into disposable hazmat suits and got to work cleaning the kitchen crime scene, collecting clothing and incidentals and eliminating the mess the body left behind.

Two phones chirped at the same time, Max and Wilkes. They answered them in unison, Max pleasantly, Wilkes sticking with his M.O., grim and business-like. Their calls ended nearly simultaneously. Wilkes spoke first.

"Langley. We have a positive ID on the gun, gentlemen. They went to Mossad with the photos. Israel intel confirmed it's the stolen prototype that's been bouncing around the dark web. My hope is whatever digital currency info those thumb drives hold will tell us how much money changed hands for it and the directions it moved."

"My call was from Renee," Max said, "about Gilles Khalifa. There's more than one Gilles Khalifa out there. But ours is in a corporate phone book. Her facial recognition software matched him to—get this—a Fleetwings Europe Industries exec."

"Jasem bought the FW50s from Fleetwings Europe," Wilkes said.

"Sure, they're Fleetwings planes," Max said, "but Jasem didn't do the deal. His admin Jundiin said he did it on Jasem's behalf."

Another phone chirp, Wilkes's again. He listened to the call, hung up.

"More from the agency. Renee was right, Max. Recognition software has him popping up all over the place through a string of aliases, but nothing in the last decade."

"Right how? She'd pegged Nomad as following an obscure pattern in his travels, like a Formula One groupie or maybe someone on a surfer tour, but she couldn't match it to anything."

"Neither could Langley," Wilkes said. "His last time on the intel radar was in France, where he was fingerprinted for a ransom shakedown. Bribes freed him. Never heard from him again until now, where he pops up as a new exec at Fleetwings, but with Khalifa as an alias."

"So much for Fleetwings' business reference checking process," Max said.

"Interpol has him as French-Palestinian. His real name is Ives Hanania. In my book, his ethnicity makes him especially keen to disrupting the Israeli peace deal."

It made a world of sense. Gilles Khalifa-slash-Ives Hanania. An exec with Fleetwings, the aircraft manufacturer who provided the new FW50s. Plus two of Jasem's mechanics as accomplices. Plus the missing uncle. All were involved. Maybe Jundiin as well. And a smoking gun with *Star Wars* technology was the, um, smoking gun.

"This guy... is Nomad," Wilkes said. "We need to go." Phone chirp. "Just got a text from Qatari State Security, who's been on standby. They'll be here any minute."

"Their country's intel unit? Here for what?" Max said.

"We'll take Nomad, but they plan on finding the uncle."

Wilkes ushered Max and Trent out of the room. They were met in the hotel hallway by three plainclothes Qatari agents, one in the process of escorting a gawking hotel guest interested in the hole in the suite's door back to her room.

Trent led them to the elevators. They staggered their trips down to the parking garage in separate elevator cars. In the well-lit but quiet garage, Wilkes pointed at a white Ford pickup truck with a black truck bed cover.

"We wait next to that truck," Wilkes said. "Things are about to get busier." He stayed buried in the data reader Trent gave him, reviewing thumb drive info line by line while they waited for his team to arrive with the body and the gun prototype.

"The motherlode is on these drives, Max. Quite a trail. We'll piece it together, but the uncle is in way deep here, pulling the strings. Transactions, emails... plane sabotage. Another fuel snafu planned for the last leg with a fake trail traceable to Israel. A lot of money to the mechanics. Plus using this gun to frame the Israelis for Jasem's father's assassination. A shame Uncle Saeed got so impatient, wanting the throne now. And our guy here—"

Three CIA agents arrived on foot at the truck, one pushing the suitcase with Nomad's body in it, two carrying the weapon in the black trunk. They lowered the lift gate and slid their spoils inside.

"... our bad guy is twenty-five million bucks richer for agreeing to do the deed, ten million paid in advance, the money out there somewhere. Nice work when you can get it, and if you aren't already dead." He stopped talking to check his phone again. "Another text from Qatari intel. Their domestic police force just stormed the uncle's jet. He's not onboard. And they're closing in on the two rogue mechanics. We'll hear more about them in a minute. Max, we need to talk with Jasem."

"And Jundiin," Max said. "His airplane purchase deal for Jasem, with Khalifa, or whatever his name was, puts him in the middle of this. I vote we keep this quiet until tomorrow morning. We can roust everyone for a debriefing then. Tell me about the airplane mechanics, then I'm going to bed."

Wilkes popped out one thumb drive, inserted another, was preoccupied with the data as it came up onscreen. "I haven't heard anything more yet. Patience, Max. Fascinating reading here..."

"How hard can it be to find them? They work at night in the hangar and get their sleep the next day on a private jumbo jet while flying to the next location."

"That 'patience is a virtue thing,'" Trent said, "is crap, Wilkes. One virtue among many that I don't have. Max, let Renee know I'm on my way up to your room to crash on your sofa again. Good night."

Max finished his text to Renee. "Now, reward my patience, Wilkes. I'm exhausted."

"Hold on."

Wilkes retrieved a phone from his pocket, eyed a new text. "The wait's over. Qatari intel wants me to call them."

Max eavesdropped, but Wilkes spoke quietly. The call ended, and with the phone and thumb drive reader away, Wilkes shared.

"The two mechanics are dead. They felt sick, returned to their sleeping berths on their plane, and never came back. The Qatari agents found one in his bunk, bloody foam streaming from his mouth. Looks like he was poisoned. A second one was found just inside the hatch. Same bloody foam M.O., but he was also shot through the head, was maybe trying to leave the plane."

"Loose ends," Max said. "Someone cleaning up after himself."

"Maybe. Plus another surprise. Evidence of a third person squatting on the plane. Someone who left in a hurry. No mention of an additional person on the passenger lists the uncle's crew filed. Good chance she'd been invited by one of the mechanics, not the uncle."

"*She*?"

"A companion. Left behind enough identifiers to out her as the co-pilot for the Pakistani team. Memona Qureshi. Former Pakistani intel. You know her as Bibi."

"But she and her co-pilot quit the race in Cairo," Max said.

"He quit the race, she apparently didn't. They think she hooked up with one of the mechanics, stayed out of sight."

"Renee," Max said, thinking aloud, and ahead. "I need to text Renee and Trent, *now*."

"Nomad's dead, Max. The threat's been neutralized."

"Sure, I get it, we got him," Max said, unfazed. He found his phone and spoke while texting. "But they need to be aware. For this to happen now, Nomad had to be close to completing his assignment. Finding that gun here... we're only two hundred twenty-five air miles away, no more than an hour from Dubai."

"For Nomad, more like seven hours away," Wilkes said. "I just saw a car rental reservation agreement in his travel itinerary. He was going to drive to Dubai. It would have been an easy, no-hassle way to get the gun there."

22

———

Max stumbled into bed, into Renee's arms. This was the softest and the warmest that her comforting body had ever felt next to him, with him beyond thankful that she was here, that she was fine, and that they were together. Max recounted what had happened. The headshot that took out the bad actor, the evidence trail, the smart gun, and what the agents did with the body to force-fit it into the luggage. Disquieting images all, making sleep elusive.

Next morning, Max's call to Jasem was to have him gather their shrinking group of air race participants together for a debriefing. On the phone, Jasem registered an audible gasp when Max mentioned Nomad's alias. "He's... he's Fleetwings?"

"Afraid so."

"But he'd also been invited to be part of the race's closing ceremony in Dubai. He would have been on stage with my father and I..."

That, Max hadn't known. "Jasem, my guess is, at that ceremony, some unwelcome event, at the behest of your uncle, would have been Nomad's Plan B."

Max and Renee entered Jasem's penthouse suite for the debriefing, only doors away from where Max and his CIA associates had eliminated the single largest threat to Middle Eastern stability in years. They joined Jasem and Camille and Israeli co-pilots Ozzie Katz and Talia Vaknin in the living room, bodyguards posted in the hotel hallway and on the terrace. Jasem spoke first, to tee up the drama that Max had related to him when he'd told Jasem to pull them all together.

"Max, fill everyone in, please."

"Here's what we know. There was another threat against Jasem's life by an assassin known as Nomad. He'd bribed his way into acquiring accomplices close to Jasem and the royal family. The threat has been neutralized, but I suggest we cancel the last leg of the race given what's happened."

"Describe 'neutralized,'" Ozzie Katz said.

"He's dead. Shot while U.S. operatives attempted to capture him. He had ties to the Emirati air race maintenance team. Two of the maintenance mechanics are also dead, and my U.S. State Department contacts tell me it was by this bad actor's hand. And there is one other development we are still piecing together. Qatar police say there's evidence our Pakistani pilot friend Bibi was on the maintenance team's jumbo jet. They didn't find her with the two mechanics, but she was traveling with them."

"Assumed to be alive?" Israeli pilot Talia Vaknin said.

"No evidence otherwise. She'd dropped out of sight after our Cairo stop. After that, she managed an audience with Jasem's uncle, maybe a dalliance of some sort. Jasem, please fill them in on your uncle's involvement."

Ozzie Katz pushed. "Wait. How did these people die?"

Jasem intercepted the question. "Let's not talk about—"

Max overruled him with a raised hand. "It's okay. The mechanics were poisoned, my people say."

"Wow," a surprised Ozzie said. "Was he identified?"

"He went by Gilles Khalifa, an alias. Facial recognition, although the image was somewhat compromised. Not going into detail."

"Khalifa? The Fleetwings executive?"

"Yes," Max said. "You can dwell on his Fleetwings involvement later, but the manhunt for Nomad is over. Not the hunt for Jasem's uncle, however. Jasem, let's hear about your uncle please."

Jasem laid out Uncle Saeed's alleged involvement. Infighting about the Dubai monarchy, the jealousy, the misplaced Middle Eastern country allegiances, and his desire to cling to the old ways of the kingdom at all costs.

And a mention of what had generated what was now an Interpol world-wide "red notice" for his arrest, plus arrest warrants for him in Dubai: the payments to a contract killer for the assassination of a king.

"So where is Jundiin?" Ozzie said, his head swiveling. "Why isn't he here?"

"We're not sharing this with anyone else yet," Jasem said. "We must exclude Jundiin for now. He is as close to Uncle as I am. He needs to be out of this loop until we get a handle on things. The Qatari police ripped apart Uncle's jet, looking for places where he might have concealed himself. They're not letting the jet leave until they're sure he's not on it. The police have blanketed the city, are visible at each airport gate, and have checkpoints at all the major roads out of Qatar. Chances are he's already slipped their grasp, but they will keep searching locally regardless. My friends, this is about to have major repercussions within the royal family. I ask that you each remain here while I contact my father the king to update him on what we learned today. Excuse me."

Renee joined the Israeli pilots in the galley kitchen. Max prepared a cup of coffee for himself, eavesdropping on their assessments, the discovery about the Pakistani pilot, the things that brought them all to this moment, like the best of intentions on the part of a young Arabian crown prince that had devolved into three murders, multiple poisonings, and airplane tampering that could have cost innocent lives. Plus, in Max's head but not a part of their discussion, was that high-tech piece of sniper hardware that the CIA now had in its possession. He left the kitchen with his coffee and found Camille on the terrace, the morning air cool and breezy. She was smoking a cigarette.

"A few things are wrong with this picture of you, Camille," he said, leaning against the railing. "First, I wasn't aware you smoked. It will stunt your growth, by the way."

She smiled, took another drag. "Yes, and I have lost that battle already, have I not?"

"Second," Max said, "this is a non-smoking establishment. I am sure that, as we speak, the cigarette police are on their way up here to arrest you."

Her glare at him was a congenial one. "Be aware that your weak attempt at persuading me to quit my vice has failed, but because I have enjoyed enough of my French cigarette for today—it has calmed me—I will now be rid of it."

She stared him down while she butted out her cigarette like a military person did while in the field, looking confident that this would impress him: an index finger tap and hold to the cigarette's tip until it stopped burning, the ashes flying away in a windy updraft. She tucked the unlit butt into her jeans pocket. "Know also that I am an environmentally conscious person. I will dispose of the cigarette properly. So, *Monsieur* Max, you have seen fit to engage me out here. Let me share one thought I have about these events.

"Jasem wants his uncle to be found not only to punish him for what he has done, but also because his uncle is now in grave danger, and from what I can tell, Jasem is too much a romantic. I believe that regardless of his uncle's poor behavior, he would like not to lose his uncle forever."

"In grave danger? I see the uncle maybe getting hurt if he doesn't cooperate when he's found, but the *uncle* was the danger, for having engaged Nomad. What other grave danger do you see for him?"

"Is it not obvious? *L'état d'Israël voudra sa tête sur un plateau.*"

"In English, Camille."

"Sorry. The state of Israel will want his head on a platter."

Jasem emerged from a bedroom, waved everyone back together.

"I have spoken with my father, and I have some news. He and I would like us to finish the race. The threat is eliminated, but we really haven't made things right. By not finishing, it would be a poor reflection on our diplomatic efforts. What say you, my friends?"

"Max?" Renee said, her look expectant, her vibe the one that was usually his to project, not hers, with Renee maybe needing to talk him out of a careless leap, not the other way around.

"Hold on, Renee. Jasem," Max said, "are you sure about this? Why tempt fate here?"

"We feel the peace agreement will benefit immensely from our race having weathered this obscene attempt to sabotage it, and by association, the treaty itself. So, if the other teams would like to finish this, and I hope you would," he said, making eye contact with each of them, "then my family will be waiting to crown the victors in Dubai."

"Other teams?" Ozzie Katz said. "There are only two teams left, yours and the Americans. We were eliminated on this leg."

"Ahh. Yes, that is correct, Captain Katz, but it is my race, and I have decided to un-eliminate the Israeli team. What do you think about being part of a three-way sprint to the finish? It will be dramatic and extraordinary. But there would need to be some race modifications. And the one major change is," Jasem explained as a declaration, "the Israeli team needs to win the race, Captain Katz."

"Come again?" Ozzie said.

"To make amends for what Nomad has done, and had planned to do, to your country's reputation. You, sir, and your co-pilot will win."

"Okay, a wonderful idea, Your Highness, but..."

"Our efforts to forge a partnership with your country... I think it appropriate for an Israeli single-engine plane to be the first of our air race planes to touch down in Dubai. It will be the first private plane from either side of the treaty to cross all of UAE's sheikdoms and land inside the other country's borders. Captain Katz, and Talia Vaknin, your plane will be that plane. I can hear the cheers from your Israeli social media followers congratulating you both on your victory while my followers, heh, come completely undone over it. But I will earn back their respect one way or another. I always do."

"An honor for sure," Ozzie Katz said, "but that means you are going to throw the race."

"Yes, that is my intention. I realize it might not be as simple as me merely making this declaration. There are other pilots in the race, including my own very accomplished co-pilot. While I hope you will all cooperate, that is not a guarantee that we will all follow through. I therefore want to handicap my plane and the U.S. team's."

Max understood the prince's intentions, and could sympathize with them, but where was this going? "What do you mean by handicap, Jasem?"

"We will add ballast, and by ballast I mean a third person to each cockpit," Jasem said. "The Israeli team will still fly their two co-pilots only. The extra weight in our planes will put us at a distinct disadvantage if any of us reneges on the plan. What say you about this, Max Fend?"

Caught flatfooted, Max stammered his answer. "I, ah, does this mean I need to look for a third pilot? That's not reasonable at this point, Jasem."

"Not a third pilot, Max, just a third person. I will do the same, perhaps give my personal assistant Jundiin an unusual perk. A reward for having coordinated this entire affair. He will be thrilled."

The alarm went off in Max's head. Jundiin was the joker in the deck. A question mark because of his possible allegiance to Jasem's uncle.

Batman. Joker. A question mark, the calling card for another Batman nemesis, the Riddler. A trifecta of life imitating comic book art. Still, how could Max talk Jasem out of using Jundiin?

Max turned to Renee, looking for help, but Renee was already on it.

"Jasem," Renee said. "That is a wonderful plan. Max, knowing you will ask me, I'm telling you I am good with it. But Jasem, there is one modification I'd like you to consider. Instead of having your personal assistant Jundiin fly with you, would you consider me as your additional ballast?"

Jasem's smile was billboard-worthy. "Of course, Renee. Fantastic. But wait. Camille, what do you say?"

This was moving too fast for Max, but he didn't know how to stop it. Renee had thought well on her feet, saw the opening that would keep wild card Jundiin out of the air with them and went for it. Max had reservations that they could discuss later, but this sounded like a winner.

All eyes went to Camille. After a beat, she reached out her hand to Renee.

"*Mon nouvel amie* Renee, welcome aboard."

"Jasem, that is a tenacious approach, and a gracious offer," Ozzie said. "Talia, what say you?"

"I am good with it, too, Captain."

"Then it is done," Ozzie Katz said. "Count us in, friends."

Jasem declared the plan fit. "People, let's finish this most excellent adventure today by gathering to celebrate our bipartisanship and sportsmanship together at the race's final stop, in Dubai."

Jasem clapped Max on the shoulder. "So tell me, Max, who will your two passengers be?"

Max had his phone out and was texting. "I'm in the process of figuring that out."

He already had, but there was no reason to mention them here. Trent and Lou Dotto would be his plus-two. Trent's bulk on its own might be handicap enough, but he couldn't ignore Lou, who would be thrilled to fly with his boss, or so Max imagined. Max would settle it as soon as he could make the connections. They'd need to get ready quickly.

"You know, Max, according to our rules, changing our flight crews during the race technically disqualifies both our teams as soon as we get in the air," Jasem said, "not that anyone will keep us from going up."

"Make sure that doesn't happen. Our race, between you and I, will now be for second place, and I intend to beat you," Max said, enjoying the trash talk. "See you in my rear view at the airport."

The three FW50s had their hatches open outside the hangar, the race participants in the process of boarding. Max and Renee faced each other between Max's plane and Jasem's, Max speaking, his voice low.

"So proud of you, Renee, keeping Batman out of the air like this. Wilkes likes it, too. But my work is now cut out for me. Three pilots in your plane against me and four hundred pounds of freeloading hangers-on in the other. Not fair."

"You'll manage, Max, you always do." Renee's arms surrounded his neck for a goodbye hug.

"And you'll get to see Jasem and Camille operate as a team. Report back, tell me if you see anything juicy going on between them. Inquiring minds want to know…"

"None of my business, or yours, Max honey. Here's what you should be thinking about…"

Their embrace was tight, the only race team romantically involved with each other, or at least the only team open about it, and their kiss was worthy of its audience.

"Max, I know this short flight is supposed to be a slam dunk," Renee said, "but please be careful." She glanced at the plane that had carried them this far, had weathered dust storms, bad fuel, and an emergency landing. "Rose deserves a relaxing trip. Please take good care of her."

Max agreed, nodded, and eyed her shoulder bag. "Phone and laptop in there?"

"Of course."

"Keep me posted. I want to hear their reaction when I pass them out there over that beautiful Arabian Gulf," he said, smiling. Another kiss between them, then Renee boarded, joining Jasem and Camille already in their seats, Camille piloting, Jasem alongside.

Max climbed inside his ride, Trent sitting shotgun, Lou in the rear row, their personal gear already onboard. They strapped in.

"I appreciate you gentlemen joining me for this junket," Max said, checking the instruments. "But don't get big heads about it. Much as I like you both a lot, today you're nothing more than my ballast."

"Happy to be aboard, Captain," Trent said, "and you can bite me."

Lou was more diplomatic, revisiting the employer-employee arrangement that got him to say yes to the trip. "My fat Italian buttocks are getting paid triple-time for this, boss. My RV on order gets a few more options. You want me as ballast anywhere else, I'm good for that, too. Maybe I get a new condo."

No media or press on hand. All were prohibited, to keep the composition of the teams under wraps for this leg. Excluding takeoff and landing, the two hundred twenty-four air miles of the route would be over water. The three planes taxied up to an imaginary starting line that stretched across two parallel runways, the Jasem with Camille and Renee plane and the Max and his merry duo plane on the same runway, the Israeli team plane separate. Lined up across from each other, pilots and passengers alike were head-geared up, listening to the tower. Not a starting gun sendoff as originally imagined, but close enough.

"Pilots, ready now, on my countdown from ten. Ten, nine..."

Max's phone, set to earthquake mode in his shirt pocket, jolted him, then stopped. "Who the hell—"

Trent interrupted him. "It's Wilkes. He texted me too. The text is in all caps, it says 'Pick up your phone, Max.'"

Max called him back. "This is a really bad time, Wilkes..."

"... five, four..."

Cockpit noise, the tower countdown... Max could hear Wilkes's voice but couldn't understand him. Max yelled back at him, into the phone. "You'll need to text us! Gotta go!"

The *three, two, one, go!* from the tower had come and gone, with a distracted Max starting later than his competitors, him watching the Jasem plane shoot ahead, mirroring the Israeli plane's jackrabbit start. Trent read Wilkes's newest text, his head now swiveling in all directions as Max accelerated.

"No—Max—you need to shut her down—something's up—"

A white pickup truck rocketed alongside their plane to parallel them on the runway, accelerating to move past them.

Another text; Trent read it. "Wilkes again. He's in that pickup. We need to shut this thing down now..."

"But Renee... Jasem..."

"He's flipping out. He wants you to abort the takeoff. Let's live to see another day, Max. Stop the plane now! We'll just need to figure out a way to catch up—"

Max cut the engine and the pickup screeched to a stop in front of them. Wilkes exited the truck's shotgun seat, trotted to the fuselage, waiting impatiently for the hatch to open. Max climbed onto the wing, Trent did likewise, Lou staying put, watching from a window. They both dropped onto the runway.

"Wilkes, this better be good, damn it. This leg's head-to-head, no staggered start, and now we're at least a full minute behind. Wait—is that the Feds' truck, the one with the—"

"Listen to me carefully, Max," Wilkes said. "Yes, this is that truck. The gun is in the payload. The man Trent shot wasn't Nomad. Nomad is still active."

Max and Trent traded glances. "You know that how?" Max said.

Wilkes went into it. Something from the raid on the hotel room hadn't sat right with him, but he couldn't put his finger on it. Too easy maybe, and how was it that this zephyr who had evaded authorities for over two decades had suddenly become that stupid and left behind a trail of such damning information about himself and Jasem's uncle. But the biggest problem Wilkes had with him had nothing to do with what looked like uncharacteristic incompetence.

"The CIA's computer models. The analysts usually get a ninety percent-plus match against all the data, provable after the fact. There was a discrepancy on one of the physical traits."

"C'mon, Wilkes, you're killing us, just tell us what didn't match."

"Ives Hanania, a.k.a. Gilles Khalifa—his height. Way off. Too tall per the computer modeling. All the scenario models have Nomad at below average height."

A gruesome image on Max's part: the agency unpacking the body from the luggage, laying it out, straightening out the mangled parts after rigor had set in. Height, weight, dental records, other measurements... maybe even an autopsy, the reason there were coroners on the payroll.

"The game is still afoot, gentlemen," Wilkes said, "and the uncle is still at large, and unfortunately the Dubai royal family might still be in danger. We need to regroup."

The racing planes passed overhead only a hundred feet above them, the two planes banking at a discomforting G-force, the pilots of both teams showing off before going into their climbs. Max squinted, watched as the Israeli team zoomed into the lead, Jasem's plane a short distance back, the distance a safe one, but the lead had already opened. As the Israelis left the airport's airspace, their plane dipped a wing at Max to acknowledge him and his plane still on the ground. A wave goodbye, or a playful jab? Or was Ozzie Katz leaving with maybe an eat-my-dust taunt?

Or worse. An unflattering image hit him: Max behind the Israeli captain at the urinal in Athens. Tall, lanky Max, waiting behind the shorter Ozzie Katz. Half-a-head-shorter Ozzie Katz. Below-average-male-height-or-shorter Ozzie Katz. Israeli Intel Ozzie Katz.

And maybe double-agent, maybe *Nomad* Ozzie Katz.

"How close did you look at the Israeli team, Wilkes? Did Langley run them through the models?"

"The Israeli Air Force Captain? He's Mossad, Max. We checked him out—"

"He's the right height, short like Nomad, he's in the spy game already, and he's no stranger to world travel. He deserves a revisit. I say you should recheck his movements over the past ten, fifteen years, like, *now*."

Wilkes spoke while pressing numbers into his phone. "Fine. We'll revisit him. In the meantime—"

"In the meantime, I need to alert Renee and Jasem, and we need to get into the air asap."

23

Jasem, in the passenger's seat, took his turn piloting. Camille's serene face said she was in full-scale awe of the bluest expanse of the Arabian Sea below them, their plane cruising at nine thousand feet at a speed that had topped out at 165 knots, restricted by their added weight. The Israeli team's plane had left their viewable air space, was "... ahead of them by two minutes," Camille said, "but we can still make a run at them when you let me have the controls again, Your Highness."

"Relax, Camille," Jasem said. "It will be good for us to make them earn it, but as we all agreed, they will be first to touch down. That is best for our message of regional goodwill; best for everyone involved. I am enjoying this experience. A few more minutes, then you can have the plane back."

Renee, her laptop open, wasn't so sure where the Israeli plane was. Had they increased their lead by that much, or had they simply veered off to the left or right, out of their sight? A text popped up. This would be Max calling to explain why he hadn't taken off with them.

Nope, not Max, but rather a message from one of her hackers. It bore multiple exclamation points in its first line and contained a data download about Nomad's travels, except the message was already three hours old. Frustrating. She opened the file to read the data even though it was moot, considering Nomad had already been neutralized.

On it were the dates of the crimes credited to Nomad over the past fourteen years. All old news. Then came the results from running these dates against major events taking place in major cities give or take a week, close to the same time. Sporting events, celebrations, festivals, anything repetitive year after year. She'd gone with Langley's speculation, that Nomad worked around a yet-TBD pattern of special events that put him in these places for legitimate, professional reasons. Not there for the commission of these crimes and assassinations, but there because his lawful profession or pursuits had required it, and the behind-the-scenes wetwork contracts he'd executed had fit that schedule. Here were iterative runs made by laying in matches between the crimes committed and the approximate timing of the recurring events.

Fourteen years of criminal offenses in cities around the world. Then came the surprise. Nearly all the crimes were hits when matched against various aerobatic shows and one overlooked recurring event: the defunct Red Bull World Air Race Championships.

A phone text arrived on her laptop screen, from Max. *Good*, now she'd get to the bottom of what had kept him from departing Qatar. She stopped her data review to open the text, her fingers poised to respond to it. They stayed raised, Renee dumbfounded as she read each message.

Nomad is still alive Langley says dead man in hotel room was too tall

No announcement coming out on this let him think we still think he's dead

We'll get Dubai to increase security for the landing ceremony

Tell Jasem & Camille they need to return to Qatar. Dubai ceremony might still be a target

FYI I radioed your plane but was cut off then I couldn't get through again

Her anxiety kicked in as hard as a punch to the gut, fueled also by the new hacker info. Red Bull's race in Acapulco, Mexico, 2007. Her godparents killed as collateral damage nearby, from a verified Nomad hit.

Other locations, other dates, other assassinations, all matches.

Another text from Max.

Langley's rerunning models strong possibility Ozzie Katz is Nomad. Shorter stature, lighter weight, both are fits. Checking his movements now

In Renee's head, the hacker data was wreaking havoc, crisscrossing

Max's pronouncement. Something niggling—a detail about Camille the pilot. Camille the military pilot... the aerobatic pilot... the air race pilot...

Fiery Camille. Short-tempered, also short in stature. Sharing, boasting about piloting races from Abu Dhabi to...

Acapulco.

The blood drained from Renee's face.

With Jasem still piloting, Renee and Camille enjoyed a spectacular view in all directions. Camille's glance out a side window absorbed Renee's face mirrored in the glass. Renee managed a small, nervous smile meant to mask her shock. Camille's grin at her turned into a thin line.

"You're awfully quiet back there, Renee. What's going on, *mon chérie*? Worried about your Max? He will get back to you, although he is effectively out of this race, I'm afraid. Which works to our advantage, heh, now that he is out of the way. How do the Americans put it? 'No worries, it's all good?'"

Renee composed herself enough for a broader smile and delivery of a light pleasantry in French, which gave her breathing room. She keyed a response to Max's text, her fingers trembling.

Ozzie Katz isn't Nomad. Camille is.

24

Max stared at Renee's text in disbelief. "Sonovabitch."

He read the text aloud to Wilkes and Trent, the three of them in the middle of the runway outside Max's plane, the hatches open, the airport tower coming through on the radio saying they needed to get the hell off the tarmac and take their plane with them immediately.

"Trent, get back in the plane. Wilkes, get in. I'm taking it back to the hangar. Have your pickup meet us there. We don't have much time."

Max climbed into the cockpit and restarted the engine. "Lou, I'm gonna need your help."

Another text from Renee. Max tossed his phone to Wilkes. "Check it out and text her back."

"It's a file. She highlighted passages on it." Wilkes stayed silent while he read. "Her hackers connected the dots. There's a statistical probability exceeding ninety percent that Nomad was a part of these air competitions in some capacity. And one of the races was in Abu Dhabi."

The plane screeched to a stop inside the hangar. Max yelled at Lou in the rear seat. "We need your magic here, Lou, right now. Get out and make this plane go faster any way you can."

"Not enough time, boss..."

"Figure it out. We need more horsepower. Wilkes, I'm calling Jasem's plane on my headset. I've got a question for him."

Wilkes objected. "Not a good idea, unless you want them all to hear what you have to say."

"Exactly."

~

"Max. Good to hear your voice," Jasem said into his headgear. "Are you airborne yet?"

Max, headgear on and speaking from inside his plane, still in the hangar, was fired up but remained calm. He needed to play this just right.

"No, still on the ground. A mechanical issue might keep us here. I thought I'd keep you company and distract Camille a little, so she doesn't get any ideas about trying to overtake the Israelis, competitive as she is. Mademoiselle Gagneux, are you behaving yourself? No heroic measures, I hope? No aerobatic magic planned?"

"*Mais non*, Max, but of course not. I do want to make it my best effort, but I also understand the expectations. The Israelis must win. *Très* important to promoting Middle East peace."

Max would look at everything Camille said in a different light now. "Works for me," he said. "Keep your eye on her, Jasem, heh. That Red Bull race in Acapulco, and another one somewhere in the UAE... nearby terrorist events almost spoiled the festivities, but no matter, Renee told me Camille still turned in kickass performances in both races."

"Ha! Good memory, Max," Jasem said. "I hadn't heard about Acapulco, but the Emirati race was in Abu Dhabi. It was where I met Camille. Where I saw how gifted she was as a pilot."

"Right, Abu Dhabi, how could I have overlooked that? One of the pilots withdrew before the last heat; the race leader, I think it was. See, now that I'm in the aerobatic race game I'm schooling myself where I can, playing catch-up. It makes me a better sponsor. What was it, Camille, food poisoning? After this recent brush with it—I mean, hell, they might start calling food poisoning the Air Race Disease," he said, chuckling.

"Ah, *Monsieur* Fend, you are terrible," Camille said, "but frankly, I do not remember."

"Oops, my bad," Max said. "Sorry, just talking a little trash. Look, guys, stay safe, enjoy the ride, and take care of that precious cargo you have in the back seat. Renee, we're with you all the way, honey. Signing off, everyone. Bye."

He hoped Jasem heard it, hoped Jasem would piece it together: in many of the cities where Camille piloted races, people were poisoned or murdered or both.

Max hopped off the plane wing and barked at Wilkes: "Text Renee. Let her know we're coming after their plane. With Jasem in there, no way Camille's not planning something horrible to end this thing. Lou?"

"Yeah, boss?"

"Tell me you figured something out that will give us more speed."

Lou was beaming. "Bad news is, nothing I can do will give you more horsepower on such short notice. But I did make one adjustment that will help. I—"

"Great. Tell me later. By the way, you're not coming with us. We can't afford the weight."

"But what about—"

"Shut it, Lou, sorry. I'll still pay you either way. You're costing me a fortune. Trent?"

"Here."

Max waved him over to the pickup truck, Wilkes trailing them. "The sixty-four-thousand-dollar question is, this whiz-bang *Star Wars* gadget in here—" Max lowered the tailgate, exposing the black carrier with the precision-guided rifle in it, destined for Langley. "Can you use it?"

"I can, and I would be delighted."

"We're going up, Wilkes. The only way to stop her now is to take her out while she's flying the plane."

"Max. Whoa." Wilkes had his phone to his ear. "Not so fast. I just alerted the Navy."

"You *what*? To scramble a jet? No—"

"This is too big a gig for two guys in a small aircraft. Who knows what she's going to do with that plane—"

"No, you can't, Renee's in there, damn it."

"Then we'll need to get her out," Wilkes said. "No jet, Max, the military is preparing a Stinger. They have an air defense team on high alert."

The specs on a Stinger in Max's head: surface-to-air heat-seeking missile, handheld, two-man team, low altitude range twelve thousand feet. It would need to be in place within a few miles of the airport.

"We can't let them get anywhere near that airport, Max. It will be an international incident if they take out the king. That gun stays on the ground, is going back to the Israelis, and *you* stay on the ground. Let the military handle this..."

"They'll shoot them down, Caleb!"

"They'll shoot *it* down, Max. Message Renee and the Crown Prince to tell them to get the hell out of the plane."

"Really? Camille's an ace pilot. You think she'll let them parachute out? We need to stay quiet, act like all is well, and you need to let Trent and me go up with that gun, move into position, and take Camille out. Let us go, *now.*"

Wilkes sharpened his gaze at them both. Max waited for an answer, Trent was next to the pickup, looking for the word to rip open the truck's payload cover and commandeer the rifle.

"I'll make some calls and have the higher-ups deal with the Israelis looking for their gun," Wilkes said. "In the meantime, while we wait for permission on all this, why don't I go inside the hangar and busy myself and leave you guys out here to busy yourselves."

This was Wilkes turning a blind eye. They wasted no time. Trent popped the payload cover up, yelled to Max. "Give me a hand and we'll board this bastard." They dragged the trunk with the smart rifle in it to the edge. Wilkes had a parting comment.

"Max, know this, because it can't be any other way—"

Max and Trent hoisted the gun carrier onto the wing. Trent tossed out their luggage from the hold behind the rear seats, onto the tarmac.

"... there are protocols for supporting our interests..."

They moved the trunk onto the rear seat, climbed aboard, and strapped in.

"Make it good, Wilkes," Max said. "What is it?"

Wilkes spoke over the noise of Max cranking the aircraft engine. "I'm not unscrambling that air defense team. They will be out there with that Stinger, awaiting orders to engage. If you and Trent don't get it done—"

Wilkes's jaw locked up on the implication, his eyes narrowing, meeting Max's stare. "I'm not going to finish that sentence. Just make something happen, Max."

25

―――――――

Renee eyed Jasem in the co-pilot's seat. Did he know? Did he now realize the monster he'd teamed himself with? Renee knew the feeling. She, too, had been sucked in, played by Camille's strong, silent, take-no-BS act. Charming, confident Camille. Friendly Camille, comforting even. And too short, too female, on no one's radar as dangerous. No consideration as an assassin, certainly not anyone as prolific as Nomad. Not big enough to be effective in a murder-for-hire profession that screamed strength and dominance, or so the assumption would always be. She had a chip on her shoulder, much like Renee. That's why they'd hit it off. That's why Renee had closed her eyes, blinded by her resume and her celebrity, oblivious to the signals and the circumstantial evidence plaguing Camille's presence here.

Renee's nerves tingled, some with fear, more with adrenaline. She was never more aware of the concealed Ruger pocket pistol under her loose-fitting top than she was now. This French fly-girl, she reminded herself, had taken away two of the people dearest to her.

But her stark new awareness reminded her that Camille also liked loose tops, same as Renee did, and for probably the same reason. A good probability that there was a concealed weapon under Camille's top as well.

A veil of silence settled into the cockpit, a quiet worthy of sights as incredible as these, the great big expanse of the bluest of blue seas, the sky fettered with only a few clouds. Or was it the tensions of three people in a small cockpit with each knowing something was off, a cloak of deceit and death hanging over them. Had Jasem pieced this dire situation together? Was Camille aware that Renee had?

Camille's hands… only her right hand was visible, gripping the yoke.

"Jasem," Renee said into her headset.

This would be it. Renee would gauge Jasem's awareness of their predicament by how he responded, his voice inflections, his facial expression, his eyes…

"Jasem? Jasem?"

"He's napping, Renee."

Renee leaned between the seats to see for herself. Jasem's eyes were closed, his head and shoulder against the side window, but his mouth was moving.

"Mgglmpffdg…" came back to her through the headgear, incoherent rambling from Jasem's uncooperative lips.

"By now, *chérie*," Camille said, "I expect you are wondering, with us in the air for only, how long has it been?" She checked her watch. "Fourteen minutes? You wonder what is it that could have made him so tired so quickly?"

Renee unholstered her handgun, a secretive move, unsure what she would do with it in such close quarters, inside an airplane cockpit, where a stray bullet could send their plane into a tailspin in an instant. She had no choice other than to use it if necessary, then deal with the consequences. They were nine to ten thousand feet up; there would hopefully still be time to drag a dead Camille out of her pilot's seat into the rear with her, then go for the yoke and take over the plane. She checked outside the windows, all of them—left, then the windshield, then right—keen on how two-hundred-seventy degrees of the horizon was still ever so blue, in the middle of an ocean, except…

A faint, dark, ragged edge moved into view in the right-side window. It had to be the Emirates coastline. Camille was slowly taking them right, off the water, moving toward land, and from Renee's knowledge of Max's flight plan for this final leg, this wasn't the most direct route toward the finish line. She was going off course, putting the plane over terra firma.

Renee faced forward. Camille's left hand stayed on the yoke, her right hand now free and on her knee. It was closed around something.

"I... what happened?" Renee said, checking Jasem out, feigning surprise. "Did he take something to calm himself? The thrill of this last leg too much for him?"

"*Mais non*," Camille said. "He does not use drugs. He is a wonderful person, Renee. His persona visible to the outside world, what you see of him, it is real. It made this... circumstance difficult for me. It is why I want this last leg, this glorious flying experience, his last, to be as least anxious for him as possible."

A genuine appreciation for him, but also a coy, calculating comment.

"I don't understand," Renee said, even though she did.

"He is sleeping because it is best for him. Because I like him. Because regardless of his culture's façade about fraternizing with non-Muslim women, he has, in fact, been a good lover to me. No reason to hide that now. I like you, too, *l' amie*, and it will be easy for you as well, if you let me make it that way."

Camille opened her hand. Her fingers held a short vial with a covered tip.

"A single dose. Like a flu shot at the doctor. A quick jab anywhere, and all your worries about what is about to happen will float away."

26

At his rotation speed, Max began pulling back on the yoke, bringing the aircraft into a steep climb. Strapped in next to him, Trent was nothing like a co-pilot: game face on, grim, in full focus mode. His head swiveled, searching the horizon like a gun turret.

Max got on his phone via SATCOM interface with Lou. "What do you suggest, Lou? We need an altitude that will work best."

Lou spoke from outside the Qatar hangar, his laptop resting on a piece of luggage, his butt planted on another. "*Solo un minuto, per favore*, I am checking. The tower says prevailing winds make it best to be at ten thousand feet. For your beloved FW50 Rose, that sounds right. Plus—"

Max reached the suggested ceiling with Lou still speaking and leveled Rose off. "We're there, Lou. You said 'plus.' Plus what?"

"Do you feel it, boss?"

"Not sure what you mean."

"Check your RPMs. They should be running higher. Two hundred or so RPMs higher. Higher speed for you, boss."

"How many knots faster?"

"Maybe seventy-five."

"Nice. How'd you manage that?"

"I played with the governor. It lets you run higher RPMs. The engine won't be in good shape after this flight, but you'll get great performance out of her for a short time. Max?"

"Yeah, Lou?"

"You can catch them, but just don't go crazy with it. That would be bad. Speaking of bad: by any chance did you already authorize my OT, 'cause, you know, things don't always go as planned—"

"Copy that, Lou. Yes, I authorized it already. Thanks for the vote of confidence, you morbid SOB. Out."

Jasem was still breathing but was no longer making any sounds, incoherent or otherwise, leaning forehead-first against the gull-winged door in dreamland. Renee had moved to the center seat in the rear row, her shoulders square, readying herself. For Camille's reach, or for Camille to produce a concealed firearm, a taser, or whatever, she didn't know what to expect. Renee's own weapon, her small pistol, was in her hand, tucked under her right thigh. Its alloyed steel felt hot there, an imaginary effect. Or was this how all guns felt just before you killed someone with one? She'd need to pull the diminutive Camille out of her seat by her hair, then between the seats and into the center console. She'd shove the gun barrel against her skull and pull the trigger, with the bullet's exit hopefully not ricocheting into any vital aircraft instruments. She could pull this off with brute force, overwhelming the shorter, less bulky woman, or so she told herself. She just needed to stay away from whatever pinprick needle or syringe Camille held in her right hand while she did it, or it would be la-la land for her. One other issue: Camille would need to be out of her shoulder harness for Renee to pull her out of her seat.

And a gun, if Camille had one, would be a bigger problem, for all of them.

A text came through to Max while he switched back and forth between checking the radar and visually scanning the horizon and their speed. On his mind, the delay in their start. It had cost them ten, maybe twelve minutes. How well was their plane tracking against the UAE plane, how far behind were they, were they gaining...?

Waiting on info from Wilkes. Had the U.S. brass been able to herd the UAE royalty away from the race terminus in Dubai? Was that even where Nomad was headed?

He stopped to read the text. It was from Renee, not Wilkes. He wasn't sure what to make of it. "Trent, look at this."

The text read, *Nearing coastline over land soon Jasem drugged out cold love you max*

"Too soon for them to fly over land," Trent said. "Nowhere near the destination."

Max processed what this meant. What did Camille have in mind?

He had it. "Camille's going to abandon the plane. She's giving herself a soft landing in the desert with a chute."

"Yeah, but what about Renee and—" Trent caught himself, realizing the implication. "This can't be good, Max."

"Agreed. She can put it on autopilot and let it go wherever it's supposed to go. As long as Renee and Jasem are in no condition to do anything about it."

Max goosed the yoke right, altering their course, looking for the coastline. He flipped on Rose's autopilot so he could text Renee back.

We're coming we will catch you say nothing. Get behind the rear seats in the cargo section make her work to get at you

Autopilot off. "Trent, call Wilkes, let him know."

"Roger that. If she's looking for a soft spot she won't have to look far. Dubai's ninety-five percent sand."

Another visual scan of the horizon, up and down, plus a radar read, left Max bordering on frantic. "Where are they, damn it? C'mon, Rose, faster..."

Trent got off the phone. "Wilkes says we've deployed someone overland who will track her down if she jumps. Radar picked up their plane and is tracking them. We're behind, but this is still doable, bud." Trent unbuckled his harness and climbed into the rear seat.

"Trent?"

"Yeah, Max?"

"I don't want to lose her."

"Roger that."

Trent raised the heavy top to the black trunk with the Hebrew writing on top, kept it open, and admired its contents. "We're not going to let that happen."

~

"In my hand, Renee, is the answer to your anxiety, and mine, too. One little jab anywhere with this prickly vial and you will rest comfortably just like Jasem, numb to what's coming."

Stay out of her reach, Renee told herself. *Engage her, keep her talking—*

"This makes no sense, Camille." Renee discreetly returned her handgun to the holster on her hip. She needed both hands. "Why do this? You are, what is it they call French fighter pilots, an *'asso volante'*? A flying ace...?"

"First, shame on you and your lousy French, Renee. You mean *'un as de l'aviation,'* in honor of all the great World War One French pilots. And second, we both know who I am to you and your agency. To all the agencies. Your name for me... it's something I rather like."

"Nomad."

"Yes! A wonderful name! And I am also, of course, *un as de l'aviation, un as de l'assassinat,* I am all that and more. I am also *un génie acrobatique...*"

An aerobatic genius. Camille took the plane into a steep climb, the G-force shoving Renee back against the seat, Jasem's unresponsive frame flopping backward, almost out of his harness. At the top of the climb, she stalled the engine. The plane dropped silently down, gathering speed, the back end of a controlled loop before Camille started the engine again.

Renee's stomach moved into her throat, but she managed to keep its contents down. The groggy Jasem wasn't so lucky, his mouth erupting at the end of the loop, vomiting on himself, the spray drifting down his chin and neck, but he was still incapacitated, oblivious to his predicament.

Camille, showing off, was full-on ecstatic after completing the move, proud of herself.

The crazy loop move was worth the slight discomfort to Renee.

Anything that slowed them down would help. Renee used the time to unbuckle her seat belt and slip into the small baggage hold behind the rear seat, already tight with luggage. At this moment, her life depended on creating space between her and Camille.

"Oh my," Camille said, noticing Renee's defection, "you are afraid of me. Fine. But be careful. My carry-on back there isn't what it seems. It is secure, but it is a bit, um, explosive. You can stay back there with no seat belt, but here's what you should worry about if you do—"

Camille spun the plane over, riding them upside down, the spin lifting Renee off the floor of the hold as gravity reversed itself, her body pressed against the ceiling, the luggage secured to the floor with straps. Another touch of the pilot controls and the plane nosed downward, with Renee starting to slip forward on the ceiling, sliding out of the cargo area. She pushed against the back of the rear seat with both hands, trying to stay in place and not spill forward, nearer to Camille.

Quick as the plane had gone topsy-turvy, Camille righted it again. Renee dropped from the ceiling face first, hard enough to draw blood from her nose. "...aghhh—!"

"I can hurt you much worse than that anytime I want, Renee, so you should sit still and listen to me—"

"No, Camille, *you* listen to *me*. What Jasem's uncle wanted from you, or your boss—I don't know what the hell Gilles Khalifa was to you—was ludicrous. Kill the king? Kill Jasem? Blame the Israelis? Why would you need to destabilize the peace? And now the uncle is on the run. How do you collect from a man in hiding, or who might even be dead?"

Camille smirked. "Sorry, so sorry, Renee, ha-ha, but no. My-my, such puppies, all the intel agencies are. So easily led. Gilles—Ives—was my middleman, Renee, my recruiter. *He* worked for *me*. For the contract killing side of me. I am due one last monetary installment, a large one, which I intend to collect. I do owe him a lot—*so* much—but I detest him because he also ruined me—"

A new text arrived on Renee's phone, in her pocket, Camille still pontificating. She unpacked her laptop instead and flipped it open on the seat. She glanced at the text notification on her screen. From Max.

"... he ruined my life. He saved me from myself, from my drug addictions, took me off the French streets, but what he did after he got me clean —what he turned me into...

"Murder gives me a rush better than any drug, *mon amie*. He taught me to fly, but better yet, he taught me to kill. My double life as a contract assassin is *incroyable*. But it is a worse addiction. I have killed for money, but now, I also kill for sport."

One minute behind you Renee per Max's text.

"I do not need him," Camille declared. "I need no one. I set him up in Qatar. I led your intel people to him. I left that beast of a gun with him, told him to sell it again. I left the plans, the fake itinerary, and the dark web info, all of it, to frame him. That weapon attracted too much interest.

"All those communications were from *me*. I had access to Jasem's phone and laptop. And I hacked his uncle's devices. I sent messages from Jasem to his uncle. Sent messages from the uncle to Jasem. Sent messages I wrote to *me* as Nomad from the uncle. The ground signal from Nomad to Jasem? It came from inside our plane. And I sent Jundiin messages from Jasem, like the one that directed your plane into the sandstorm, not away from it. I expect your agencies got none of it right. The uncle—he wanted only to embarrass Jasem, not kill him. And he certainly did not want to kill the king. The king is old, and he will die soon anyway. Killing him would make the uncle a pariah, unable to rule. The uncle wanted the king to recast his Crown Prince selection after seeing how naïve Jasem had been. He wanted to show Jasem as incompetent, about this race, about the treaty, about the Israelis, about everything."

This was where Renee wanted Camille to be: talking.

Look at me, look how smart I am, no one smarter than me...

But where Renee also wanted to be was up close and personal with a gun to Camille's head. She instead kept it holstered, Camille still too dangerous for her to do otherwise.

Another text from Max. *Click on this link a surprise for you. Spoiler alert turned my transponder off Im trying to get close*

"I had such a good thing going, Renee! The Prince, Jasem, promised me great sums of money to pilot his planes in these new aerobic plane races. It all changed with the peace deal he negotiated. He suddenly became a target. He made new, powerful friends, became adored by the world, but the deal produced enemies for him that were far more dangerous than he'd ever seen as a playboy prince. A large—very large—assassination contract emerged."

A disgusted Renee zeroed in on Camille's betrayal. "You were friends. You betrayed him."

"Oh, *mais non*, it was not me, Renee, it was the uncle, he wanted to teach Jasem a lesson. Jasem just became the, what would you call him in your movies, the 'fall guy?' The spy agencies, yours, all the others, they all got it wrong."

Renee discreetly opened Max's new text. His online link showed a picture of an airplane, an FW50 from behind—no, not a picture, a streaming video, and not just any plane, the UAE plane that she, Renee, was a passenger in per the call letters, in flight and in real time. It tempted her to look out a window and around the UAE plane—behind them, she'd see Max—but she stopped herself to remain focused on Camille.

With Max's transponder off, their TCAS did not get an alert.

"The uncle, he was a pigeon, a patsy," Camille said. "My recruiter Ives saw the potential of making the contract so much more consequential, more lucrative financially than what the uncle had in mind, because now it would be politically charged. It could promote an incident..."

Renee squinted, saw Camille had reactivated the plane's GPS, also saw a blinking red dot on the radar screen. That had to be Dubai International. They were closing in.

"*Iran*, Renee! Who wants destabilization more than anyone else in the region—*Iran*! Ives, my recruiter, he is French, but he is also Palestinian. He so abhors the Israelis. Or he did. The uncle gave us—gave *me*—a payday I can retire on, payable by Iran, if—when—I execute the Dubai royal family. And it shall be blamed on Israel. So, here we are, approaching zero hour—

"Do not move from your space back there, and I will not spin the plane to maim any more of your extremities. There was time for you to fade into the comfort of tranquilized oblivion, to not suffer any of the pain that I can deliver to you with flicks of this yoke, but that time is past. And now, *mon cher*, it is time to say *au revoir*."

Camille removed her headset and reached under her shirt, not to liberate a weapon but to lift it over her head. Underneath she wore a tight, neck-to-ankle jumpsuit in black. Sleek. She unbuckled her seat belt, allowing her to turn around to speak directly at Renee. She settled in with her arm over the seat and a big smile.

"My dearest Renee from Montreal, Canada. You speak only passable French, and you are a poor excuse for *une femme Française*. What else is there that I should tell you? Well, there is this one more thing—"

She spoke while removing the rucksack from under her seat. "A custom parachute for me, Renee, sporty and aerodynamic. I am ready. And you are, as they say in *l'anglais*—"

The plane also had standard parachutes stowed under each seat. Camille climbed into her backpack with the custom chute and strapped herself in.

"... so screwed. You chose no medication, that is fine with me. With the autopilot engaged, the plane will follow the signal. No interruption to the signal, my luggage stays intact until impact, otherwise my luggage detonates. Oh, I forgot to tell you about the signal! There is a homing device that should be moving into place, right about"—she checked her watch—"now. At the celebration platform at Dubai International. Excellent timing. It will provide quite a display of fireworks when a certain FW50 does not stick its landing on the tarmac at the finish line, but instead follows the signal, and destroys the stage and anyone near it."

For a device to be "moving into place," it had to be attached to something, or someone. Renee would show her smarts now, too. "You attached it to Jundiin, correct? That little shit is involved, isn't he?"

"Oh, *mais non, chéri*, Jundiin is incorruptible. *Non, non, non,* it is with my newest girlfriend, former ISI spy, Bibi. Poor woman. Unemployed now. I've given her my credit card. American Express! She is in Dubai on my tab, and it thrills her. I convinced her I am only one step removed from the DGSE, *Direction Générale de la Sécurité Extérieure*. France's intel agency. She has inserted herself incognito among the well-wishers at the front of the stage, and she is keeping her eye sharp for any covert air or ground activity that might threaten the festivities. 'Do this, my dear friend Bibi,' I said to her, 'and I will give you a superb personal reference to French intel. They might even give you a job *tout suit*.' Ha! Can you see this little red dot here, Renee, on the GPS screen? This is Bibi, and it means she and my credit card are close to where they need to be to make this happen. *Magnifique!"*

~

Max was hard-wired, his eyes bulging, blinking less, the yoke moist with sweat: their target was directly in front of them. He backed off their speed and looked for Trent's input. "So what do we have? Are you ready?"

Max checked over his shoulder, watched Trent in the rear seat attaching the hefty scope to the Israelis' precision-guided long gun, putting sophisticated technology at Trent's fingertips. He held it up to his shoulder, leaned his face into the scope, brought the gun back down. He cradled it in his arm, then reached into the gun's carrying case, rummaging around.

"What are you looking for?"

"The instructions pamphlet. Did you see one anywhere in here?"

"The what? Are you crazy? I thought—"

"Just screwing with you. I found what I'm after."

Trent readied the rifle, now loaded with .30 caliber rounds. He expected that he'd get maybe two shots. If he missed, Camille—Nomad—would be alerted and her flying skills would negate a second approach.

"Okay, brace yourself, Max, it's going to get windy." Trent slid left, into the left-most rear seat.

"Wait. You still belted in?" Max asked.

"For now."

"Gun video active?"

"Affirmative. The gun's scope is streaming live."

"Your chute on?"

"Damn it, Mom, yes, my chute is on. I'm also tethered to the seat with straps and clips, just in case."

"How you gonna—"

"Directly overhead. You move us into position, I lean out, shoot straight down. The round pierces the airframe, then her skull, explodes her head, enters her torso, hopefully ends up no farther south than the seat cushion and stays inside the cockpit."

"You're counting on it being a perfect shot? That's your plan?"

"Yes, that's the plan. The rifle's onboard computer adjusts for the wind, the barometric pressure, our speed, the other plane's speed, and the rifle's cant. If that all happens, it lets me take the shot. If I can get the right angle, we win."

"It's all gotta happen, Trent. You need to make it happen."

"I know. Now shut the hell up while I break this window. There's gonna be some flying glass in here."

Trent grabbed a fire extinguisher. One swing, two... four, five, the window splintered, seven, eight—

The glass pushed out then came flying back inside, breaking into little pieces engineered not to be shards, floating around the rear of the plane on the rushing air, then settling on the seats and floor. Gloves on, he picked the window perimeter clean, removing the remaining chunks. Head out the window, then shoulders, then his torso down to his waist, Trent forced himself outside the plane, no gun yet, the wind resistance bucking him backward. Could he lean out far enough to get enough clearance over the wing...?

"Clearance is acceptable, Max. Let's creep into position above their plane so we can neutralize this bad actor."

27

The visual popped up on the link. While Camille talked, Renee could see the inside of Max's FW50 from her laptop, saw herky-jerky clipped shots as the rifle scope's camera calibrated each image it picked up: the ceiling of Max's plane, the back of a headrest, the back of a head. Then the head turned around and she saw Max's grim face, him pushing the rifle's barrel away from him. The image moved to the side of the interior, faced the window inside the rear gull-wing door. The picture turned azure blue into infinity with no definition, the rifle sight looking at sky. An abrupt jerk of the gun barrel moved the streaming video back outside, again transmitting only the blue of the sky. The barrel lowered to the window ledge, rested there, with white numbers and markers surrounding the perimeter of the screen, flashing, recalibrating, searching.

She was seeing what Trent was seeing: images on the rifle's high-tech scope, tracking its target, her plane.

Sharpshooting Trent, preparing to take Camille out from... somewhere. Renee needed to be out of the cargo area when that happened, in the rear seat, closer to the pilot's seat.

Renee moved into the rear seat row, now saw what Camille wanted her to see on the plane's GPS: the red dot.

"You are going to kill your accomplice Bibi, too? This is madness!"

"*Mais non*, not madness, this is business," Camille said. "Survival of the smartest. And I am the smartest of the smart in this deadly jungle."

"Look, Camille, I'm not part of this, you can let me parachute out of here." Renee removed a tightly packed rucksack from under a rear seat.

"*Au contraire*, Renee, I have made you so much more a part of this now. You now know *tous les details*." A disdainful look behind her, Camille seeing Renee climbing into a packed chute. "Oh my, no, no, I cannot let you leave this plane..."

The plane rolled hard left then hard right, the unsecured Renee bouncing against one wall then sliding hard against the other, her laptop airborne. The jostled rucksack with Renee's chute floated in midair. Camille snagged it, pulled it forward, then stuffed it at the feet of the still slumbering Jasem. Renee resettled the laptop.

"Try that again with any of the other chutes, you will get a similar jolt, *chienne*..."

Enough. Renee exploded over the back of the front seat at the French slur, grabbed Camille by her auburn hair, then connected with a right cross to her cheek, stunning her. Renee worked at the pilot's seat belt, snapped it open, freed Camille, was dragging her out of her seat...

... where is that vial? Does she have a gun...?

No, Camille didn't have a gun, but now she had Renee's, a deft move that slipped the small pistol out of its holster on Renee's hip. It was now under Renee's chin, Camille's finger on the trigger. Renee released her grip on Camille's hair as Camille leaned into the center console, shoving Renee back down into a rear seat, the handgun now pointed at her face.

"Agghhh! You are strong, Renee, but you are *stupide*! You will now join Jasem and sleep your way through your final moments. I must ready our approach..."

Camille flicked off the cap to the vaccine vial with her thumb and forefinger. Renee got a good look at the tiny needles in its base, all glistening with a paralyzing agent or a sleeping serum or an opiate worthy of great incapacitation.

"I am tempted to push these needles directly into your face, Renee, but I will instead shove them into your arm. You do not deserve this relief..."

Renee's unattended laptop had resettled, was open next to her in the rear seat, silently transmitting a streaming image that wavered, kept recentering itself, on the tail of an airplane, now its fuselage, now its roof, then wavering again, then refocusing, all of which caught Camille's eye.

"What the hell is that?" Camille said. She squinted to see and hear better. Her eyes sprung open. She looked up at the roof of their plane and listened.

~

Max inched them forward, his hands surrounding the yoke, wondering how long they could fight the air currents, keep the plane steady, ten thousand feet up, thirty feet of altitude separating the two planes, twenty-five feet separation dropping to twenty-three, twenty-two...

Trent was half outside the window, the smart rifle poised against his shoulder and pointing south, the scope against his eye socket. He was still on an angle, not absolute north, waiting for Max to take them farther forward. He had a mental image of where the pilot would be sitting in the seat like Max sat in his: the distance away from the door, the distance from the console in the middle of the front row, all mental coordinates allowing him to paint an imaginary X on the roof of the FW50 directly below them...

Concentrate on a spot on the roof, then fire an armor-piercing bullet through it, into the pilot's head...

But it wasn't working. He spoke to Max in the headgear.

"I can't keep the gun steady! The air, it's too much, it's pushing the barrel around. No way the gun's onboard computer will let me fire the shot..."

An upset Max whined, spoke to his plane. "C'mon, Rose, help us out here, what do we do..."

Rose bucked through a wind gust. Max had to roll her slightly left, then he leveled her again.

He had it.

There was one way to give Trent and the gun the protection from the elements he needed to fire the shot.

"Trent! Get back inside—anchor your ass across all the seats, your feet behind me—"

Max explained and Trent complied. He lay across all three seats, wrapped and clicked the seat belts around his long body, and gave Max a thumbs up. Max increased their altitude, thirty feet above the other plane, forty, sixty, seventy, then began rolling Rose left, pointing their left wing down, making it perpendicular to the roof of the UAE plane. Trent's strapped-in body automatically moved into an upright position as Max continued the plane's roll.

He decreased their altitude a few feet at a time, moved them closer with surgical precision. Trent spread his legs wide, now had both feet on either side of the rear door's broken window beneath him, straddling it, staying upright, remaining safely inside the plane with the rifle, able to point it due south, between his legs. Max inched them closer, the wind entering and exiting the interior still making it a struggle for Trent to hold his position, but with the gun inside the cockpit it was manageable. Now the only thing impacting his aim would be Max's ability to keep the plane steady, and the target plane remaining on its current course.

Max called into the mouthpiece. "How you making out?"

"Locking onto the rivet I want to punch a thirty-caliber cartridge through—just about there—the scope's computer likes the coordinates—"

"Wait—stop! I see Jasem in the co-pilot's seat drooling on himself, but I don't see Camille..."

Camille trained Renee's gun on her but backed off, disgusted, tossing the vial on the floor in front of Jasem. "I gave you a chance to get a pinprick that would give you ecstasy like you've never had before, right up until impact. You wouldn't have cared what was going to happen. But because you won't cooperate and your lover is hanging around above us, I will send you to hell the hard way."

Camille slipped back into her seat, the gun in her lap, and did not strap herself in. "I am done. I have activated the autopilot. I am leaving. Good-bye."

Renee would take no issue with this. Once Camille was gone, she'd take control of the plane and land her. How could Camille have overlooked this—?

Camille gave her a sly smile. "I almost forgot." She produced Renee's gun. "Thank you for this. It will be a great help."

She checked the gun magazine to confirm it was loaded. "There are two ways I can do this, Renee. I shoot you, I leave, and the plane goes on its merry way into the awards celebration where kaboom, one royal family is obliterated. Or I can do this."

Camille stuck the barrel of the gun against the autopilot on-off interface and pulled the trigger, repositioned it, then pulled the trigger again. The bullet holes sparked, the plane sputtered and bucked but returned quickly to its prior course. Next, two rounds into the fuel dump control panel, then the same with the on/off toggle switch.

"There. I have left you with no way to stop the autopilot, no way to jettison the fuel, no way to turn off the engine. Which leaves you with the impossible task of rousting the Crown Prince, getting a chute on him, and leaving before his plane kills his family. Adios, Renee."

The pilot's gull-wing door lifted, pushing up and away from the fuselage. The plane stuttered from the change in cabin pressure, *woosh*, the air pulling at Camille before it restabilized. She pressed her back against her seat to ready for her jump, gave Renee one last look over her shoulder. She puckered up to blow Renee a kiss.

Renee was ready for her with a full arm extension that shoved her laptop screen in front of Camille's face. The screen streamed its video showing a length of rifle barrel from a shooter's vantage point, aimed between cinched cuffs of Trent's camo pants and paratrooper boots at the white roof of an airplane that the rifle scope said was thirty-two feet, four inches away. A bullseye with the words *Target Acquired* blinked at the bottom of the screen.

"Yes, adios, Camille."

~

"You see this, Trent?"

"Sure do." Their target plane's door had jerked open. Someone was about to bail. Trent kept his eye in the scope, still liking that one rivet on the plane's roof a crazy lot. "Gun's ready. Fighting the wind but we're handling it. I press the trigger, the gun genie takes over and hopefully lets her rip. Can't hold this all day, Max… Can I go? Max? Max?"

Max received a text from Renee.

Now back in her seat she knows you're up there do it max do it now

"Go!"

Trent stared into the topsy-turvy distance between the two airplanes that started outside their broken window and ended forty feet away at the white roof of his target. He gritted his teeth, brought the gun barrel down, steadied it close to the windy abyss that separated them, as close as he could without sticking the barrel outside. He pressed the trigger and held it, one second, two seconds, three, four…

A flash across the gun's scope: *Target acquired*

The barrel erupted with a .30 caliber cartridge locked onto its target. The shot pushed Trent's shoulder back, a slight tug. The bullet found the rivet, punctured the roof, made the plane waffle in the air before righting itself and spilling one person out of the open door with a parachute. Camille's limp body rocketed upward past them, the chute deploying, except this wasn't a jump, it was more like a sleepwalker's step off a short plank. The open chute did its job and was ready for its parachutist to take its sporty reins and fly the heavenly air currents that would guide it softly into a sand dune, but the parachutist, legendary contract killer, jet pilot, and aerobatic flyer, was bleeding fore and aft with massive holes in her skull, her lower torso, and organs in between, the wind-blown blood splattering the white underside of the chute.

Max raised the wing and uprighted the plane too quickly for Trent, who lost his grip on the rifle. No harm to him, but the weapon was now out the window and airborne, seconds into a twisty, topsy-turvy descent of nine thousand feet or so to a sand dune.

~

Renee heard a thump against the plane's roof, then watched Camille's head take a bullet just before she leaned outside the cockpit, her hand wrapped around the ripcord. A chunk of skull and gray matter jettisoned cross-cockpit onto Jasem's cheek. He squirmed, emerging from his tranquilized, euphoric state.

"Whaaat is thisss," Jasem slurred, gumming through his words while wiping sleep out of his eyes plus a piece of auburn-haired scalp. He gagged.

Renee slid forward between the center console with her laptop in hand, into the pilot seat, grimaced at the mess that surrounded her: the spray of blood on the instruments, the plane's windshield, the yoke...

"Jasem! Hold on," she screamed, "we need to close this door..."

She found a button and pressed. The gull-wing door fought the air currents but soon retracted, fitting itself snugly back into the frame, locking them in. She started keying feverishly on her laptop.

"Listen—Jasem—you need to focus, there's not much time. Put on a parachute. This plane is a guided missile. I... I'm looking at this navigation system online. The autopilot is jammed. I could override it if we had more time, but we don't. That red dot is where we're headed, an entertainment stage at the Dubai airport. Your father, all the spectators waiting for us on the platform, they are evacuating now and searching for cover—"

"Camille—?"

"Dead. Tried to parachute out, didn't make it. This was all her doing, Jasem. All her. She's not your friend. She's..."

"Nomad. I know now."

"Indeed. Or she was."

"What about the Israeli plane? And Max?"

"Texting Max now. The Israelis are on the ground, they finished the race. Max's plane is still in the air. He and Trent are the reason we're still alive, Jasem. Get into your parachute, we need to bail!"

As soon as Max turned Rose's transponder back on, Dubai air traffic control came through the headset with a warning that an FW50 was unresponsive on approach to the Dubai airport.

Max pounded the dash. They were ten miles from the airport. "They know about Renee and Jasem, damn it." He handed Trent his phone. "She can't disengage their autopilot. We'll shadow her and Jasem, stay close to them."

"I texted Wilkes first and told him Nomad is neutralized. Also told him we lost the gun."

"Wilkes's ground team will hopefully find it before the desert swallows it up. But they'll look for Camille's body first."

Max's phone rang. Trent answered it. "Renee. Great. Stop, hold on, Max says to go to the VHF safety channel."

Renee's voice floated into their headsets. She went directly at the hysteria of the moment. "Max, they need to find Bibi Mizka *now*—"

"Who? *Bibi?* She went missing back in Cairo."

"Bibi, er, Memona Qureshi, yes, her, the Pakistani spy, remember? She's not missing anymore."

"You know this how?"

"From Camille. Max, she's carrying a homing device of some sort. The signal is on her somewhere, probably on Camille's Amex credit card. Bibi's there with the card, thinks she's ad-libbing some protection work for the French and has no idea she's carrying a homing device. This plane's GPS knows where Bibi is. Camille's baggage is loaded with explosives that will kill her and everyone around her. Max, I can't stop the autopilot!"

"No time to find the device. Renee, you and the Crown Prince need to get your asses off that plane. Dump the fuel and shut her down. Get the chutes on and jump."

"Max, Camille shot up the instruments! We can't dump the fuel and we can't turn off the engine. Getting the chutes on now."

"Ah, Max?" Trent looked at his phone. "A text from Wilkes. They know about the homing device."

"Which means they now know the plane is a bomb." Max checked the distance to the airport. Seven miles. Stingers had a range of a few miles. "Renee, it's important that you bail *now*."

"Okay, got it, Max, but why—?" She stopped herself. "Oh."

No need to mention that the plane wouldn't make its destination. Renee had figured it out. "Just do it, honey."

"Roger that, Max."

"Max." Trent tapped him on the shoulder. "We need to give them room to jump, bud. Pull back."

"Yeah. Don't want to, but yeah."

The stage area at the airport was being evacuated per Wilkes, the king being moved to a secure area, but they also needed not to take any chances. Someone had to find the homing device.

Max put more space between them, took them up a hundred feet and banked right, where they watched and waited. Then came Max's brainstorm. Not about Renee, about the homing device.

"Dubai International tower, this is *November three-six-eight Romeo Juliet.* Come in!" Max shouted into his mouthpiece. "Dubai tower, do you copy? Come in, please. This is an emergency."

The passenger gull-wing on Renee's plane opened. From the co-pilot side, one passenger jumped. Trent pointed, Max nodded, and they watched Jasem drop end over end until the parachute opened and its freefalling passenger jerked into a swaying descent. He settled into a pronounced swing back and forth beneath the chute, heading for a landing in the desert.

"*Aircraft calling Dubai tower, what is your emergency?*"

Max gave his name and repeated the plane's call letters, then gave a very specific message, spitting it out almost incoherently, preoccupied by trying to will a second chute to jettison from Renee's airplane.

"Tower! Broadcast this everywhere outdoors on the runways—loudspeakers, baggage handlers, everywhere! This is a life and death message for Memona Qureshi, a Palestinian pilot on foot. Memona! Bibi! You must find Camille Gagneux's credit card on your person, get rid of it, and anything else on you that looks suspicious, then *run!*"

"*Mister Fend, what is wrong?*" was the tower's response.

"Someone on the ground is being tracked by GPS. It's a pilotless plane loaded with explosives. A homing device is on her somewhere. She doesn't know it..."

Max squinted, eyed Renee's plane, seconds passing. It was descending, but it was not slowing down. He checked their distance to the airport. Under three miles—within the Stinger's range. He spoke to himself. "Renee. Jump. Get out. Jump *now*..."

Max's phone rang, Trent answered. "Wilkes, this is Carpenter. Max is busy."

An out-of-breath Wilkes spoke. "Crank up the volume and put me on speaker."

"Ready. Go ahead."

"I'm with the ground game now. We found Nomad. Our second unit is hunting for Jasem and Renee."

"Wilkes!" Max shouted. "Jasem's out there somewhere, but Renee's still in the plane. I don't know what's holding her up..."

"Not good, Max," Wilkes said. "I'm checking with the other ground unit right now. Hold on."

Renee's plane was descending, Max and Trent following her down. Three thousand feet, twenty-eight hundred... Dubai air traffic control was now in contact with them.

Max eyed Trent, whose binoculars were up. Trent shook his head; no second chute yet. They both stayed focused on the other plane, with Max trying to will Renee's exit from it. "C'mon, Renee, c'mon..."

Wilkes's "other ground unit" was the one with the Stinger.

"Max." Wilkes's voice broke their trance.

"WHAT?"

"One Stinger ordnance on the way. Make yourselves scarce."

"Shit! No—"

Trent shouted, "There! Her chute. She's out!"

The second parachutist left the plane, dropping straight down until the chute opened. Renee jolted into a sway beneath the chute's lines and would also land in the sand, but her landing would be miles away from Jasem.

Max shouted at the phone. "Renee parachuted out, Wilkes! When your unit gets to her, call me."

"Debris field from the plane will hit near an airport runway, Max, but not on it. And Max?"

"What?"

"There's a naked woman running near where the debris will hit, near the stage set up for the celebration. We believe her to be the missing Memona Qureshi, ex-Pakistani ISI. When you land you need to find her—it shouldn't be too hard—and detain her. Suffice it to say, Max, I'm glad things turned out this way. Closing our call."

Max eyed the airport runways in the short distance and was readying them for their approach when the Stinger's screaming surface-to-air missile hit its target, obliterating the small plane. The airborne explosion erupted into a fireball, visible to the tower and across all the runways. Flaming debris showered a fence and an airport vehicle next to it, but as Wilkes promised, it missed the tarmac, and it left intact the stage that had been set up for the celebration.

Max's descent onto his assigned runway had them pass a woman bent over in the grass, naked head to toe, her hands on her knees and breathing heavily, her head raised, watching airplane debris burn about a hundred yards behind her.

28

Two runways. One was out of commission while airport security and its crash recovery crews cleaned up the mess next to it, with minor fiery debris catching updrafts and drifting onto the tarmac. The second would be able to function with a normal load the rest of the day, flights arriving, flights departing, flights not crashing and burning anywhere on its thirteen-thousand-foot length. At the end of the runway, near another fixed-base operator's hangar, the Israeli team's FW50 rested intact as Max taxied his plane up to it. He shut down, and he and Trent vacated the trusty Rose in a hurry. They trotted inside the hangar.

The way things were going to go from this point—what was on Max's mind, the things that all needed doing ricocheting inside his tense head like radiation off pinballs in a microwave—none of it would relent, none of it would allow him to relax a muscle until he could close each of them out: commandeer a vehicle, hit the sand, find Wilkes, find Renee. Patch Renee up and fly her home.

Trent found them a Hummer, a civilian model, and they were off.

"What about that naked woman back there?" Trent said. "Wilkes wants—"

"Let Wilkes get someone else to pick her up. We're busy."

After jockeying around peaks and valleys on the open sand with Trent shouting course corrections, they arrived alongside an emergency vehicle and screeched to a stop. Max got out, ran to the rear of the ambulance. Sipping water on a gurney, his arm in a sling, Jasem lowered his cup when Max poked his head inside. The look they shared said everything. The prince hopped off the gurney, kissed Max on both cheeks, and said, "Your other rescue team said they have her. It just came through on a walkie-talkie. I know where. Let's go."

The CIA unit that recovered the Crown Prince, plus Trent, fended off the prince's bodyguards, but his smarmy little admin who meant well, Jundiin, was waiting at the SUV.

"Your Royal Highness, this is not good, you must stay here," Jundiin pleaded. "You are injured, the king wants you airlifted to a hospital—"

"Be right back, Jundiin, this is family business," Jasem said. "I'll be fine."

"But—"

Jundiin's hand disappeared inside a fold in his robe. Trent and Max simultaneously drew their guns and pointed them at Jundiin's head. "Do not—move," Trent said.

A startled Jundiin froze, spoke with a trembling voice. "Please, it is a phone..."

Max nodded for him to proceed. Jundiin removed his shaking hand slowly, the cell phone in it, and raised it above his shoulders, matching his other hand. "Your Highness," he said, his body quivering, "I only wanted you to have a phone... so you can update the king and your followers. They are worried..."

Max lowered his weapon, Trent didn't, and Max quickly relieved him of the device.

"You are a good and loyal chief of staff for the Crown Prince, Jundiin," Max said, tossing the phone to Trent, who handed it to Jasem. "I'm sorry I doubted you."

"Please," he said, "I am, and will always be"—his lips curled into a nervous smile—"His Royal Highness's *most* loyal servant."

Max gripped Jundiin's head, pulled him into his chest for a catch-and-release hug. "I forgot. You're Batman."

"I'm Batman."

Jasem eased his way into a rear seat of the Hummer, behind Trent. Max floored it, fishtailed into a U-turn, and they were gone.

"I owe you my life, Max Fend," Jasem said, bettering the engine noise. "You and Renee both."

"You'll tell her that in person, Jasem," Max said, winding the SUV up to a speed that almost took them airborne across the hardened dirt and sand roadway. Less than five minutes later, mostly all off road, and after bettering the two miles of sand and sun and the rising and falling dunes, they were there. Max saw the other emergency vehicle, and on his approach he nearly hit an EMT on foot before making a hard stop.

Out of his seat, Max burst into the back of the ambulance where Renee sat on the edge of a gurney attached to a drip. The drip came loose when Max lifted her up. They hugged, a ferocious clutching of arms and shoulders and faces and mouths, with no room between them, and no declarations needed except for this:

"After I get this drip, I can go," she said.

"Screw that, we'll take it with us."

Trent drove with Jasem as shotgun. Max held Renee in the back seat, the drip hanging from a headrest, their destination a Dubai hotel for as much caring and feeding and pampering as Renee could handle, before retiring to as much sleep as the two of them would let each other get.

29

Wilkes debriefed them over lunch delivered to Max and Renee's room. It was their first meal of the day, a large spread, and they were ravenous.

"Nomad and her recruiter planned all along to assassinate Jasem in Dubai at the end of the race, just not necessarily crash the plane to accomplish it."

"Why not just crash his plane early and be done with it?" Renee asked. Max cut up a piece of cantaloupe and fed her a slice.

"I'd say it's easier shooting someone in the head from a distance, which is what Nomad had originally planned with that Israeli smart rifle, before all these curious people and intel folks from different governments got in the way during the race."

The plane tampering, however, was all the uncle's doing and his followers, not Nomad, Wilkes said.

"Uncle Sheikh Saeed wanted to make the race a disaster but not necessarily kill anyone in the royal family to do it. Incapacitate some of the teams, cut the race short, damage some aircraft if necessary. Whatever it took to make Jasem look foolish while framing the Israelis for all of it. Money buys the best help, and he found Nomad's recruiter, Ives Hanania, via darknet connections. The family knew him by his clean Gilles Khalifa persona, embedded inside Fleetwings Europe's management team, perfect for the uncle's plan. Except Hanania a.k.a. Khalifa brought with him quite a crazy underground resume. Eastern European gang hits, Mexican cartel assassinations. They masked his terrorist work and his political connections to Iran, plus his secret weapon, Camille Gagneux. Nomad."

"Iran and Israel," Max opined. "A death wish for anyone to get in between them. And that's where you put us."

"Max, please," Wilkes said, the "please" a cross between an apology and asking their forgiveness. Two places Wilkes rarely went with them. "We didn't know at that point that this was an Iran thing."

"You *never* figured out it was an Iran thing," Renee said. She stopped chewing her toast. "*I* told you it was. Or rather I told Max and Trent while we were in the air, only because Camille told *me*. She blabbed, spilled her guts on that nightmare of a final leg, thinking she was home free."

The conversation skipped a beat, pausing right after Renee's "spilled her guts" comment. A figure of speech too close to the actual outcome. Her eyes filled up. Camille's horrific elimination was already surfacing as PTSD material. Max held her hand.

"Please make sure that gets in there, Wilkes," she said, following up. "The agency missed it. That's why you need friends in low places as well as high, with reach. Like me and my network of hackers."

Wilkes jotted a few words, took a breath, put his pen down. "Duly noted," he said, then held up his notepad for Renee to see: *No intel on Iran connection. Came via civilian interface. Why. Need to fix. Need more reach.*

Wilkes again: "With Hanania and Nomad under contract with Iran as well as with the uncle, they were letting the uncle have his fun. The bigger picture for Iran was to diminish the new UAE-Israeli peace agreement by making a big splash in Dubai at the end of the race: kill the king and Jasem for the large bounties they put up. Last-man-standing protocols would have put the uncle in charge. Not the way he would have wanted to be installed, though. He'd be open to extortion for his peripheral involvement in the murders. Iran would have quite the leverage during his new reign. And knowing the uncle's dissatisfaction with the peace treaty, the agreement would suffer, maybe fail, making Iran happy, and Nomad and her recruiter quite wealthy."

"Okay. Two questions," Max said. "One, who would help Camille get out of Dubai after she dropped out of a plane into the desert, and two, where's her money?"

"Iran's Revolutionary Guard. We already had an altercation with them. An IRGC helicopter versus our Stinger ground unit. We had permission to be on the ground, they didn't have permission to be in the airspace. No confrontation, we think only because the Iranians realized Nomad had been neutralized."

"The money?"

"About their purses. An interesting development. They're out there, in Bitcoin and the other digital currencies, floating around the darknet somewhere. Anyone close to Camille Gagneux or her recruiter at the end might be able to learn enough to corral the remaining payment for themselves. The cash and equivalents pieces, the agency is tracking that down also. Short answer is we don't know, yet, where it ended up. If you'd picked up Memona Qureshi on the runway—"

Max turned to Renee, fed her more fruit. "My dance card was full at that point."

"Yes. Well, if we'd found her, and found her things—found that credit card—we might have been able to reverse-engineer it to trace things back and find that money."

"She still missing?"

"APB out on her, from our agency, the UAE's intel, and others," Wilkes said.

"Whatever. Worst thing that could happen is it turns into an online treasure hunt," Max said. Then he took out his phone. "I'm calling Jasem. We can't let him stream any of the footage from this last leg. None of it. By now, the world knows something went wrong with the race. The royal family can release a few statements, cite that the video is too graphic, etcetera, but the footage and audio from all three teams for that leg needs to stay concealed."

Max relayed his message to Jasem over the phone and he acquiesced. Wilkes wrote while the two talked. Renee had a question for Wilkes, fishing while he took notes. "I gather that we will want that footage."

"You gather correctly, Renee. We will get it."

"If the royal family balks about handing it over," she said, "I'll have my guys find it for you." She gestured at her laptop occupying a side chair.

Wilkes's long stare at her computer said something just hit him. "Your plane exploded, almost with you in it, from the airstrike."

"Meaning?"

"Your laptop. How is it that it survived?"

"I was inside the autopilot code, close to unlocking it remotely via SATCOM. In the zone, Wilkes. Just so—damn—close to turning it off..." Her look was fierce, stubborn. "Besides, my laptop hard drive—it knows things. It needs to stay with me. I stuffed it down my pants before I jumped."

"We almost lost you, Renee," Wilkes said, his expression nonplussed, but the words and the sentiment were real.

"But you didn't."

How Renee and he could get back on a plane the next morning, Max didn't know, but they decided to, and they booked their flight. Nonstop from Dubai to DC. Fourteen hours, first class, to minimize the inconvenience. They cuddled in the first-class airport lounge nursing their mixed drinks, waiting for their call to board.

"We need a vacation," Renee said.

"Roger that."

She scanned the news on her laptop. "The Israel-UAE peace deal—is it still on good terms?" she asked.

"No worse, no better," Max said. "Jasem's got his hands full. But handing the race over to the Israelis' air team, declaring them the winners, that didn't hurt. And it gave a soft landing to Ozzie Katz and his co-pilot Talia back home. It might keep him in good stead with their intel agency for life. Although they could send him back out to clean things up."

"Things? What kind of things?"

"To find Bibi. If they find her, she has some explaining to do."

"I liked Bibi, Max, a lot. She got played. I wish her well."

"We all got played, Renee." He squeezed her hand. "Alaska. That's where I'm taking you. Somewhere that isn't hot or muggy or sandy. I'll book some time for us in Alaska. We'll take a train overland from DC, see the western states, travel north, get on a cruise ship, maybe pan for gold…"

Bibi pulled her embroidered headwear closer around her face while at a table in the Windows Café, a restaurant on an upper deck of the Azamara Quest cruise ship. Whom she would contact when she arrived at port of call Mumbai, she hadn't decided.

Two weeks at sea were ahead of her, Dubai to India, Sri Lanka, Indonesia, with the cruise terminating in Singapore, where Memona "Bibi" Qureshi hoped to stay for a while.

She'd had to go underground to find contacts from her past life, to have them spirit her out of the airport. It wouldn't have happened if not for:

… hearing her name blasted through the airport terminal's runway loudspeakers, the announcer pleading, telling her to separate herself from a certain plastic credit card or she would face a spectacular, movie-climax-worthy death.

… the debris from the destroyed air race FW50 crash-landing close to, but not on her.

… completely disrobing because she hadn't known where the credit card was on her person.

… seeing the American race plane fly overhead after the explosion, the plane she knew had the U.S. spy onboard.

… piecing together that Camille Gagneux had betrayed her, had turned her into an unwitting lynchpin in an international incident.

… recovering all her clothes from the tarmac, putting them back on, and walking the empty runway until she found an American Express credit card that ten minutes earlier had almost gotten her killed.

… plus additional technical systems expertise.

She'd called in some favors, had contacts in India, would find what she needed. She needed hackers. She needed talented but desperate people willing to take chances to earn top dollar on secret à la carte requests from a new acquaintance, her, with questionable ties to the espionage world.

Requests for filling in back histories on decades-old assassin identities that would never be used again because the person they belonged to, a zephyr called Nomad, was dead, unless she could figure out how to use them herself. Her hackers would create a map for her, would identify the tricky routes that had many stops at many financial institutions: traditional brick and mortar, online, and digital. They would take deep dives into the dark web for digital currency balances and hidden bank accounts until they could find the motherlode that Nomad would have tapped if she had lived. It was out there somewhere.

And when she found it, she would use it to bankroll herself. No one wanted to hire her, but she knew there was a market for the things she could do and the services she could provide, *for* the fringe elements, or *against* them. Nomad had thrived in it; now Nomad was gone. She could fill that space.

She moved her embroidered veil away from her mouth to sip her drink. Tapping Nomad's Amex card on the table, she pondered how long it might take her new friends to trace everything back with only this card as a roadmap. Weeks? Months?

But it could be done.

Cobalt
Book 1 of the Maximum Risk Series

A high-stakes battle erupts over a game-changing cobalt deposit in small-town America.

When billionaire Max Fend and his hacker girlfriend Renee LeFrancois are enlisted by the FBI and CIA to search for a cobalt deposit in rural Pennsylvania, they're plunged into a race against time and international forces. Cobalt, the precious metal powering lithium-ion batteries, has the tech world scrambling for control, and the discovery of a new source ignites a frenzy. But as domestic and international stakeholders mobilize, the local community finds itself caught in the crossfire.

As adversaries close in, a deadly contract killer, a former Philly cop, a single mom reclaiming her identity, and a band of vigilante townspeople join the fight. With secrets unraveling and danger mounting, Max and Renee must risk it all to protect a community and their nation from unbridled greed.

In Cobalt, the quest for power and control collides with the will to protect, resulting in a thrilling, explosive showdown.

ABOUT ANDREW WATTS

Andrew Watts graduated from the US Naval Academy in 2003 and served as a naval officer and helicopter pilot until 2013. During that time, he flew counter-narcotic missions in the Eastern Pacific and counter-piracy missions off the Horn of Africa. He was a flight instructor in Pensacola, FL, and helped to run ship and flight operations while embarked on a nuclear aircraft carrier deployed in the Middle East. Today, he lives with his family in Virginia.

Sign up for Andrew Watts' reader list at
severnriverbooks.com/authors/andrew-watts

ABOUT CHRIS BAUER

"The thing I write will be the thing I write."

Chris wouldn't trade his northeast Philly upbringing of street sports played on blacktop and concrete, fistfights, brick and stone row houses, and twelve years of well-intentioned Catholic school discipline for a Philadelphia minute (think New York minute but more fickle and less forgiving). Chris has had some lengthy stops as an adult in Michigan and Connecticut, and he thinks Pittsburgh is a great city even though some of his fictional characters do not. He still does most of his own stunts, and he once passed for Chip Douglas of *My Three Sons* TV fame on a Wildwood, NJ boardwalk. He's a member of International Thriller Writers, and his work has been recognized by the National Writers Association, the Writers Room of Bucks County (PA), and the Maryland Writers Association. He likes the pie more than the turkey.

severnriverbooks.com/authors/chris-bauer

www.ingramcontent.com/pod-product-compliance
Lightning Source LLC
Chambersburg PA
CBHW012013050726
47590CB00009B/3165